Foolish Desires

An April May Snow

Southern Paranormal Fiction Thriller

By

M. Scott Swanson

April May Snow Titles

Foolish Aspirations
Foolish Beliefs
Foolish Cravings
Foolish Desires
Foolish Expectations
Foolish Fantasies

Seven Title Prequel Series

Throw the Bouquet

Throw the Cap

Throw the Dice

Throw the Elbow

Throw the Fastball

Throw the Gauntlet

Throw the Hissy

Never miss an April May Snow release.

Join the reader's club!

www.mscottswanson.com

Well raise another round boys and have another glass

Be thankful for today knowing it will never last

Still let's leave this world laughin' when our eulogies are read

May we all get to heaven 'fore the devil knows we're dead

Turnpike Troubadours-

"Before the Devil Knows We're Dead"

Chapter 1

When I was eight, Grandpa Snow took me aside one day at the farm and said, "Let me tell you a secret, Lady Bug. Sometimes you need to relax, spread your wings, and ride the breeze."

I spent the rest of that summer holding my arms out, attempting to catch a summer breeze and float. When my brothers and I returned home for the start of the school year, I realized it was just another one of Grandpa's silly sayings.

My sophomore year in high school, Grandpa floated up to heaven. I thought about his words that day, and I finally understood their meaning.

I wish I were capable of floating with the breeze.

I'm the high-strung, high-drama person in my family. Nobody ever says that to my face, but they must be thinking it. I know *I* realize I'm too emotional.

Consequently, I've been working diligently on "April's four-point improvement plan." Don't get upset over things I can't control, don't say anything before thinking, don't judge, and chill out.

How's it going? Meh.

But, hey, Daddy says it's about constant improvement, not perfection. With that bell curve scoring method, I'd say I'm right on target.

It would be hard to notice my incremental improvement,

though. I live in the most laid-back community in America: Guntersville Lake in North Alabama. So, until I'm in a coma, everyone will probably continue to think I need to slow my roll.

The pace here is uber chill, everybody knows one another, and eccentric personalities are not only tolerated, they are revered. Life here is like a slice of heaven on earth for everyone … except for me. I can't escape the gravitational pull of my hometown, and it's making me nuttier than squirrel poop.

Calm. Deep breath and smile, April.

Seriously. Things have been marginally better. I recently helped my brother, Dusty, successfully complete another *Southern Haunts* novel. It did so well that Dusty secured a contract for another six books. In appreciation, he and my other brother, his fraternal twin Chase, restored a 1985 Z-28 IROC for me.

I know, I would've been absolutely thrilled to have cash instead so I could have replaced my ten-year-old Prius with a more suitable vehicle. Lord knows the Z is not helping my carbon footprint. But it's sort of a Snow family thing. All the men in our family are gearheads.

The only person in our family who doesn't drive a restored or modified vehicle is Mama. She prefers new vehicles, and Mama always gets what she wants.

I must admit, driving into work this morning, windows down with the crisp autumn air caressing my face, it is hard not to feel on top of the world. A shiny red sports car does wonders for the spirit.

The feeling I have right now is close to what Grandpa meant. Relax and enjoy the moment.

I wish it were that easy for me. I really do, but it is a struggle. Because I'm the anomaly in town.

Folks in town take the long view on relationships and take everything with a grain of salt. Me? Gnats have a greater attention span than me, and my patience is all but nonexistent. So, I don't exactly fit in.

I knew early on, to maintain my sanity, I would have to leave my hometown. Someone with my type of personality needs the constant stimuli that only a large metropolitan city can offer. A city with open minds, diverse thoughts, and progressive attitudes.

I have never been afraid of hard work to facilitate my goals. I excelled in school and finished in the top ten percent of my class at the University of Alabama School of Law.

Did all that happen because I was just brilliant? No, it happened because I worked my butt off, and I knew the alternative was living in Guntersville for the rest of my life. The most significant motivating factor I had through all those years while getting only four hours of sleep per night and eating caffeine and ephedrine tablets like peppermint candy? I knew that it would allow me to move to one of the big cities and make my mark.

Well, my mark is more like a splat. I should've easily gotten a position at a law firm with a fast-tracked partnership. Unfortunately, I accepted an offer from an unscrupulous firm. Before I signed my insurance paperwork I was out of a job.

Since then, I've been back home saving money and, more importantly, nursing my wounds.

I'm still actively searching for employment in a metropolitan setting. I'm optimistic that, eventually, I will get what I'm looking for. Unfortunately, to date, all the interviews I've had with prospective firms have been ... let's just say, not acceptable.

When I moved back to Guntersville, I honestly thought I might be staying only for five days—five weeks in the worst-case scenario. I've now been here five months.

Surprisingly, I am not stark raving mad yet.

Why?

Because I'm trying desperately to float with the breeze. I'm still not good at it. I still get wound up and face plant on the concrete when I quit floating, but it gets easier and more intuitive with each passing day.

Grandpa, God rest his soul, tried to explain it to me nearly twenty years ago. If I had been able to comprehend it then, it would have saved me a lot of anxiety.

Still, better late than never. Right?

I pull up to the law office of Snow and Associates. I can't help but grin at the skeleton wreath on the front door and the cobwebs strung across the black-and-gold awning.

You would think since I see *real* ghosts, Halloween wouldn't be my favorite holiday. Yet there is something perversely comforting about the rest of the world believing in apparitions and other assorted monsters, too, even if it is for only one day a year.

That's another positive "floating" aspect of my life. With the help of Nana, I'm not fighting my "gifts" as much as I have in the past. I'm not embracing them like she wants, but I have decided to own them like someone with twelve fingers would have to own their situation.

It's how I'm made. Get over it.

Of course, my weirdness requires more effort than just coming to the point of acceptance. That's why I meet with Nana each Thursday evening for dinner.

Nana is a talented witch. She has been helping me understand and harness my powers. Mainly to make sure I don't accidentally fry somebody—or me.

Still, that is for Thursday evenings and today is Monday morning. Which means I get to do what I trained for all these years. I get to put on the hat of my chosen profession and be a normal person. Well, as normal as I can be when my pool of potential clients is from Guntersville.

I enter the office and hear my uncle talking to someone inside.

Uncle Howard offered me a part-time job when I found myself back in Guntersville. It has turned into a full-time gig.

That's good for April's pocketbook but will make it difficult when I do leave town. I worry he has designs on me taking over the business when he retires.

Sliding my purse into my bottom drawer, I try unsuccessfully to identify the voice. It is male, but not the district attorney, Lane Jameson. He would be the usual suspect at this early hour.

My overactive curiosity is one of my strong points. I used to label it a weakness, but in the interest of keeping a positive attitude, I now call it a strength.

I'm not sure how the whole positive attitude thing is going to work out long-term. It's a lot more challenging to be Little Miss Ray of Sunshine than what it is to be a brooding cloud.

I ease toward the door of Howard's office while I think up a pretense. I knock on the doorjamb and peek my head inside.

Howard stops talking, cocks his head to the right, and says, "Oh, I didn't hear you come in, April."

"I've only been here a couple of minutes."

The man in front of Howard turns, offering a faint smile as he dips his chin.

He is military, in full dress Army uniform. I forget the ranks. But from his rugged, weathered face and the amount of paraphernalia pinned to his jacket, I can tell he is an officer, likely close to retirement.

"April, this is Colonel Sullivan. Mark, my niece April."

The colonel's eyes are an intense brown with gold flecks. His nose and jawline are angular and unyielding. "Ms. Snow."

"Miss." Where did that come from?

The sides of his lips curl up as he nods his head.

"What can I help you with, April?"

I turn slowly to Howard's voice. "Sir?"

He frowns slightly. "What did you need?"

Ahh, I forgot to come up with the excuse for interrupting them. "I was wondering if you're going to the costume party this weekend."

"I always go."

"I was just making sure." I quickly duck out of Howard's office.

My uncle and I have this rule at Snow and Associates. My

clients are his clients too, and his clients … well, they're his clients. That means that if I'm going to find out what tall, dark, and intense is having Howard work on, I'll have to do my own reconnaissance.

The intensity in Col. Sullivan's eyes reminds me of Vander. This makes sense. Vander is former military. Well, Vander might still be military for all we know. He is a local private investigator Snow and Associates uses for research projects when he is available.

Come to think of it, Vander would be the perfect person to ask about Col. Sullivan.

I fire up my laptop and review my calendar. I have a couple of contracts to finish out and file with the county clerk. Other than that, it looks like a light week. Which doesn't bother me since the big Halloween party is coming up Saturday.

Howard walks Col. Sullivan out the door. Mark isn't as tall as my brothers, but his long, lean frame and narrow waist made him appear lanky.

I'm not interested, but I scan his left hand for any band. Surprisingly, I don't find one.

So, sue me. I'm overly curious about people's status.

Howard comes back into the office and arches his brow. "Nosy much?"

"I know the base is just down the road, but you have to admit we don't get many Captain Americas in here."

"Colonel."

"Colonel America." I smile.

"You'll be running into him at the grocery store and around town now. He just bought a house on the lake," Howard informs me before disappearing into his office.

There could be worse things, I suppose.

Chapter 2

I finish my contracts and am surfing the web looking at slutty Halloween outfits. I usually prefer the more conservative ones, but I'm in sort of a dry spell on the dating scene, and I have a lot of pent-up energy.

Sexual energy.

I'm not saying I want to be slutty. Still, it would be nice to pretend I was for a night.

Howard steps out of his office. "It's meatloaf Monday at Mrs. Bell's. Would you like to come with me?"

I hesitate. "Is this a business lunch thing or is it, like, do I want to tag along with you?"

Howard shakes his head. "We'll call it a business thing, and I'll buy."

"Nice." I pull my purse from my bottom drawer.

Mrs. Bell's is four blocks from our office. Given the beautiful autumn day, we walk to the familiar meat and three.

It is barely eleven in the morning, and there is already a significant line building inside the café. There will be a line outside the door by noon.

I order the meatloaf, green beans, and a double order of mashed potatoes with gravy. Not the healthiest selection, but at least it's not French fries. Right?

"I was just thinking, have you heard from Vander lately?" I

ask.

Vander saved me from getting involved with the *wrong* sort of client during the summer. I have not seen him since.

Howard stops butchering the meatloaf he covered with ketchup. "He's out of the country right now. He stopped by to tell me before he left."

"Where'd he go?"

Howard grins and shakes his head as he turns his attention back to his plate. My uncle has the client privilege thing down pat. The only thing is, we are Vander's clients, not the other way around.

"What's the story with you two anyway. Vander even told me that Daddy knows him."

"That would be a true statement."

I roll my eyes. "I think you can trust me."

"I didn't say I couldn't trust you. Still, I've made a promise." He points his forks at me. "Your word is your bond."

"Spare me the theatrics Sir Snow of the Gunter." I wait for a response.

Howard continues to cut all of his meatloaf into bite-size portions.

"You promised Vander?"

"More or less," Howard says.

Now, this just gets my goat. As if Vander isn't sketchy enough, now my uncle wants to emulate him.

"You're not going to tell me anything, are you."

"Nope," Howard confirms as he pops a piece of ketchup-slathered meatloaf into his mouth.

"You'd be able to taste the meatloaf if you didn't put so much ketchup on it," I say as I run a bite of meatloaf through my mashed potatoes and gravy.

The crowd has doubled in the small amount of time we have been in Mrs. Bell's. Mondays usually are second only to rib Friday for crowd size.

"So, what's with G.I. Joe?" I ask.

Howard renews his interest in the fried okra on his plate.

I huff, "Okay, Colonel Sullivan."

"I'm working on a limited partnership with him."

That's cool. We haven't had any new businesses open in town recently. "How many folks are in the partnership?"

"Just two. Mark is retiring from the service next month and will be the operator of the business. He needed a partner for financial backing."

"Is he starting a security company or something?" I ask.

Howard laughs. "Not unless Pizza King has branched out into personal security, too."

"Pizza King?" That is a Southern regional pizza chain best known for tomato paste on cardboard delivered cold and late. "Well, I guess you'll be drawing up some bankruptcy papers in a few months."

"I hope not. I have a sizable chunk of money sunk into it now," Howard says.

My jaw drops. Which is particularly embarrassing because I have mashed potatoes in my mouth. "You're the financial backing?"

My uncle's lips tighten into a thin line. "Don't look so surprised. I keep a modest lifestyle, and I've made decent money over the years. I've got a nest egg to invest."

"But Pizza King? Why would you invest in that?"

Howard finishes the last precut bite of his ketchup-lathered meatloaf with a flourish. "I don't see it as me investing in Pizza King. I see it as me investing in Mark Sullivan. The man's got true talent in logistics and operations. If anybody can straighten the franchises out, it'll be him."

Franchises? As in plural? "How many franchises did you buy?"

"Nine."

"Why?" I cry.

Howard snorts a laugh. "It's not like I can be a lawyer forever."

"Yeah, you can. People are working into their eighties all the time."

"I have better things to do with my time. Maybe if we were closer to the coast, I could *coast* into retirement." He grins at me.

"Stop it."

"I'm just saying I've been doing this for over thirty years, and if I can figure out a way to draw a little income..." He flashes two fingers. "Deuces!"

I shake my head. "Don't."

"Listen. I love what I do. Still, those drives down to Mobile are long, and it's where I want to be at this stage of my life. Can you imagine waking up and being able to go out your back door onto the beach?"

Of course, I can imagine it. It sounds like heaven. But Howard has responsibilities. He has a company to run and clients to service. "What about Snow and Associates?"

He slouches back in the booth. "Hopefully, there's some young person who wants to buy into a firm rather than start at a mega-firm. If not, I'll close it down in a few years."

I sure hope he isn't thinking I want to take it over. The last thing I'll do is get caught in Guntersville, chained to a business nobody wants to buy. He also has to know there aren't any young lawyers coming into town looking to buy a partnership.

None of this makes sense to me. It also seems highly irresponsible of my uncle.

"But that building has been a lawyer's office for decades now," I say.

Howard sighs. "You know what it was before I bought it?"

"No, sir."

"A florist's shop. There are very few people left in town who could tell you that. That helps me put it into perspective. See, in a few years, after I have moved to Mobile, nobody will remember there was ever a Snow and Associates."

"That's not true."

"It is true, and I don't have a problem with it." He laughs. "For one thing, I'm going to be down in Mobile enjoying the sunshine."

"I would've just thought you'd be tied more to the community. That it would be too difficult to leave," I say.

"That's rich coming from you, young lady. I could easily say the same thing about you."

Touché. I'd never admit it to him, but Howard makes an excellent point. I have made no secret about the fact that at the first real opportunity I have to move to a large metropolitan city I would be, to coin Howard's term—deuces. But I don't have any responsibilities in the town like my uncle.

"You don't have to worry about your job. You'll be long gone by the time I decide to close the door. Well, assuming you quit taking on crazy clients." Howard laughs.

"Just a special talent of mine."

"Amen. But it is aging me unnecessarily."

I'm happy for my uncle. I know his heart has been in Mobile these past few months.

I feel it's more than the beach. Howard always says he is going to visit friends—and I'm always waiting for him to share her name. Which he doesn't.

Still, the news leaves me uneasy. Which is illogical since it has nothing to do with my situation.

It's the change. I've begun to notice all the changes around me.

I've always been a proponent of change. It was my belief you have to change things to make them better. Even when something was working for me, I would think a change would be a good thing.

It excited my senses and made me feel alive.

Now I'm not so sure change for the sake of change is a promising idea. Solid and steady predictability is beginning to effectively litigate its merits in my mind. Safe and comfortable might be okay?

It's nothing I would have even considered a few months ago. But, bless it, time melts away like ice cream on a hot summer day lately.

"Are you alright?"

I exhale loudly. "Yeah. I just ate too fast and have a bit of indigestion."

"I have some antacid back at my desk," Howard offers.

"Thank you." I'm confident antacids will not help my situation. As Granny used to say, "I need to poop or get off the pot." Right when I should be doubling my efforts to secure a position with a large firm, I've halted my job search until the start of the year.

If that doesn't exemplify conflicted, I don't know what does.

Walking to Mrs. Bell's was the right decision. At least I'll be able to walk off five percent of the calories I consumed. Besides, the belt of my skirt doesn't cut into my stomach as badly when I'm standing.

Howard is a terrible influence. He is a full-fledged, card-carrying lawyer over breaking bread attorney. This means we never miss a lunch.

That sounds like a good thing until I realized how few calories I really need to sustain myself through the day. I'm not a professional dietitian, but I did some quick calculations a month back on my caloric intake between business lunches and Daddy's cooking. I was horrified at how far over the maximum recommended level I am daily.

Last week I considered taking up running—for a few minutes. Then I decided I would take all the clothes hangers off Mama's treadmill and exercise for an hour every morning.

Did you know an hour on the treadmill only burns two glasses of sweetened tea? I mean, really, what's the point?

I shouldn't be too terribly concerned about it at the moment. Especially since nobody is looking anyway.

Still, I found the most adorable Tinker Bell outfit on the website I was looking at this morning. As it is, I'll need to shed five pounds by this weekend to make sure Tinker Bell isn't grounded by the ballast in her backside.

"So, what are you going to the party as this year, Howard?"

"Aargh … I thought I would go as Captain Hook this year."

I can't help it. My head jerks as my blood chills. There is a grin on his face.

This isn't funny. It would be, at best, awkward if my uncle is dressed as Captain Hook while I'm dressed in a Tinker Bell outfit. He's just trying to get a rise out of me. He must have left the costume site up on my computer to bait me.

Or he's on my wavelength. Mama always said I think too loud.

"Look at what the cat dropped at the front door," Howard says.

His voice brings me out of my trance, and I look toward the office entry. Lane Jameson is leaning against the door frame, scrolling through messages on his phone.

In his mid-forties, Lane looks like old Southern money in a new Italian suit. He is above average height with broad shoulders and a block jaw sporting a dimple in the middle. Lane is easy on the eyes for an older guy, a perfect gentleman, occasionally a good mentor, and frequently a royal pain in the butt. He is intelligent, driven, and quite oblivious to the fact that not everyone comes from money and runs in his social circles.

Howard and Lane are long-time good friends. This is partly because of their profession, their passion for golf, and deep down, they truly believe in the rule of law being essential for a community to survive.

"It's early for the football pool, isn't it," Howard says affably.

"I wish it were a social call, Howard." His eyes lock with mine and the left corner of his mouth raises. "April."

"Lane."

Howard unlocks the front door. "Do you have an assignment for us?" he asks.

"I suppose you could call it that. Although it's pretty hard to defend stupid."

"Nah." Howard gestures with his thumb toward me. "April specializes in defending stupid."

I don't take offense. My uncle may tease me a lot, but in this instance, he's just stating the obvious and most likely paying me a compliment. Since I have been working with him, I am a total stupid magnet.

I have scars on my tongue from biting it, so I don't interrupt them and ask, "So how did you think that was going to end?"

Yet here I am. Still standing and sane—mostly.

"Are you familiar with Jayron Freeman, Howard?"

Howard shakes his head. "I know some of the Freemans, but not Jayron."

Lane frowns. "You might remember Marcy Freeman."

I walk over to my desk and turn my laptop on while they talk.

"Jayron is Marcy's youngest son. The game warden brought him in a few hours back, and the detectives are holding him for interrogation. He has asked for an attorney."

"Game warden?" Howard asks.

That perks up my attention. We haven't been involved with the game warden since I've been working.

"Yes. Currently, Jayron is being held for suspicion of terrorism."

Howard shifts his weight. "Terrorism, Lane?"

"Wayne's fit to be tied." Lane shrugs his massive shoulders. "Caught the boy dropping explosive devices in the lake."

Howard squints his eyes. "I know that's illegal. Still, how's that terrorism."

"Jayron isn't the sharpest tool in the shed. When Wayne caught him, he was only forty feet away from the base of the dam."

The assignment sounds eerily familiar, and I slide into a dark place.

A few months back, I defended a not-so-bright client who had taken an action that resulted in an unintended consequence. Specifically, he accidentally burned his house down.

I was able to negotiate a liberal plea bargain for him. The only problem being he was distraught over his wife having left him. Just hours before he was set to be released, the security guards discovered him hanging in his cell.

I'll never be the same. That's the sort of loss you never expect and surely can't clear from your mind.

"They can't think the boy did that on purpose, Lane," Howard continues.

"I don't think so. But there have been those reports of gunshots around the dam. And now this. Neighbors in the area are already jumpy, and now we have a boy endangering the dam? It's just bad optics.

"We can't just give him a slap on the wrist and let him walk. He's too much of a liability now that the news has gotten out about what he was doing."

"I'll take it." Ugh. What happened to think before you talk?

"Are you sure, April?"

The concern on my uncle's face flips a switch in my mind. I know he is concerned for me. Worried that I wasn't past Jethro hanging himself. Still, I need this. I want a case where I can help someone who has put themselves in a bad position unintentionally. If I can help this young man, maybe it will balance the loss of Jethro.

"No, I've got this." I turn my attention to Lane. "Besides, it sounds like Jayron could use some help. And like my uncle says, I excel at stupid."

Lane appears dubious, which piques my temper. "With it being treated as a terrorist attack, the FBI will want to question him."

"It seems like a long drive from Huntsville for a boy being a boy," I say.

"The Gadsden office. Huntsville pushed it off on them."

"That proves my point. Huntsville didn't believe it worth their effort." I pull my purse out of my desk and shove my laptop into my backpack. I stop in front of Lane. "Shall we?"

"Certainly." He opens the door for me.

Chapter 3

The courthouse is two blocks from Snow and Associates. Our police station is catty-corner to it.

I love this time of year when the heat has finally released its tight grip, and we will have weeks of low humidity. I prefer to walk a block without feeling like I ran through a battery of water sprinklers.

Most importantly, the break in the heat signifies football season and the coming of Halloween. Those two reasons alone make it difficult to beat fall in Alabama.

That's also why six weeks ago, I put the brakes on my job search. It isn't going to hurt to spend one last football season in Alabama before heading off to my next career. Besides, Coach Saban has put together another stellar team, and I'm excited to see the Tide win the SEC again.

"Are you positive you're alright?"

I shoot Lane a sideways glare. "Why wouldn't I be?"

He shrugs as he slides his phone into his pocket. "I don't know. You seem extraordinarily quiet—for you."

Now I can take that as concern on Lane's part or that he thinks I talk too much. "I was just thinking about my mama's party Saturday night. Are you coming?"

"Oh yeah. I wouldn't miss it for the world."

"Really?"

"Don't look so surprised. I've attended Vivian's open houses the last six years without fail."

Who would imagine Lane would be a regular at a "fun" event? Specific factoids about my hometown continue to catch me by surprise. I've been back six months and find I'm still catching up on the seven years I was in Tuscaloosa.

"So, what will the district attorney be dressed as at this year's event?"

"I'm going as the hangman."

I wait for the punchline as we continue our walk toward the courthouse. Stealing a glance, I see he does not plan to elaborate. "That's sort of morbid, Lane."

"Why do you say that?"

Has he lost his mind? "I don't know. Maybe because given your profession, you should pick something happier."

He pushes his lower lip out as if he is contemplating my opinion. "I suppose I could go as a clown."

Yeah, I don't like that idea much either.

"I've seen some clown masks complete with fangs and blood smudges. They're quite elaborate," he continues.

"That's just messed up."

He chuckles as he shakes his head. "I was just messing with you, April. I've already rented an American Superhero costume."

Lane has dark hair, but he will make an excellent American Superhero double, other than that minor detail. I'm sure he can rock that costume.

"I won't be able to stay the entire night. I have tickets for the game in Tuscaloosa Saturday, and it's a noon kickoff."

Oh my gosh. "You got tickets to the Mississippi State game?"

"Yes. I have a friend who graduated from State. We intended to make it a weekend, but his wife broke her ankle last week and has to have surgery. He'll need to stay home and help her since she can't get around. I figure I'll go down and see if I can sell his ticket."

"Man, what a waste. That's going to be a great game. State's quarterback is for real, and their defense is stiff."

Lane's brow furrows. "Would you like to go?"

My heart does a fluttery number. Partly because I really would like to go to the game. Also, even though I know Lane is asking as a friend, I worry about what people will think and say in town.

He reads my expression. "If you're not comfortable, that's fine. I just got the impression you might enjoy the game."

"I would." I wince as I ask, "Are you sure you wouldn't mind?"

"Not at all. I'd enjoy the company. The ticket would go to waste otherwise."

"I can pay for it." I think. I don't even know what a ticket costs when you're not a student.

"Don't be silly. I've already purchased it. I'd rather the ticket go to someone I know rather than me sell it on the cheap to someone I don't know." He wrinkles his nose. "Sitting by strangers isn't my strong suit. Besides, you can buy the hot dogs if it will make you feel better."

That seems fair. "Well, if you don't mind, I am going to take you up on the offer."

Lane opens the door to the police station. "Good. Then I won't feel quite so guilty about you accepting to defend Jayron. See, we all win."

"He can't be that bad, Lane."

"I can only hope you feel that way after you've spoken with him."

Lane brings me into the viewing room before we enter the interrogation room. Detective Dorsett is standing in the small room.

"Anything new?" Lane asks.

Dorsett frowns. "No. The boy is not very bright, but once he makes up his mind—he sticks to it."

"I will need you to turn the speakers off, Detective Dorsett," I instructed him.

"No problem, April."

I move toward the viewing room door.

"April."

I turn to Dorsett's voice. "Yes?"

"There's no way that boy made those bombs. Which can only mean there's someone out there who knows how to make explosives—potent explosives. We don't have a clue who it is."

I understand what he is asking. Still, I shrug my shoulder. "Sorry, Dorsett. That's your job, not mine."

Anger flashes across Dorsett's face telling me I might want to work on my tact for delivering the truth in the future. But I can't concern myself with another self-improvement project right now. I have a client who needs my help.

I open the interrogation room door. Jayron's mind leaps to me. He is not a particularly deep individual, but he is sincere.

This has to be a misunderstanding. There is no way someone this open meant to endanger anyone.

Energy reads can be extremely helpful. More helpful, because they add context to the energy disposition, are the mind's obsessions. The events that play over and over on a closed loop in a tortured soul's mind.

I get only the energy read from Jayron. That of a protector. Other than that, it is as if his mind is a freshly scrubbed chalkboard.

Smiling as I take a seat across from him, I ponder this new occurrence.

Most of us walk around in our own insulated bubble. Our time is primarily consumed by the most wonderfully important human in the world—us. Since the sun of our universe is us, there isn't natural energy that penetrates our own bubble.

That's why to get a read on people, I usually just wrap my own energy around theirs, be still, and listen. When I still can't read them, I may pierce their bubble with my own energy if it is important enough.

I refuse to do this unless it is imperative. One, because it is as intrusive as it sounds. Two, because if the person is crazy, it is like plopping yourself into a house of horrors movie with a homicidal maniac screaming for your head.

Seriously not cool.

With Jayron, it flowed—no—leaped to me. This indicates to me he is so desperate to connect and be accepted by the rest of humanity he has turned his energy outward like a beacon, leaving no energy to nourish his own ego.

Or, which is the danger of reading out of context, Jayron could be an incredibly intelligent sociopath. An evil man who, on some fundamental level, is aware of his energy "pitches" and how they affect others' perception of him.

Continuing to smile kindly, I center my breathing and clear the initial read of "protector" from my mind. Even though it is analogous to telling a jury to disregard something a prosecutor says during a trial.

Jayron is a gaunt young man, almost anorexic in appearance. His severe overbite and thick brow leave him with a less-than-stellar-student appearance. He wears a Miami Heat basketball jersey and a Cleveland Cavaliers cap.

So, he likes basketball. That must be tough at less than six feet tall.

His bright white arms sport a rebel flag.

I do a double-take at the odd tattoo, realizing the flag's staff is crossed by the forearm of a raised black fist. That seems to be a special kind of stupid. Still, despite the preposterousness of the artwork, it doesn't exactly surprise me.

Boys like their symbols. It's how they identify their tribe.

Love within their tribe can't be conditional. When they identify with multiple tribes—well, let's just say the love can be *conflicted*. Couple that with not having the required intelligence to truly understand the historical relevance of said symbols...

On second thought, it's a special kind of stupid.

"Hi, Jayron. I'm your court-appointed attorney, April Snow."

The young man sways his shoulders to and fro as he looks up into my eyes. He lowers his eyes and stares at the back of his hands.

"I'd like to talk to you about what happened today. Before we start, do you need something to drink, or maybe to eat?" I hope he'll accept something since eating lowers your defenses. Also, Jayron looks like he could use a sandwich—or three.

He shakes his head, then fans his left hand over his eyes.

"Do you have a headache? Do you need some aspirin?"

"No. I just need to get outta here."

I can understand that. I've been on the other side of this table in an interrogation room before, and I can attest to it being unenjoyable. "Okay. Well, the sooner you tell me what happened, the sooner we might be able to work out your release."

"This is stupid. I didn't do anything wrong," he mumbles.

"I hear you. Tell me about being on the lake today."

Jayron frowns and looks away. "I was just fishing down by the dam. You can get some good-sized catfish there sometimes."

"Sure can. I've seen catfish as big as thirty pounds out there," I say.

"There's some down there pushing a hundred pounds."

"Yeah, I have to wonder if a hundred-pound catfish would taste good."

He looks back and smiles at me. "Put enough hot sauce on it, and it would be fine."

Jayron makes an excellent point. I'm not the biggest catfish eater in the world. Especially once I learned they were bottom feeders, i.e., poop eaters. But yes, if you're eating fried catfish, if you put enough hot sauce on it, the taste of the fish will improve regardless of who cleaned or fried the fish fillets.

"Did you see the game warden?" I ask.

"Yeah, I saw that crazy douche."

"He claims you were setting off explosive charges next to the dam."

Jayron tilts his head while screwing up his face. "Explosives, that's a laugh. It's more like M-80s."

"Well, some people think M-80s are explosives."

He fidgets in his seat. "Are you going to get me out of here or what?"

Jayron is missing the scale of the trouble he is in. "That's my intent. But I'm going to need a favor from you if you can help me."

He makes direct eye contact. His expression turns serious.

Good. Jayron appears willing to help. I either read him correctly as a protector, or he is a highly adept sociopath.

My gut remains firmly in the "low IQ, high need for affirmation" camp.

"Jayron, as much as I want to help you, I can't do anything for you if you don't share the truth."

His lips tighten as if he is deep in thought. I decide it is time to push. "Why do you want to lie to the one person who can get you out of here?"

His eyes open wider. "I haven't lied to you."

"M-80? Really? You expect me to believe a game warden as seasoned as Wayne Swain is going to bother bringing you in here over dropping a few firecrackers into Guntersville Lake?"

Jayron's nose flares. "I don't care what you believe. It's the truth."

I stare at him. Clicking my tongue, I collect my notebook and shove it into my backpack. As I push my chair back and begin to stand, his eyes widen as he comprehends what my movement indicates.

"Where are you going?"

"Me?" I point to my chest. "I have better things to do with my time than being jerked around by someone who won't work with me."

"But you're my attorney."

I push my lips out as I shake my head. "Not this girl. I got better things to do."

"But they have to give me an attorney."

"Oh, they'll assign you another one. One who can sit next to you and do nothing while you end up getting the maximum sentence for your stupidity."

Jayron's ears redden as he narrows his eyes. "Don't call me stupid," he growls.

"Then don't lie to me like *I'm* stupid."

His eyes divert downward as if he is considering my words. My hope is there are a few active brain cells in his skull.

I'm relieved to see he has a faint grin when he looks up. "You're right. I'm sorry."

I make a massive production of huffing a breath of air as I pull out my notebook, plopping myself back into the chair. "So, what sort of explosive device was it since we've established it wasn't M-80s."

Jayron exhales, taking a moment to answer. I arch an eyebrow, and he looks to the tabletop. "Pipe bomb," he grumbles under his breath.

Holy fudge! "Why are you setting pipe bombs off so close to the dam?"

He looks up and snorts as if I asked the dumbest question he ever heard. "I told you. That's where the catfish are."

I try to fight it, but my curiosity which I can never control, and my geekiness which I usually can conceal, roll to the front of my personality. "Jayron, it's seventy to a hundred feet deep at the face of the dam. How are you expecting to get the pipe bombs down there?"

"For reals? Pipe bombs are metal. Metal sinks."

Right, pardon my stupidity. "I meant did you have a fuse or some other means to time when they went off?"

He raises his chin in acknowledgment of the *correct* question. "They had fuses. I just did a couple different fuse lengths until I got it right."

Good Lord, how many of these had he made?

"I got others I can detonate with my cell phone. But I don't have one right now."

I'm not sure if he is telling me he doesn't have one of those types of bombs or he doesn't have a cell phone. Still, I want to know more about the construction of the bombs. "What sort of load and fuel are you using?"

"You know, some diesel, some fertilizer." His voice trails off.

One of the last criminal classes I took in law school reviewed the Unabomber case. I found myself doing research online for homemade bombs strictly out of curiosity. For months I was paranoid the FBI would raid my house for me having visited the bomb-making sites.

"What percentages did you use?" I ask.

"Like half-and-half." His eyes dart back to the top of the desk.

Something isn't feeling right. "What was the shot load?"

"Like buckshot and ball bearings."

What? "Buckshot? Do you know what that would do to fish?"

He sits up straight. I swear I can smell the gears turning in his head as he considers my question. "Birdshot. I meant to say birdshot."

Uh-huh. "You didn't make the bombs, did you?"

"Yes, I did."

I let his lie hang in the air for a second. I ask very slowly, "From your calculations, what's the kill zone of the pipe bombs?"

"He said twenty to thirty feet. But I think in the water, it ends up being less."

"Who is he?"

Jayron appears completely confused. "He?"

I raise my brow. "Yes. You said, 'He said.' Who is he?"

"Did I? That's weird." Jayron laughs nervously and looks toward the one-way glass.

"What I find weird is that you just lied to the one person who can help you get out of here, not once but twice, in just a few minutes. What do you expect me to think about that, Jayron?"

His face screws up with tormented concern. "It's not like I want to, lady."

"Then don't."

"It's not that easy."

"I am so losing my patience with your little game." Not

really. I have him talking, and I want to know who made the bombs for him.

"If I tell you, he'll get in trouble, and he was just doing me a favor."

Odd favor by my standards, but I'm learning not to judge. "Jayron, do you understand what it means that I am your attorney."

He shrugs his shoulders. "Sure, I do. It means you're supposed to try and get me out of this dump."

His elevator keeps getting stuck in between floors, as Daddy likes to say.

"Right. But more importantly, to do my job, I need to know as much information as you can remember. You can't hold back. We never know exactly what bit of information you tell me will be the piece that sets you free."

"I promised him," he interjects.

I hold up a finger. "Let me finish. In return for you telling me everything, I promise you I will not say anything. To anyone."

"Seriously?" He tilts his head.

"Yes." He contemplates my promise and frowns. "I don't know. It's not that I don't believe you. It's just I made a promise not to tell. Not *only* to tell a lawyer. A promise is a promise."

Jayron, the protector, considers literal meanings to be a black-and-white affair. The problem is the courts are very literal as well. Presently, Jayron is labeled a terrorist. If he has any hope of a successful life moving forward, he must have the terrorist charges dropped.

"Jayron, without a name, they're going to assume you made those devices, and with you being right next to the dam, that you were attempting to blow it up."

His mouth opens in an "O." He blinks rapidly. "Why in the world would they think that? That would flood people's homes. It might even kill some people."

He is honestly surprised. "I don't know, Jayron. Maybe because you were right next to a dam. And like you said, if it failed, it would flood a lot of expensive property and kill some innocent people?"

"But I was at the dam because that's where the catfish—"

"Are," I finish for him.

I allow him to sit in silence before I try again. "Listen, you're going to have to trust me. I won't tell anybody where to find your friend. But if you look like you're a lone wolf, doing this on your own, they're going to try *you* as a terrorist."

"Well, he's not either. He's no terrorist."

That's what I already figured. If I were to guess, one of Jayron's friends likes to build things. Specifically, things that explode.

That doesn't automatically make him a criminal. Still, it might make his friend reckless. If you're intelligent enough to construct explosive devices, in my book, you should understand handing out fifty bombs to your friend for a fishing excursion is not the best decision you can make.

"Come on, Jayron. I don't have all day."

He swallows hard. "It's my older brother, Kenny."

Thank goodness. Maybe I'm getting through to Jayron. "Why was Kenny making pipe bombs?"

Jayron shrugs his shoulder. "I like the big boom?"

I believe that, but it doesn't feel right—complete. Something in Jayron's energy signals to me he is lying again.

"You're lying to me again. You need to tell me what the real reason is, or I'm outta here."

Jayron throws himself to the back of his chair and groans. He says something unintelligible.

"Speak up. I can't understand you," I say.

His eyes lock with mine. "There's no meat in the freezer. If we want anything besides the vegetables we grow, we have to go hunt it down."

Typical. Here I'm worried about my Tinker Bell pseudo-hoe outfit I'll squeeze my chunky butt in and if my uncle will ruin the effect by coming as Captain Hook, and Jayron tells me he and his brother Kenny are hungry.

I know I am blessed, and I try to be grateful for it, but does everything in my life have to point it out?

"I'm going to go talk to your brother right after I talk to Wayne Swain," I say.

"No! Kenny will be pissed." He gestures toward me. "You said you wouldn't tell."

"I'm not telling anyone who doesn't already know."

He covers his face with his hands.

"Hey, look at me, Jayron."

"What?"

"I'll do my best to set things right for you. At the very least, I'll get the terrorist charges dropped. I'll be back to fill you in with the details as soon as I can. In the meantime, just be patient and stay out of trouble."

As God is my witness, I hope I can deliver on my promise.

Chapter 4

Thanks to my big mouth, the pleasantly slow day has turned into a high-risk situation for a new client. All I needed to do to coast into Friday and the Halloween party was keep my mouth shut when Lane mentioned Jayron's case. Could I do that? *No.*

I need to talk to Wayne Swain, the game warden. It is always best to get the arresting officer's version of the case.

The sweet tea I drank at Mrs. Bell's forces me to detour to the ladies' room before I leave the police station.

After relieving myself of the discomfort, I wash my hands.

Bless it. If there were one place you would think folks wouldn't create graffiti, it would be the police station. Right?

Yet here I am with the majority of Guntersville's finest within shouting distance, and someone had brazenly written on the women's restroom mirror.

Taking a paper towel from the roller, I swipe at the letters across the mirror, erasing most of the message.

The black bags under my eyes seem to have popped up in the last few minutes. I guess it's some sort of stress-induced thing. Having a client below the average-intelligence curve is taxing.

A point on the surface of the mirror wavers. A drop of metallic liquid sweats out of the mirror.

Intrigued, I lean forward to examine the reflective droplet closer. It reminds me of a drop of mercury.

Against all good judgment, I reach to touch the foreign liquid with my finger.

The bead loops wildly across the face of the mirror. I draw in a sharp breath and take a step back.

The bead, resembling a silver pearl, swirls in a coiling motion across the surface of the mirror. It leaves a raised, embossed trail of silver in its wake.

I'm not panicked—yet. Thanks to my intense curiosity that demands I identify what I'm witnessing.

Two long sticks with a perpendicular line connecting their midsection followed by a round, looping circle appear. A crude sketch of a grapevine, I guess, or possibly a hastily drawn clothesline with a basket next to it.

Another parallel loop traces outward from the "basket," and I realize the bead is not forming a childishly drawn sketch. It appeared foreign to me since I have not used cursive handwriting since the seventh grade.

Other than for signatures, does anybody use cursive writing anymore?

The revelation makes the hairs on the back of my neck stand up as I reexamine the bead's work. Hel ... I'm hoping for "Hello," but I feel things are turning south despite my desires.

My gut clenches as the bead heads toward the top of the mirror as if it will form a loop to make another "l." The droplet stops its upward progress, circling out and back to create a "p." I exhale in relief.

I suck in a quick breath as the new word registers.

Help? The muscles in my thighs twitch. I suppose my mind is checking their readiness in the event I need to exit the ladies' room like my hair is on fire.

Still, my curiosity keeps me rooted where I am. I watch the bead travel back to the left of the mirror without leaving one of its silvery, embossed trails.

I am completely captivated. All my senses are wound right up to the breaking point, but I have never heard of this phenomenon before, much less seen it.

The bead appears to be finished with its inscription. I reach out to touch it with my finger. I have a burning desire to confirm if it is a liquid or a solid.

It must be a liquid. Right? To leave a trail.

The bead starts its travel across the mirror again, and I pull back with a gasp. With a better understanding of what it is doing, I watch patiently as it continues with maddening slowness. It writes "M" and then finally an "e."

Me. Help me. Well, peaches.

That's a little on the ambiguous side, don't you think? I mean, I'm not a mind reader. Well, actually, I am. But I still need to know who the heck "Me" is and the issue that has them asking for help.

I have half a mind to ignore the message. It isn't my fault if I can't understand the cryptic message from a ghost.

Still, refusing a plea for help is not as easy as I think. The thought of it feels like a piece of my humanity being stripped away.

Maybe so, but the least I can do is satisfy my curiosity. I reach out and touch the "e" in help and let out a yelp as the electrical current snaps from the mirror to my fingertip. It feels like someone thwacked the tip of my finger with a rubber band.

Man, what was that? Another first.

"Whatever. You're going to have to do better than that for me to be able to help you," I grouse.

The tiniest speck of green smoke puffs from the mirror. I draw back. I take a backward step toward the exit. I'm ready to run, and my self-preservation is just about to kick in.

The smoke from the mirror dissipates. A sickly green orb floats from the back of the mirror, as if it is hundreds of yards in the background, toward the forefront. Shifting from left to right, it slows and speeds up in spurts.

Finally, it comes to rest at the left of the "H." It sits there. A large, wavering puke-green orb.

Fine. If it needs help but is unwilling to give me any helpful information, it can sit there like a giant green mushroom for the next person to find. I've got more than I can say grace over now even without this diversion.

As I turn away from the mirror, a face appears momentarily in my peripheral vision. I think.

I turn back to the mirror and stare at it through squinted eyes. "Show yourself or go back from where you came."

The orb swirls, tilts, and breaks into a thousand particles of slime-green sparkles. Slowly, the elongated face of a woman surrounded by a light-green mist takes shape.

A year ago, I would have left the premises in a rush. Now, sad to say, these occurrences are all too commonplace for me.

"What do you need?" I ask.

The green, opaque woman's eyes roll up in their sockets until only a muted white shows. Her jaw opens, causing her mouth to elongate as if something is caught in her throat and she is gagging.

The piercing shriek catches me entirely by surprise. I stumble backward, nearly falling as my mind orders my legs to run while my feet stayed planted firmly on the old tile floor and cause my legs to buckle.

I catch my balance by grabbing the bathroom door handle. I steal a quick look over my shoulder.

Gone.

The woman, the green orb and mist, even the mercury bead, and the "Help Me" request ... all gone.

Well, that is just the rudest!

Perhaps I daydreamed the entire interaction.

As much as I want it to, that doesn't ring true for a couple of reasons. I'm still standing, and I'm anything but sleepy.

There must have been something in the meatloaf at Mrs. Bell's. That is the only answer I can manufacture.

That's the trouble with weird happenings. My explanations tend to sound as bizarrely improbable and unbelievable as the actual events.

Unsure of what transpired, I have one choice available to me. I put the weird interaction behind me like it never happened so

I can keep my sanity card.

Chapter 5

I get into my Z-28. The engine rumbles to life while I dial the number I have for Wayne Swain."

"Ranger Swain."

"Ranger Swain? My name is April Snow, and I'm doing some investigating on the explosions near the dam today."

"Okay." He draws it out into a four-syllable word.

"I wonder if you would mind getting together to discuss the details of the arrest of Jayron Freeman."

"I'm swamped, Ms. Snow. Did you not read the report?"

"The DA has not released it to me yet."

I hear a disgusted breath on the opposite end of the line. "The kid is guilty. I caught him red-handed. There is no disputing that. But I suppose he needs real representation. Can you meet me at Jasper's to go over the case details at four this afternoon? I can probably spare you a half-hour then."

"Oh, that would be wonderful."

"Don't mention it. Even idiots deserve well-prepared legal representation."

I can go back to the office to finish an hour's worth of paperwork before meeting Wayne at Jester's. Instead, I decide to go early and hang out at the bar.

Jester's is what would commonly be referred to as a roadside bar, between Guntersville and Boaz. Jester Warner owns the bar and his son Winky manages it.

Winky was my first boyfriend. We were nine.

I walk into the dimly lit bar and am greeted by the smell of over-fried chicken strips, cigarette smoke, and stale beer. As my eyes adjust to the decrease in lighting, I hear, "What do you know? It's snowing in October."

Some voices make me smile automatically. Winky's voice always has that effect on me.

"You better put something over those guns, Winky, or you're going to catch your death of cold."

His broad smile flashes a dimple in his right cheek. "I can't cover them up, doll. They won't give you a concealed carry permit for guns this big." He slaps his right bicep with his left hand.

Winky's upper arms are the size of my thighs. No one has ever been accused of saying my thighs are petite.

The size of Winky's arms isn't the only thing scary about them. He has inked every inch of available skin with graphic tattoos that appear to be from nightmares induced by a bad LSD trip.

"Besides, I like to keep them on display to keep the criminal element at bay." He bounces the biceps in his arms a couple of times for effect.

To a stranger, Winky is one *bad*-looking, thick-muscled man. The type you go out of your way not to insult.

He doesn't scare me. I know he has a heart of gold, and in a pinch, he is an excellent confidant.

Winky slaps a stained bar rag over the left shoulder of his dirty tank top. "Tough day?" He makes a point of looking at the Jim Beam clock. "It's a little early for a young professional like yourself to be starting a tab."

I sit down at the bar. "I'm supposed to be meeting Ranger Swain here at four."

Winky's brow furrows. "Dating them a little older now, are you?"

I scoop a couple of peanuts out of the dish in front of me and flick them at him. "Get your mind out of the gutter, Winky."

"I'm just saying if you need a date that bad, I might be able to hook you up with one of my friends. They don't have jobs—for that matter, they don't have any teeth, either. But I guess a girl can't be picky."

I attempt to glower at him and burst into a laugh. He can be so stupid. "How about you bring me a *clean* glass of water, and I won't talk about the girls you go out with."

Winky shrugs as he turns his back to me. "As long as you remember that 'clean' is a subjective term."

"Wow, subjective. A fifty-cent word. Very good, Winky."

He smiles over his shoulder. "I've been saving that one up for you. I knew it would get you all hot and bothered."

"Yeah, I'm all worked up now."

He sets a glass of ice water in front of me. "Seriously, what do you want with old Ranger Swain, anyway?"

"One of the locals got caught doing something they're not supposed to do on the lake. I need to get the warden's side of the story to compare it to my client's."

Winky shakes his head. "I feel sorry for the guy. Whoever it is. I'd rather get picked up by the sheriff or the po-po before one of the game wardens. Those boys play for keeps."

I have never had any dealings with the game wardens. However, their reputation does precede them. They have been known to lower the hammer on anyone stupid enough to break the gaming rules.

In this part of the country, the position is highly coveted. I mean, what self-respecting country boy wouldn't love to cruise the forest or lake all day and make sure everyone is playing the game according to the rules?

"I've got some leftover chicken fingers and fries I can warm up if you're hungry," Winky offers.

"No thanks. I ate meatloaf at Mrs. Bell's today. You know how that stuff will stick with you for forty-eight hours."

He snorts a laugh. "True that."

"Maxwell!"

The booming voice makes me cringe. Winky hangs his head in a defeated manner.

"Maxwell, get your butt in here now."

"Is that your dad?" I ask.

Winky meets my eyes and his lips thin. "Yeah. He's gotten worse in the last year."

That is saying a lot. Winky's dad was a sergeant in Vietnam. He came home after three tours because the Army made him go home, but he never quit being a fighter.

Winky's mom hung in there for the first fifteen years after his return from the jungles, but eventually, she left him. Sgt. Jester Warner then began a deep dive into the Scotch whiskey and took to blaming Winky for everything that was not right in his life.

Winky, bless his soul, is too kindhearted to leave his father to drown in his alcoholic misery.

A small, gray-haired man limps through the kitchen door leaning heavily on a gnarled hickory cane.

I'm horrified. I have not seen Mr. Warner in a decade. The intimidating middle-aged man with the rock-hard body I remembered has been replaced by a frail, sickly looking old man. The only thing that remains of the man I once feared is his cutting, ice-blue eyes that have an unfathomable intensity about them.

I would hope someone so close to death might change their ways at the last minute in hopes of conning their way into heaven. No such luck with Mr. Warner, I suppose.

Winky corrals Mr. Warner with one of his massive arms and leads the old man back into the kitchen. Winky handles his father with incredible gentleness while still being firm. It is grace under fire personified to me.

Well, that's twice today I have had it demonstrated to me how fortunate I am. A friend offers me chicken fingers when

I have a client being charged with terrorism because he was hungry, and my family may drive me crazy some days. Still, they have never been abusive toward me.

I spin around in my bar seat to face the tables. It is still too early for the construction workers who visit Jester's after their shift.

Three truckers are eating a late lunch. Two together and one by himself.

How hungry do you have to be to eat chicken fingers fried in grease that smells so old? Still, it smells no different than the grease at the convenience stores that serve potato wedges and corndogs off the highway exits.

"Ms. Snow?"

The voice to my right startles me out of my thoughts. "Yes?"

A man with skin the color and texture of leather extends his hand toward me. "Ranger Swain."

"Oh. Of course." I shake his hand. "Thank you for coming on short notice."

He takes the stool next to me. "Thank you for being on time. I wrapped up what I was doing a little bit early and wasn't sure you would be here already."

I gesture with my thumb toward the kitchen. "Winky and I know each other from school. I thought I'd come in and catch up with him."

Swain nods, his face is solemn. "Winky's a good man. His daddy, Jester, he used to be better."

Awkward. I'm hoping that is a rhetorical comment.

"It sounds as if you drew the short straw and got the honor of defending Jayron Freeman," Swain continues.

I can't help but grin. "Somebody has to do it. I think I'm the girl for the job."

The wrinkles at the corner of his eyes deepen. "Lane can be quite the prick at times. This case will be a fool's errand for you."

"But it pays the bills."

Ranger Swain shifts on his stool. His gaze holds my full attention. "You got a little fire to you. Don't you, girly?"

There are times a comment like that would spark anger in my gut. I can tell from Ranger Swain it is actually a compliment, possibly even a statement of admiration. "I've heard that on occasion."

An easy chuckle rumbles from the old man. "You're a character, Ms. Snow. I like you." Exhaling, he asks, "What can I do you for?"

"Today, I interviewed Jayron Freeman and got his statement of events, but given the situation—let's say something still feels out of sorts. I feel getting your account of this morning might help me clear up whatever is missing in the story."

Swain leans his elbows onto the bar. "I suppose you first need to realize your client is as smart as a box of rocks. There's no way he made those devices."

"I might've found a way to say it a little more delicately, but yes, I do realize that. Do you have any thoughts as to who may have made them?" I thought while I was here, I might as well do a little *fishing* myself.

Swain's gaze shifts from my eyes as he peers over my shoulder. His lips narrow.

He does a push-up onto the bar, plants his butt on the oak top, and rotates, swinging his legs over to the back of the bar. "My thoughts are I'm thirsty."

I watch the man with what I am sure is a dumbfounded look as he pulls a Budweiser out of the ice bucket behind the bar. Swain is deceptively fast and agile for his apparent age.

"You want something while I'm back here?" he asks as he pulls a second beer out of the tub.

"No, thanks. I'm set with my water for now."

His butt lands on top of the bar. This time without the aid of the barstool. He rotates his legs back across the top of the bar, resuming his seat.

"You were saying?" he asks as he twists the bottle cap off the beer bottle.

"I suppose what I'm trying to piece together is why you

charged him with terrorism."

"I had to."

The habit of rolling my eyes is something I've been attempting to curb. I fail miserably this time. "Really, terrorism? You seriously believe that's what Jayron was up to?"

Wayne's face draws together. With his skin texture, he looks uncannily like a shrunken head. "Heck no. That stupid boy is out there trying to blow a few catfish to the surface."

"If you believe that—why the terrorism charge?"

"Look, I don't like having to arrest folks like Jayron anyway. I can't fault a hungry boy. And that's one *hungry* boy. Still, you need to understand this isn't the first time I've caught him with explosive devices."

I'll want to have a discussion with Lane. This tidbit of information would've been helpful to know.

"The times before, I gave him a stern talking to and confiscated his gear. I thought it would end there. Instead, I've had to pick him up three more times, and each time, the explosive devices are getting more and more sophisticated and powerful." He pauses for effect as his expression conveys the seriousness of the matter. "I kid you not. If Jayron had been six feet away from the dam rather than the fifty feet he was with the devices he was using today, he very well would have cracked the dam."

Swain lifts his hand while tilting his head. "And before you go and tell me, 'Well, he wasn't six feet from the dam,' I'm telling you it was only a matter of time before he was that close. The boy's got the attention span of a gnat, but once he gets to a task, he is all tunnel vision come heck or high water. Believe me, we were too close to high water for my liking."

I consider what Swain is telling me as he draws another sip of his beer. There is still one underlying issue he is not addressing. "But there was no intent. How can you charge Jayron with terrorism if there was no intent to commit a terrorist act?"

He favors me a sideways grin. "I never said I expected him to be convicted of it. The idea being to spook him enough to spill the beans on who is producing the pipe bombs for him.

So far, he's been closed-lipped about the person I really want to charge.

"I'm concerned. If he doesn't tell us soon, one or both of them will accidentally blow themselves up—or worse, unintentionally blow up the dam or some fellow anglers. There's nothing you or I can do for the boy if he ever accidentally creates a disaster or hurts someone. Once that rock starts rolling, it only picks up speed regardless of the Freeman boy's intent."

I recognize there is truth to what the warden is saying. I must admit I appreciate his approach of trying to keep everyone safe.

"You have a theory on who the bomb maker is." I frame the question as a statement on purpose.

Swain drains the last of his first beer and smiles. "I'm not much into theories. I do know for a fact it's his brother, Kenny."

I already have this information firsthand. Still, it startles me that he has such a level of certainty when Dorsett is still pressing Jayron for the bomb maker's name. "Really? What makes you so certain it's his brother?"

"Those two have been thicker than thieves their entire life. Kenny is smart as a whip, has a real knack for physics and chemistry. Jayron—well, you spoke with him. Let's just say he doesn't have the same talent.

"What Jayron does have is an unquestioning belief in his older brother Kenny and a lot of white-boy crazy." Swain scrubs a hand across his gray stubbled chin. "The list is long and varied, including stuff like impossible bicycle jumps and brownies that would give you continuous gas for twelve hours."

I can't help myself. "Why would you want gas for twelve hours?"

Swain laughs as he holds an imaginary lighter to his backside, toggling his thumb up and down. "So, you can light green fireballs out your butt."

I do an internal eye roll as I think of my brothers. The stupidity they will concoct to amuse themselves is boundless.

"The most recent was, I ran into the two of them after they had stolen a WaveRunner from the Adams family out of Birmingham. They only make it up to the lake a couple weeks during the summer. Long story short, Kenny souped up the WaveRunner, and I see Jayron blurring across the lake at what I guesstimate to be ninety knots."

"No way!" I interject.

Swain's eyebrows shoot up. "True story."

"I'm calling bull. That's over a hundred miles an hour. There's not one that goes that fast, and if it could, you couldn't hold on to it."

"That's what I knew." Swain removes his hat and scratches his gray flattop. "Until I saw that stolen WaveRunner flying down the channel with a skinny boy hugging it like a rocket.

"I never would have caught him if he hadn't ran out of gas."

"But I thought they are poor. Where would the brothers have gotten the tools and equipment for the improvements?"

"Poor, but resourceful. Kenny has a natural curiosity and aptitude. If it were funneled correctly, there is no telling what he could accomplish. Jayron? That boy is crazy fearless. He does not know the meaning of the phrase 'can't be done.'"

"But I don't understand. If you know the bomb maker is Kenny, why don't you just pull him in? It sounds as if you could convince him of the danger."

Wayne drains his second beer, pulls out a ten-dollar bill, and sets it under one of the empty bottles. "Ms. Snow, I think it'll come to you once you talk with Kenny. I'm assuming that is who you'll be wanting to speak to next."

I nod my head in affirmation.

"You'll understand better once you talk to him. To answer your initial question, I charged Jayron with terrorism in hopes it would convince him to pull Kenny into it, so I can have this discussion with him.

"I know it is Kenny. It's simple reasoning. But I can't prove it, and one thing about those two boys, they'll be loyal to each other until death.

"It's my own fool's errand, but I had to try something." He shrugs. "Who knows. Maybe you talking to Kenny will be enough to make him stop."

He pauses, seemingly lost in his thoughts about the Free-man boys.

"I appreciate you taking the time to meet with me, Ranger Swain."

He glances back to me. "Wayne. Call me Wayne now that we've shared a beer together—well, beer and water."

"Thank you, Wayne."

"The pleasure has been mine." He winks at me and slides off his bar stool. "I wish you the best of luck with the case, Ms. April. I'll be rooting for you."

He tips his cap to me before leaving me to my thoughts.

This has been one of those days where I know everybody is trying to tell me something, but they won't just come out and say it. Like they want me to guess it. Read between the lines. Yeah, I hate that game.

One thing is true. The answers to my questions lie with Kenny. Like the game warden suggested, he will be my next stop.

Chapter 6

The Freemans' plot is five miles out of Guntersville on the south side. Property on the south side is more "rocky mountain" than actual "land." For this reason, it was some of the last pieces of property claimed by the early settlers.

Nowadays, you see an occasional random Mac-mansion stuck up on the mountain with a three-thousand-foot gravel driveway. Still, for the most part, people with small means live out this way.

The tall cedars shade the crumbling blacktop as the sun has begun its descent to the horizon. The day has passed quicker than I realized.

I am clueless about what I want to ask Marcy Freeman or her eldest son, Kenny, when I arrive at their property. Mama tells me I tend to lean on my improv skills too often. I believe I'm just one of those people who works better under pressure.

Coming around a tight corner, I nearly miss the turnoff to Spencer Lane. I take a right onto the heavily pocked county road and avoid the largest of the potholes. My IROC's stiff suspension complains with every bump I manage to hit.

A hail-battered single wide sits on a half-acre clearing to my right. I double-check the address on the mailbox and turn onto the hardpacked dirt leading to the trailer.

I step out of my car and take in my surroundings.

It's tranquil. I can't hear the traffic from the state highway this far off the road. On the positive, as secluded as they are, they must be able to see every constellation at night.

On the negative, their housing speaks to the desperate situation of their family finances. The home is little more than an oversized aluminum soda can that has been kicked down the road a few too many times.

My car is the only vehicle in the drive. I wasted my time by not calling first.

Still, the odd sensation of being watched that hit me the moment I turned onto Spencer Lane continues. I swallow hard as the alarms begin to go off in my mind.

Foolish, foolish girl for having come out here by myself. I should have brought Jacob or one of my brothers.

I debate whether I should knock on the trailer door since I've already made the trip, or if I should get back in my car and leave.

Standing with my hand on my car door, I make a note of the well-tended vegetable garden to the right. The half-acre field is filled with vibrant pole beans climbing bamboo canes, tomato plants supported by intricate latticework still bearing fruit, a late crop of corn taller than me, and a few pumpkins creeping along the corners of the plot. Along the back edge are the most enormous, beautiful sunflowers I believe I have ever seen.

As impressive as the vegetation is, that is not what draws my continued attention to the garden. The figures standing eight feet tall in the field are what have caught my interest.

"What in tarnation?" I whisper as I walk toward the garden.

At each corner of the plot, a mannequin is mounted on a post. Their arms are outstretched with an American flag in either hand. In the center of the garden are two mannequins two feet apart, each holding a metal rod in their hand.

The words of Warden Swain ring in my head. "Poor, but resourceful." I wonder if resourceful in this instance meant the mannequins were stolen or if they were scavenged out of an old dumpster.

Walking closer to the garden, I'm able to identify each of the four corner mannequins as female versions, dressed in bikinis and old wigs. The mannequins in the center are male and are only wearing shorts.

Not the oddest thing I've ever seen, but it qualifies for an honorable mention.

From the appearance of the garden, the fancy scarecrows must be working out well for the Freemans. I've seen gardens with three-foot fences around them with more damaged vegetation.

I notice three runs of okra in front of the sunflowers. Man, there is nothing better than fresh okra. It's tasty baked, irresistible fried, and vegetable soup isn't complete without okra. Not to mention the purple flowers are as beautiful as the vegetable is delicious.

A loud click echoes through the crisp air.

I catch a flash of color moving in my peripheral vision and swing to my left as I watch one of the mannequins twirl in a three-sixty. "What the devil!"

Stepping back, my heel hits a rock. I catch myself, and a loud clang of metal rings through the air. My knees instinctively buckle.

I end up on all fours. Jagged rock bites into my knees and palms.

What the heck was that?

Standing to a crouch, I move to the garden and squat between two tomato plants. I struggle to calm my nerves.

The laugh, so faint it's difficult to decipher if I'm imagining it or if it may even be from the other side of the veil, comes from the sunflowers. The laughter grows in volume, and I most certainly am not imagining it.

Standing, I brush gravel off my knees and hands before peering over the top of the tomato plants. I'm surprised to see a handsome young man grinning at me, his dark complexion accentuating his smile.

He holds up a hand toward me. "Sorry, lady. I don't mean to

be laughing at you." He claps his hands together as he sways his shoulders. "But that was epic timing. I wish I had a video of you. We'd get a million hits off it."

I'm not nearly as amused as he is. "You did that?"

"Nah. Well, yeah." The young man gestures toward the mannequins. "I mean, I set them up. But they're on a chain and a timer. Every thirty minutes, they do a three-sixty. The *perfect timing*, that was all you, lady."

It dawns on me. "You're Kenny."

He offers a lopsided grin as his eyes narrow. "Maybe. Who are you?"

"I'm Jayron's attorney."

I can see the levity drain from his face. "Attorney? What does he need an attorney for?"

"You haven't seen him today?" I ask.

"I saw him. I cooked us breakfast this morning." Kenny crosses his arms.

"But you haven't seen him since?"

"No. He took the boat and the truck to go catfishing today." He steps back and waves his hand in the air. "Why am I talking to you anyway. I don't know you."

"Why didn't you go with him today? Do you not like to fish?"

"I like to fish." He shakes his head and points toward my car. "I don't know what your game is, lady, but I think it best you get off my property now."

I consider pushing out and reading Kenny. I can't tell if he is deceptively obtuse. Or if Jayron didn't inform Kenny of his plan to drop a bunch of depth charges into Guntersville Lake in hopes of scoring a catfish dinner. I decide it is best to ask him point-blank about the bombs.

A car approaches up their driveway before I can ask him. I look over my shoulder as an exhausted-looking lady in her early forties gets out of the passenger side and waves goodbye to the driver.

"Hey, Mom. This lady says she's Jayron's lawyer," Kenny says as he looks to his mother before shooting me another suspicious glare.

The woman's face contorts as if she has been punched in the gut. "Are you serious?"

"Yes, ma'am. I'm April Snow."

She exhales loudly as her shoulders droop. "What's that boy done now?"

I consider if there is any gentler way for me to break it to her. There's not, so I decide to tell her the facts. "Jayron was caught setting off explosive devices close to the dam."

Marcy's eyes widen. She stomps over to Kenny and slaps him on the shoulder. She wags an accusatory finger at him as she yells, "I told you to quit making those!"

Kenny shakes his head vigorously. "I haven't made any more. I stopped when you told me to. Honest, Mom."

"Then where did he get them? Tell me that, Kenny."

Kenny shoves his hands in his pockets. "I mean, I had extras. But I told him I didn't want him messing with them. Not by himself, at least."

"You know he's not going to let you set them off with him. He's worried about your school."

Kenny yanks his hands out of his pockets and shakes them in the air. "I don't know how I'm supposed to keep up with him, Mom."

"That's rich, Kenny. How about you don't make that stuff to begin with. *You* know better." She sets her face and simmers at the young man.

"Sorry, Mom. It seemed like a good idea at the time." Kenny directs his attention back to me. "He didn't get hurt or nothing, did he?"

"No, fortunately, nobody got hurt. But he was setting the explosions off close to the dam and the game warden charged him with terrorism."

Marcy emits a whimper. "Terrorism? My sons don't know nothing about terrorism."

"Maybe not, but Jayron's case will have to be settled in court now," I say.

An eerie quiet falls between the three of us. I can hear birds in the trees behind the trailer and the last of the few remaining cicadas. Marcy and Kenny are deep in their own thoughts.

The more I know about this case, the more I realize this case just bites. I understand why Wayne charged Jayron with terrorism. I mean, he did give the boy four strikes. As the warden said, it is only a matter of time before Jayron makes a mistake and either hurts himself or some innocent bystander.

It would be easy to blame Kenny for having made the bombs. But I get the feeling to him it was just a useful science project.

Are you inherently evil because you created an explosive device, or do you have to have a specific malicious intent for the bombs to make it evil? I'm not sure of my position on that argument. I would prefer not to be involved since it seems like more of a philosophical question that would require entirely too much brain energy.

Regardless, I have a significant conundrum. I have a single mother of two, struggling to feed and take care of her sons at the core. One son is too smart for his own good. If he turns himself in, it will ruin his ability to possibly pull the family out of its destitute financial status. While having the admirable qualities of loyalty and fearlessness, the second son constantly toys with Darwin's selection model. He may ultimately remove himself from the gene pool.

In short, this family doesn't need the problem of a court case in their life.

Heck, with the Halloween party coming up Friday, I don't need it in my life, either.

"Can you get him out?" Marcy whispers.

"I'm certainly going to try." I direct a pointed stare at Kenny. "But to what end? At the rate these two are going, he'll end up maiming or killing himself pretty soon, or worse, accidentally killing somebody else."

"It's not his fault. I'm the one who made them," Kenny says. "Will they let us swap places?"

"Kenny, your school!" Marcy scolds.

"It's not right he's in jail for something I made."

Wayne was right. Nobody would ever be able to identify the Freeman half-brothers as related without knowing them. But there is no mistaking the brotherly bond between them. They are singularly devoted to one another.

I shake my head. "No. Let's not do that just yet. I'm afraid all that would do is land both of you in jail. A couple of nights in prison for Jayron might be good anyway. It might convince him that what he's doing is dangerous.

"I'll try to work with the DA and the warden to see if there is a compromise we can come up with."

I point my finger at Kenny. "If you have any additional explosives around, I think you know what you should be doing with them."

Kenny diverts his gaze to the ground. "Yes, ma'am. I'm on it."

Marcy is on the verge of tears. "That boy hasn't got a mean bone in his body. You have to get him out."

Her concern for her son causes my tear ducts to sting. I have to open my eyelids wider to keep tears from escaping.

She is right, though. Jayron is just a sweet, loyal boy.

But rules are rules. This case will require all my negotiation skills to get Lane to back down without some concrete assurances Jayron's "grenadier" days are finished.

I tell the Freemans goodbye. Getting back into my car, I notice the sun has dipped below the cedars and gnarled pines that populate the land.

Dodging as many potholes as I can, I travel down Spencer Lane and take a left onto the state highway. I'm headed back toward the lake in the dark.

The dark is apropos. That's where I am with Jayron's case, as I have no idea how I will convince Lane to drop the charges. But I need to come up with something fast.

Chapter 7

There are no streetlights on the route from the Freemans' home. Sure, it's still part of the city, but the politicians know the constituents out here don't always vote, and they don't have the resources to contribute to campaigns.

My high beams act like giant searchlights creating two coned beams slicing through the encroaching darkness. The faded yellow line to my right is often invisible, as the asphalt it was painted on has long since crumbled and slid down the mountainside.

I tap my brakes as I must steer left quickly to miss an opossum.

I've never understood why horror movies have to work so hard to make gruesome monsters. Stand an opossum up on its hind legs, make it six feet tall, and everybody who sees that movie will never sleep again.

Granny swears they're helpful creatures. That's cool, but that factoid still doesn't make them cute.

As I make the last few turns bringing me safely out of the woods and into view of the lake, my right headlight reflects off something green. The green object bounces off the pavement and kicks up into the air. It comes directly toward my windshield so quickly all I can do is stand on my brakes and raise my right forearm to protect my face.

I slide forward, the seatbelt biting into my chest. My head jerks forward as my left arm folds against the steering wheel from the momentum going from fifty miles per hour to zero in a second.

The shatter of the windshield never comes. I lower my right arm and nearly pee myself. There is a female head sitting on my dashboard.

I'm doing really well, though. I'm not hyperventilating, and I haven't screamed—yet.

When the bodiless head's eyelids fly open and its lower jaw unhinges to allow the release of a bloodcurdling scream, my heart and my ability to breathe cease to function. My eyes mimic the screaming head. My mouth is fixed open enough for an apple to be inserted without touching my teeth. I am, however, still sans the scream.

I struggle to regain my breath. My chest hurts as if a three-hundred-pound man just tap danced on it.

Catching my breath, I feel the anger working its way up in me. If somebody had been behind me, I could've been seriously hurt. What if my foot had missed the brake pedal? I could've ended up in the trees.

"What do you want?" I scream.

In response, the head lets out another bloodcurdling scream. I'll be surprised if my eardrums don't bleed.

"Tell me what you want or leave me alone!"

The glazed eyes of the head roll back until only a milky white color remains. The head punctuates this trick with a third scream that forces me to cover my ears.

Occasionally, I become frustrated enough to do something totally illogical. Something that makes no sense, but the very act of doing it just makes me feel better. That's where I am. I break.

The head on my dashboard is screaming at me. Leaning forward, I mimic the scream mere inches from its nose. The cacophony of screeches emanating from my car must sound like twenty people being butchered.

The squeal of tires is so close it penetrates the sound of our dual screaming.

Brights flash in my rearview mirror, and I look up to see the grille of a Dodge truck inches from the back of my car.

"See what you almost—" The head is gone.

It would've been better if I had seen it disappear. But the way it is no longer on my dashboard after I was screaming at it ... Well, let's just say when you deal with the spirit world, you have to sometimes wonder if you are interacting with the paranormal or if you might just be *nuckin' futs*.

Being honest with myself, I feel a little crazy right now.

The Dodge truck lays on its horn.

"All right already. I'm just having a moment here." I wave in the rearview mirror and restart my car that had died with the sudden stop.

It would be so much easier if the spirit would just tell me what it wants.

Chapter 8

It's eight o'clock when I pull up my parents' drive. This part-time gig with my uncle has somehow turned into a sixty-hour-a-week commitment.

Good for the pocketbook. Havoc on the social life and mental well-being.

I'm thankful Howard never has a problem paying for the overtime. It has made paying my insane student loan bills much easier than I ever imagined when I first moved back home.

Still, it's a good thing I have curtailed my job searches. Twelve-hour Mondays are not conducive for planning and securing your next professional move.

Howard's decision to buy into Pizza King is sitting at the back of my mind, needling me. Personally, I feel he is betting on a dog that won't hunt. But that's between him and Colonel Sullivan to work out.

The fact he plans to close the law office *does* weigh on me. It's silly for me to worry about the implications for Guntersville. It's not my issue. I'm just passing through.

I can't believe he doesn't see how much his small practice means to his community. The cases we've covered in the past few months play through my mind. I think of all the people who wouldn't have been helped. Locals would have had to wait longer for their trial because the public defenders are overwhelmed. Worse, their attorneys may have been forced to move ahead with poorly prepared and inadequate representation.

For the other services, divorces, wills, and suits, the clients would have to travel to Huntsville for representation. That wouldn't be an insurmountable obstacle for many. However, it's still different from being able to swing into town and handle your business the same day with someone you know and trust.

I don't feel he realizes how much this community has come to depend on him and how connected he is to everyone. Ultimately, it's his decision, and he must do what he thinks will make him the happiest. Still, it is incredibly sad to see how much affection this town has for him, and he can't see the love right in front of his face.

Oh well. I suppose some folks are just blind to their blessings. What are you going to do?

Man, it feels good to be home. I'm ready to put today behind me.

I see flames on the back patio of my parents' home. I squint my eyes, attempting to identify the silhouettes.

There is a cookout party going on at our home. I see Mama, Daddy, Granny Snow, and my twin brothers.

I suppose it would have been too much bother to invite me.

Briefly, I consider skulking off to my room and pouting. I would, but somehow my meatloaf lunch has finally dissipated, and I'm hungry again. The unmistakable smell of seasoned sirloin steaks grilling on the charcoal wafts to me on a cool breeze.

Bless it. I'm going to have to crash dinner and see if they have an extra plate. Besides, if I were to guess, my roommate is on the patio. He never misses a party or a free meal.

My roommate is a forty-pound Keeshond that answers to Puppy. He also responds to Bear, Fang, and Fabio.

If you have a treat in your hand, he'll answer to Sue, Carol, or any other name you care to try. He pretty much always gets what he wants. Everybody loves him, and he doesn't worry about what other people think.

Some days, I wish I could emulate my dog.

My brother Dusty notices me in the shadows first. "April." His round, full face breaks into a toothy smile as the red beard under his chin shifts. "There's still a couple of baked potatoes in the oven if you're hungry."

Chase is working the grill. "I got the last steak cooking here for you. You want it medium?"

"Medium rare," I say.

"Whoops." Chase grabs the sirloin steak off the grill with his tongs. "Then we're done. Hurry up with your potato."

I pull back the glass door and walk into the kitchen without talking to anybody else. Suddenly I feel grouchy. I'm not sure if it is because of my brothers telling me what to do or that they're all so happy.

My mood swing could also be a delayed response from seeing the head of a woman on my dashboard. It certainly made me worry that I might have put a toe across the insanity line when I began screaming at it.

Nah. The divine scent of the sirloin triggered the gnawing badger in my gut, and my mouth is watering. I'm just hangry.

I open the oven and marvel at the three large baked potatoes. They are magnificent. I select the largest and drop it on an empty plate someone left for me on the kitchen island a second before the heat would have left blisters on my hand.

As I work the butter and sour cream into the potato, I hear a most peculiar noise.

Stopping, I listen intently. It is consistent with sort of a mechanical sound to it. There is a wheezing sound, like air pulled through a pressure line followed by *chug, chug, chug*. It sounds like—pistons. What in the kitchen has a piston?

I follow the sound toward the second refrigerator. There is a piston in the compressor—but that is more of an electrical whine. Not the noise I am hearing.

The noise grows in volume. I put my ear to the spare fridge. No, that isn't it.

Crouching over, I continue toward the sound and find the source. Puppy has wedged himself between the refrigerator and the full-length picture window. He lays on his back, all four paws in the air with sour cream on the tip of his nose.

The wheeze-and-chug sound is his puppy snores.

Puppy can drop and take a nap at the snap of a finger. Something else I wish I could emulate.

Walking out with my plate, I immediately interrogate my brothers. "What did you do to my puppy?"

Chase shrugs his shoulders. "Half a baked potato and a few bites of steak is all."

Idiot. "That's way too much for him."

Chase places my steak onto my plate. "He didn't seem to think so."

"You're the adult here, Chase."

"If that's the case, we're all in trouble," Dusty says as he holds a marshmallow over the fire.

I realize it's not sour cream on Puppy's nose. "Dusty, have you been giving him marshmallows?"

Dusty points to his chest. "Me? I haven't given him anything tonight."

"Then how did he get marshmallow on his nose?" I ask.

Dusty attempts to pull the marshmallow off his stick, but it is too hot. He blows on it instead. "You'll have to talk to Pops about that."

"Daddy!"

The façade my daddy is attempting to hold on his face cracks. He laughs. "That's the marshmallow eatin'est dog I've ever seen."

"You are going to kill him."

Dusty raises a finger to his lips. "Shhh … calm down." He pats the patio chair next to him. "Come sit down next to me and enjoy your meal."

I can feel my lower lip pouting out as I shuffle over to sit next to my brother. "Y'all are going to give him diabetes or something."

Dusty sighs. "Tink, that dog is tougher than all of us put together. I wouldn't be surprised if he outlives us all."

"I'm just pleased to see how well you two have bonded," Granny comments.

I don't know if I'd call it bonding. I'm sure Granny wants to see it that way since my furry rebel was a gift from her.

I was only home a month when, in her infinite wisdom, she thought it essential I have something besides a career search, two part-time jobs, and massive student loans to worry about. In her judgment, a puppy was the perfect solution.

The funny thing is if she wanted me to take care of something, she picked the wrong dog. Puppy is about the most independent, self-sufficient dog I have ever known. I'm positive in Puppy's previous lives, he was a world-famous actor and a special forces soldier.

"Honey, do you think you'll be able to get off early Friday to help me with the last of the decorations and the snacks?" Mama asks.

"I think so. I'll have to touch base with Howard in the morning."

Mama nods her head, returning her gaze to the fire pit.

I can feel the electrical charge in the air, and the scent of ozone wafts toward me. I sometimes have the same sensation and scent when I train with Nana, and we exert energy using our "gifts."

Interesting.

I'm only tired. I'm sure I only imagined the smell.

When our patio party ends at ten, I hug Granny goodbye, wake up Puppy, and walk to my apartment above the boat dock. I open the door and take in the yellow paint and matching bedspread.

I broke down a month ago and finally painted the walls of my apartment. Mama had been trying to get me to do it since I moved back home in June.

I resisted her desires. My thought process being I didn't want to get too comfortable living at home. I viewed painting the walls as a form of nesting.

I guess I'm officially nesting.

Eventually, I will find the perfect position to kick off my professional career. I have no doubt of that.

Interviews have not been difficult to come by the past five months. Suitable job offers have.

I have cobbled together a respectable income. I earn good money between Snow and Associates, the weekend opportunities with Dusty's paranormal research team, and the line editing I now do for him. Coupled with a rent-free bachelorette pad and an occasional free dinner—did I mention I had steak and potato tonight?—those fringe benefits make it seem like the firms are lowballing me.

Call me snotty, but I don't feel I should have to cut my lifestyle to work for a big-city law firm. I mean, you go and work for the big-city law firms so you can make more significant money. Not smaller money. Right?

Another recent development, once I move away from Guntersville, I'll be too far to get training from Nana. Sure, it's freaky weird, but I have begun to enjoy our Thursday nights.

Something dramatic has changed in the "gifts" arena over the last three months. No, I still am not particularly good at controlling them, but the training has been like cutting a hole in a sandbag. The first time I used my powers, they opened up a blockage in my mind. Every day with each exercise that I use my abilities, regardless of how small the activity, more of the blockage erodes, making the power more intense and readily available.

Last month, much to Nana's surprise, I developed a version of telekinesis. It's nothing major, I can't move anything heavy with my mind, but it is incredible.

Nana was less than pleased with the development. She kept muttering that it wasn't possible. I don't consider it particularly shocking, given that *nothing* about my "gifts" would be regarded as usual.

With the increase in power and speed of regeneration, Nana had explicitly forbidden me from using my "gifts" except for a few minor exercises which focus on the control of the "gifts."

I practice the three basic controls she gave me over and over. The first is rolling a pencil six inches forward and back. In the second exercise, I flip a playing card face up, then face down.

Third, my favorite, which deals with the realm Nana is comfortable with and the most difficult to control is creating a tiny spark by snapping my finger. I can only do this with my right hand since I never learned how to snap my fingers with my left hand. On a good day, the spark will be a flame the size of a lit match head. After months of practice, I can float the flame from my fingers to the palm of my right hand.

I can do more. Lots more. I can feel it.

But I'm in agreement with Nana. It is far more critical to learn control first. Safety is more important than showing off.

I sit down at my kitchenette and start practicing the card flip. I'll practice for fifteen minutes and then go to bed early. I really am exhausted.

As I continue to flip the card back and forth, my mind wanders to the young man I met this afternoon. Kenny and I share something. We share a hidden talent. A powerful hidden talent.

When people look at me, I feel they only see a privileged white girl working as a lawyer. When they look at Kenny, they see an intelligent poor kid hoping to earn his way through college with scholarships.

But there is so much more under our shells.

There it is. That's what I need to talk to Kenny about.

Learning to control his gift and channel it. Not unlike how I am learning to control my magic.

He must learn how to direct and control his intellectual curiosity. Channel it to the good and not the destructive.

As one of my best friends, Liza, puts it, "The greater the power, the greater the pull to the dark side." For that reason, people with the most potent gifts must remain vigilant that they are using them for good.

Chapter 9

The weather is excellent Tuesday morning. I take the T-tops off my Z-28, roll up the windows, and cruise into town. Rested and refreshed with a new plan, I feel like a hot chick in a tough ride.

My euphoria crashes as I pull up to Snow and Associates.

The Gadsden Channel Thirteen News van parked outside with the satellite dish on top makes my upper lip curl. I spot Chuck Grassley setting up his camera next to our front entrance, causing me to puke a little bit in my mouth.

Chuck Grassley is a misogynistic fifty-something-year-old news reporter for the Gadsden channel with dyed hair and too many Botox treatments. Chuck, in my book, personifies slimy.

I park my car and don't bother taking the time to put the T-tops back on, opting to go directly into the office before Chuck can talk to me.

"Ms. Snow." I feel the hair on the back of my neck stand up. "Is it true you are defending Jayron Freeman, a known jihad terrorist?"

I know what I should do, but I just can't bring myself to do it. I should ignore Chuck and go on into our office. I have nothing, zero, nada, to gain by saying anything to Chuck, much less poking the bear by countering his stupidity.

Daddy always says, if you argue with a stupid person, you just end up looking foolish.

Nevertheless, I turn on Chuck and ask, "Known by whom, Chuck?"

Chuck's eyebrows, dyed an odd shade of brown, rise into his hair combed forward to cover his receding hairline. Recovering, he leans in like a starving wolf eyeing a porterhouse steak. "Our sources are telling us that Jayron is a jihad terrorist. Do you deny that?"

"Chuck, where do you even get this? What sources? Who told you?"

"Anonymous sources." He shoves the microphone so close if I didn't lean back, he would have busted my lip.

"So, you basically made that up, Chuck."

He is undeterred. "Do you deny it, Ms. Snow? Yes or no?"

I wave my right hand at him while I open the door with my left. "Bye-bye, Chuck."

"April?"

"It's me, Howard." I stomp to my desk and shove my purse in the bottom drawer.

"Your special admirer is back outside."

I plop onto my chair. "Yeah, I saw him. We had the most stimulating conversation."

"Did you give him a kiss afterward?"

"I told him he could kiss my butt."

I hear Howard laugh. It makes me grin. "You should be more careful with what you say. That pervert would take you up on it, April."

That's sound advice. I should remember it.

"Lane texted me last night. He has another case for you."

My shoulders droop. "I'm already working overtime on the Freeman case."

"You can handle it. I've got faith in you. I'm emailing you the client's name now."

I open the email. Nina Rodriguez? No, I don't know her. She is charged with filing a false report. "I've got it."

"Good, I'll be on these contracts for your mama the rest of the day. Thank you for handling it. You're a rock star."

Funny, I don't feel like one. "You're welcome."

I dial the number for Nina.

"Hello?"

"Nina Rodriguez?"

"Yes." Her voice is full of suspicion.

"April Snow of Snow and Associates. I have been assigned to your case."

I hear a derisive breath of air. "This is all just a big misunderstanding. I done told that deputy that."

"I understand. All the same, we will have to prepare for a hearing to clear it all up."

"A hearing? I don't want a hearing."

None of us ever *want* a hearing. Hearings are sort of court-ordered. "I understand, but we have to show up and give your side of the events to get the case thrown out."

"This is some sort of BS. I'm just minding my own business trying to get by, and when someone robs my place, I'm the one who ends up having to go to court. They ought to be out trying to find my stuff."

Oh boy. I've got a live one. "Ms. Rodriguez? If you don't mind, we need to set a time to meet."

There's silence on the other end of the line. Then a huff. "I don't know. I'm busy this week."

"Your court date is Thursday. I need you to make time for me today or tomorrow."

"I'm not sure I can work that into my schedule."

I want to bang my head on my desk. "Ms. Rodriguez, you do understand that I am your lawyer. I am on your side, but if you don't help me—well, I can't help you, now can I? I just need you to meet with me and give me your side of the story. I want us to be prepared on Thursday. Okay?"

"This is all stupid."

"Ms. Rodriguez." The last of my patience slips away. "Would you prefer to represent yourself?"

"Fine. You don't have to be so stuck-up about it. How about eight tomorrow morning at Tubs of Suds?"

The laundromat? "Alright. I will see you tomorrow."

I hit the red button on my phone. "Thank you!" I holler at my uncle in the most sarcastic tone I can manage.

"You're welcome," he replies.

Chapter 10

By five, I've completed several projects that had dragged out for the last week. It is incredible how much you can get done in a day when there are no phone calls or visitors.

It doesn't happen often. I'm thankful as it allowed me to wipe the board clean for tomorrow. I'll be out of the office all day to collect information on Nina's case while contemplating how to approach Lane about the Freeman case.

I poke my head into Howard's office. He's still working on Mama's contracts. "Hey, I was about to leave. Do you need any help?"

He looks up and smiles. "No. I'm good."

"I meant to ask you earlier. Can I have the second half of Friday off? Mama has sort of recruited me for the decorating squad."

Howard gives a quick snort. "I know better than to interfere with Viv's plans."

I nod in agreement and start to leave. I stop. "Do you have time for another quick question?"

"Shoot."

"This Freeman case. What do you think I should do?"

"See what sort of a deal Lane will cut with you. The boy did it, didn't he?"

"Yes. But…" I'm not sure how to explain the situation. It's

complicated.

"But what?"

"Wayne Swain is dead set on smoking out the older brother. He thinks that's who made the bombs. But Jayron keeps telling the warden that he made them."

"Jayron's not missing any limbs, so we know he didn't make them."

That's an astute observation by my uncle.

"Still, Swain doesn't know much about brothers if he thinks Jayron is going to rat Kenny out."

"That's just it. Kenny admitted it to me and even asked if he could swap places with Jayron."

Howard leans back in his chair and sighs. "That's an awful idea."

I flap my hands at my side in frustration. "So, what am I supposed to do?"

"Your job, April. That's what we do."

That isn't helpful. Not one bit. I give my uncle a confirming nod and turn to leave. "Good night."

"Good night, April."

When I open the door, I'm relieved to see Chuck Grassley is no longer in front of our law office. The last thing I need to do is rebuff an overly aggressive reporter.

It is my favorite time of year. I am in an uber-cool car and witnessing the beginning of a spectacular sunset.

I'm in a melancholy mood and can enjoy none of it.

I desperately need to talk to someone. I pick up my phone and dial Mama.

"Lake View properties, Vivian speaking."

"Mama?"

"Hi, April. What's up?"

"Nothing, I was just checking in with you."

"Well, thank you, baby. But listen, I have an agent class starting in a few minutes. Can I call you back?"

The perceived rejection cuts hard. "Yes, ma'am. I'll just catch you at home."

"That's an excellent idea. Okay. I'll see you tonight, baby."

"Yes, ma'am."

Great. I can go to the house and see if my brothers or my daddy are available. But for some reason, I feel like I need a female voice.

That leaves my grandmothers. I could call Nana. But I'll be visiting her Thursday, and I don't want to over-impose on her.

I saw Granny just last night, but we didn't get to have one-on-one bonding time. I'll head out to her place and visit with her for a while. My brothers claim they drop in on her all the time.

I get in my car, and my phone rings. When I took at the name on my screen, I nearly drop the phone.

Why I would be amazed that it's Granny calling, I have no idea. Both my grandmothers have uncanny phone habits when it comes to me. Granny is a firm believer that you can manifest things through meditation and prayer. Given that, I'm sure she would believe in the phenomenon of "talking someone up."

"Hi, Granny. What are you up to?"

"Hi, April. I'm heading over to Truncated Journeys and wanted to know if my favorite granddaughter wanted to go with."

Yeah, I obviously talked her up. Granny knows I abhor junking, and if she called, she had gotten a sense that I needed to talk to her. "Sure, what time were you planning on going over there."

"Well, now if you can. I heard Faith and Chelsie got in a new purchase from the freight line."

What the heck. Sometimes having someone to talk to comes at a steep price. "Sure. I was leaving the law firm now. I'll meet you over there in ten minutes."

"Oh, that's wonderful, sweetie. See you soon."

Guntersville has more junk stores than eating establishments. This makes it attractive to specific markets of tourists. Still, for young residents like myself, it doesn't hold any particular attraction.

I enjoy finding a bargain as much as the next person. But as a rule, I have found most of the junk stores are just that. Junk.

Faith Ray and Chelsie McDermont opened Truncated Journeys right about the time I left for Tuscaloosa. They located the business in the abandoned Rock Elementary School on the north side of town. It's a little out of the way compared to most of the junk stores, but from what I understand, they got the entire school for a favorable lease. This has allowed them to open up consignment stalls for locals who believe they will become millionaires by selling their junk to unsuspecting summer tourists.

As far as I know, no one has retired as a millionaire yet. But they're still trying.

I pull into the lot of the old school and see the silhouette of Granny's helmet hairdo in a large 4x4 pickup truck. I park next to her vehicle, and she waves excitedly at me as she climbs down from the driver's seat.

"You ever thought about getting a car, Granny?"

"I like riding high up. That way, I can see in everybody's car."

There is the nosey factor to consider.

She gives me a quick hug. "I'm glad you decided to go shopping with me."

"Well, I can't let you have all the fun, now can I?"

A knowing smile creeps across her face. "It's sweet of you to indulge me."

Funny thing, I can feel the angst and anxiety knotted up in my body from only an hour earlier dissipate. It's odd how certain people cause physiological changes in my body. Like when I'm around Lane and Nana and sometimes Mama, I feel my stress level creeping up to a fevered pitch. Like I have to *do* better.

When I'm with my brothers, Daddy, or Granny, all the muscles in my body loosen, and I'm at complete ease. Like they are Valium to my soul.

Then how when I'm around Jacob, well let's just let that be. That's sort of messed up, being we're childhood friends, and I don't have a handle on it yet.

I open the door for Granny as she tucks her checkbook into her purse.

"I have been looking for a travel trunk to put in my living room," she explains passionately. "I saw a photo in the *Southern Housing* magazine and absolutely love the look."

"From when, 1990?" I freeze.

She narrows her eyes at me.

Yep. I said that thought out loud.

Granny purses her lips as she stretches her neck like a peacock while giving me the "shut your mouth" look that I'm sure she mastered as a young mother. "It was 1997, if you must know."

Better late than never, I suppose. "Just tell me you're not going to use it for a coffee table."

"Fine. Then I'll spare you the details."

Dang. Do I know my granny or what?

One of the advantages for Faith and Chelsie of owning the store is having the entire front foyer to themselves. As we enter Truncated Journeys, we are greeted by over a hundred old traveling trunks. At least half of them scream "knock-offs." Undoubtedly, cheap imitation copies of the real thing imported from third-world countries. But many look heavy enough and sufficiently scarred to be the real McCoy.

Personally, I like new stuff. Stuff other people haven't used, and that doesn't look like it's been beaten to death and discarded for me to pick up and try to use.

Yes, I know. On some things, I am an elitist. Sue me.

I watch as Granny hurries through her inventory inspection before she lifts her hands and lets them fall to her side. "Where's the new?"

I take by the word "new" she means different old stuff. "You said they just got in a shipment. Maybe they haven't set it up for display yet."

"Well, bother." She places her hands on her hips and looks side to side as her lips narrow. "Where is everybody?"

I gesture toward the back of the old school. "If we walk back there, I'm sure we'll find them."

Granny's spirit cheers. "You're right. We might as well see what everybody else has here on consignment while we're here."

She tears off down the hallway to the left. I have to double-time it to catch up with her. It's incredible how fast she can travel on her short legs when she's on a mission.

The rest of the building is laid out in narrow hallways filled with small kiosks and large suites, which were once class-rooms. One of the suites has old metal signs and inexpensive framed posters of famous works of art.

I contemplate the purchase of a faded print of the *Boulevard of Broken Dreams* diner painting. I wish Gottfried Helnwein would do an updated version with Paul Walker, Brittany Murphy, and Heath Ledger. I'd buy that one in a heartbeat.

"That would look good in your room," Granny says at my side.

"You think?"

"Sure. Do you have anything else on the walls yet?"

Besides a fresh coat of paint, the answer to that question is a simple no. I get a lump in my throat. For some reason, it's hard for me to verbalize. It's an admission to how transient my life remains.

Great, now I can start feeling sorry for myself again.

"Not yet, Granny. I want to wait until I get settled in. You know. To make sure everything has a spot?"

Granny tilts her head. "How long do you need to get settled in before a place is a home?"

I laugh. "I meant wherever I finally end up. After I get a new job."

"Oh. I see what you mean." She points at the picture. "But, that's a pretty popular print. I'm sure regardless of where you end up, you'll be able to find a spot for it. And if you don't, I like it. I'll find a spot for it. Let me buy it for you."

Before I can protest, she's snatched it up.

"I don't need you to do that. Granny."

"I know you don't. Granny's privilege. I can do it even if you don't need me to."

And that is that. Because there *is* such a thing as Granny's privilege.

We walk through a few more of the larger rooms. The extensive collection of used glass bottles, discarded license plates, and broken farm equipment begins to run together.

"So, what's been on your mind, sweetie?"

"Ma'am?"

She casts me a sideways glance. "You wanted to talk. What's on your mind."

What is on my mind? Something is there and bothering me. I can't quite put my finger on it. "Too much."

Granny lets out an uncharacteristic loud, short bark of laughter. "Welcome to adulthood, April."

We let that hang in the air while we both pretended to inspect some door wreaths that were made by a local artist.

If this is adulthood, some days I wish I could go back to school. I had responsibilities then, too, but there were right and wrong answers.

This adulthood thing is one big gray scape. Nothing is a definitive yes or no. Everything appears to be either a selection between the worst of two evils or a case of the best you can do with the resources available.

They need to add another year to the core curriculum in college. An entire year devoted to the ambiguity you'll be confronted with daily in the "real world."

"Does it ever get easier? Or at least do you get better at making decisions?"

Granny looks over her shoulder speculatively. "No." She flashes a grin. "But I believe you begin to give yourself more forgiveness for your mistakes. That helps."

"I guess I never really thought about the human side of the career I chose."

"Oh? How so?"

I lift an ancient lead toy soldier and examine the enamel paint job that must have required an extremely fine paintbrush. "I feel sometimes I miss what is *really* going on with the people I'm working with. I mean, I know the law, I'm good there. But that seems to be only twenty or thirty percent of the job. The rest is really understanding people and what's going on with them. I feel like I really stink at that part."

"Good."

My jaw drops open as I swivel to see if she is kidding. "Good?"

She meets my eyes directly. "Yes, good. That is your job, April. It's not about how much money you can make, how many hours you can bill, or what sort of office you work in. Those things are all nice, but they are fleeting and unimportant in the big scope of things. Your job is about positively impacting people's lives." She squeezes my arm. "It's good that you are beginning to recognize that."

"Then I'm a complete failure," I whine.

"Now why would you say that?"

"Well, there's not too many attorneys who can say one of their clients hung himself."

Granny's lips thin as anger flashes across her ice-blue eyes. "Did you tie the sheet around Jethro Mullins's neck?"

"No ma'am!"

"Then quit your whining and cut yourself some slack, little girl. We all have things in our past where we wish we could go back and change something. But you *can't!*" She straightens her blouse as she draws a deep breath and appears to regain her composure.

"From what Howard told me, you did everything you should've, and maybe even more to help that poor man."

I feel tears filling my eyes. "But that's just it, I didn't. I didn't help Jethro, Granny. He killed himself. Do you not understand that?"

"Yes. I do. But I also understand Jethro would have hurt himself regardless of what you did—regardless of who worked his case. You're not God, April. You can't work miracles. But you can do your best every day to help the people you interact with." She gestures upward. "That man is gone. You worrying about him now can't help anybody. Your job is to focus on the clients you have today. Who can you help today?"

Who can I help today? I have two young men needing my help in defusing a situation they have gotten themselves into that could be ruinous for both of their futures. Granny is right. Sulking about Jethro won't help the Freeman brothers. And they deserve my full attention. Who else will fight for them?

I have the willingness to fight for the Freeman brothers, and I should have the skill. I only wish somebody could tell me what I can do to make their freedom a reality.

I consider asking Granny about the specifics of the Freeman case. To see if she has any nuggets of wisdom. But at this point, I'm sure we are nearing the dreaded "walk in faith and the path will be shown to you" sermon she favors. I'm looking for something a little more directive.

We come to the end of one of the hallways and turn right. The voices of two women arguing ricochet around the corner.

"That's the stupidest thing I've ever heard of!"

"I am absolutely shocked at you, Chelsie. You know it's the right thing to do."

"Are you an idiot?"

"I would be if I didn't do the right thing."

"Where are you going?"

"Getting as far away from you as I can."

I follow Granny around the corner. An older and very red version of the Chelsie London I remember stands with her hands on her hips. She glowers at the back of a salt-and-pepper brunette walking down the hallway away from us.

"Chelsie? Is everything okay?" Granny asks.

Chelsie gives a start. Recognizing Granny, she plasters a fake smile across her flushed face. "Why, Loretta. How are you?"

"Better than you, I take it." Granny points toward the retreating woman's back. "Is that Faith?"

I swear I can hear Chelsie swallow. "Yes."

"Were you girls arguing?"

If I had to bet, I likely inherited my insatiable curiosity from my granny. Thankfully, mine manifested itself more along the lines of continuing to investigate things until I find answers. Granny is a little more direct. It doesn't bother her one bit to ask someone a pointed question when she is curious about something. Even when it is none of her beeswax.

Chelsie manages to complete the calm façade on her face. "Oh, no. We were discussing some of the upcoming marketing plans. You know how partners are when they are both passionate about the business. Some folks could mistake it for arguing, but we were just having an enthusiastic discussion."

Granny nods her head as if she accepts the explanation, but I can tell by her eyes that she isn't buying what Chelsie is selling. I'm not either because I did not hear any mention of ads or other marketing while we accidentally eavesdropped.

"I would like to see the new delivery of trunks you advertised in your email blast this morning."

Something calculating and predatorial in nature flashes in Chelsie's eyes. "Yes, well, there's a delay in the shipment." She sweeps her shoulder-length hair to the side.

"They haven't arrived?" Granny asks.

"Nope. Not until next week."

Chelsie is lying. She is skilled at it, but there are just enough signals to confirm she is not telling the truth.

Now *my* curiosity ramps up. What on earth would possess you to lie about a shipment of old trunks?

Granny shakes her head. "I made a special trip out here to see the shipment."

Chelsie puts her hand on Granny's shoulder and turns her. I swear if she touches me, I'll read her energy. It's not like it would be my fault.

"Now, Loretta. I have some beautiful pieces up in the entry area."

Granny rolls her eyes, and I nearly burst into a fit of laughter. I thought I was the only one who did that.

"Chelsie, I wasn't born yesterday. I know y'all put all those cheap imitation imports and the pieces that are torn up beyond repair up front in hopes the tourists will buy those up before they think twice about it.

"I know you and Faith keep the good stuff back here for yourselves and friends. It's not like I'm asking you to give it to me. I just want to see what you have."

Chelsie offers another fake smile. "I know. I am so sorry that we have put you out. I assure you if I could show you the new pieces, I would. I'll call you as soon as they're ready. I tell you what, I'll give you a coupon for a free malt you can redeem at the snack bar."

Granny doesn't get worked up very often. It's a trait she passed on to my daddy and both of my brothers. But just like them, when they do get worked up, it sorta has a tendency to run on the irrational. Her powdered white face begins to look like she applied extra rouge today, and I know she is close to blowing.

"I don't need a stupid malt. If I wanted a shake, Chelsie, I would've already bought one for myself. I came to buy a chest for a coffee table. But the store owner who sent me an email this morning is now telling me that it is not available. Why?"

"Why?" Chelsie dares to look as if Granny's question is absurd.

"Yes. Why can't I see the trunks that came in on the shipment?"

"They are infested."

I thought the shipment had been delayed.

"Infested? With what?" Granny asks.

Chelsie doesn't appear prepared for Granny's follow-up question. Her face flushes red again as her eyes widen. "Beetles."

Granny waves her hand at Chelsie dismissively. "Beetles aren't any problem. I can clean that up with no trouble whatsoever. So why don't you show me the shipment?"

"Oh no." Chelsie lowers her voice. "These are dangerous,

flesh-eating beetles. Very, very deadly and extremely hard to exterminate."

I fail at concealing my laughter. Chelsie is apparently a fan of *The Mummy* series.

Whatever curiosity I had about her lying over something as mundane as a trunk shipment is waning. Evidently, she isn't going to show Granny the trunks, and I already have an excellent picture to hang in my room. I'm good to go.

"Chelsie London, I never. All the referrals I've given you girls over the years." Granny favors Chelsie with one of her patented "I'm so disappointed" glowers.

To Chelsie's credit, she doesn't melt. She is made of much sterner stuff than me.

I reach out and touch Granny's arm. "Come on, Granny. It's apparent they're having some difficulties with their business. Maybe some other time."

"Humph." Granny turns on her heel and stomps back toward the entrance of the old school.

Chapter 11

To say I feel like a complete idiot meeting Nina Rodriguez at Tubs of Suds Wednesday morning is an understatement. I've never set foot in the establishment before this morning. Having been raised in a household with its own wash maid, named Mama, I didn't wash my first load of clothes before going to Tuscaloosa.

Initially, the novelty made it great fun. Yes, like everybody else, I ruined a couple of loads of whites before I figured the whole "color versus whites" thing. About the time the novelty wore off and washing day became a pain in the butt is when I figured out how not to ruin my clothes.

At seven forty-five this morning, the only patrons are Millie Wright with her three redheaded children who look old enough to be in school and Benny Battle.

I don't believe Benny is doing laundry. He appears to be enjoying the air conditioning while he nurses the last of the big boy PBR he's holding.

There is a pervasive mildewy smell thick in the air, and the linoleum floor has a thick layer of black crust. I'm hoping Nina will be on time.

By ten after eight, I search my memory for cases where someone spontaneously spanked someone else's child in public. I'm trying not to be judgmental, but Millie seems to be raising three lifetime county jail residents, if not federal prison system inmates. The two oldest are currently jabbing a coat hanger into the detergent vending machine; I guess they are hoping to hit the jackpot.

Benny has passed out, and I'm gathering up my things to leave when a woman strolls in, smacking gum and looking disinterested. Since she has no clothes with her, I assume she is my client.

"Ms. Rodriguez." I move toward her.

"You that lawyer?"

"Yes. I'm glad you could be on time, Ms. Rodriguez." I can't help myself.

She smirks. "No trouble at all."

I go to sit down in one of the plastic chairs and stare at the congealed orange soda in the seat. Shifting down a chair, I sit while pulling Nina's folder from my backpack. "Nina, I've read the police report. You're being charged with reporting a false crime."

Nina's eyelids hood as she shakes her head side to side. "I don't know what you're talking about."

I point to the empty seat one over from the orange soda.

Nina appears unwilling to sit down.

I raise my eyebrows.

She huffs and collapses onto the chair, making it bounce against the wall.

"Let me explain this again so that we're on the same page. I am not your enemy. I am the one person who can help you in your current situation. Are we clear on that?"

"Whatever."

I'm proud of myself. I didn't hop out of my seat and slap the gum out of her mouth. Yay, April. "Do we have a problem here?"

Nina rolls her eyes. "I don't even know what we're talking about yet."

I've done this dance before. I'm not going to pretend that I understand it. Still, it becomes a little easier to play my role as the indifferent defense attorney with each client. In this case, it's not an act.

I'll never understand why so many clients are reticent to accept legal help from their court-assigned attorney. The only thing I can imagine is they are unaccustomed to receiving assistance from others. Consequently, they treat any offered service with a healthy degree of cynicism so they can't be disappointed.

"Sometimes it's easier if we simplify the situation, Nina. Would you rather spend thirty days in jail or two hundred hours of community service?"

Nina gives me a look that implies I've lost my ever-loving mind. "Neither."

I decide to fight fire with fire and shift into my "too cool for school chick" look. "Yeah. That's not happening."

A thirty-second stare down ensues.

I believe Nina is trying to convince me she doesn't care one way or the other. I'm close to being there myself. I have people who need and want my help, and I don't care to waste more time with her games.

"So that's it? You agreed to the meeting to tell me you still want to defend yourself?"

Nina rolls her eyes—again. "Look, I don't know what went down. I get back to the house that I share with my cousin Dominique, and some fool has come in and wiped out our flatscreen TVs, speakers, laptops, and my jewelry. I had two heirloom rings that my family has had for three generations. Priceless. Gone." She crosses her arms as she leans back in the chair. "So, I call the police like I'm supposed to. The next thing I know, this lady deputy gets angry with me. Then she charges me with filing a false claim."

I read the report. The deputy is Becky Gray. Becky is a little odd, but she is a strictly by-the-code law enforcement officer. "Why did the deputy get angry with you?"

"I don't know. I think that deputy lady is just crazy. One second I'm talking to my cousin, and the next second, the lady is hollering at me and slaps cuffs on my wrist."

One of the advantages of being clairvoyant is having a heightened sense of people's trustworthiness even when you're not using your "gift." Nina Rodriguez? I wouldn't trust her with somebody else's five-dollar bill.

Something is off here. There is more to this story. The disappointment is, my client isn't going to help me get to the bottom of it.

"That's it?" I ask.

"I told you from the start I didn't know what this was about."

"Okay, then I guess we're done for today."

"But you're still my lawyer?" she asks.

"Unless I find out you're lying to me." Since I plan to run Becky down either this afternoon or in the morning, Nina might be getting a lawyer change a lot sooner than she anticipates.

Chapter 12

I'm catching up on some long-overdue filing at the office when the front door opens. Col. Sullivan strides in, this time wearing cowboy boots, jeans that look starched, and a stylish pink polo.

"Good morning, April." He inclines his head toward me. "I have an appointment with Howard."

"I'm sorry. He left for the courthouse when DA Jameson called earlier."

"Ahh. Did he mention how long he might be?"

"No, sir. And there's no telling when it is Lane. It could be just a few minutes, a couple of hours, or if they get to lying about their golf game…" Did I just say that? I'm sure that goes against my new positivity pact.

The Colonel gives an easy chuckle. "Yes, your uncle loves his golf. Too bad he has to work for everything he slices off his score."

I knew I liked the Colonel. "You're welcome to wait in his office if you want."

Mark looks towards Howard's office, frowns, and points at a chair next to my desk. "Would it bother you terribly if I wait here?"

"I suppose not. I'm just doing some filing. As long as you promise not to critique my system."

"I'm sure I can pick up a few pointers," he says as he pulls the chair toward him and sits.

Filing is my mundane "don't have to think about it" chore. That's why I don't mind doing it when the phone isn't ringing and nobody is telling me to hurry and be somewhere. Yet, with Mark watching, I become self-conscious. After a few minutes, I have accomplished little as I keep misfiling items, the last folder I put into the wrong alphanumeric slot four separate times.

Mark breaks the awkward silence. "I am not looking forward to having to take care of my own paperwork."

I lean against the file cabinet. "Army officers don't have any paperwork?"

"Oh, we have paperwork to go to the latrine and two manuals instructing the proper method to wipe."

Eww. I wrinkle my nose. "That sounds inconvenient."

Mark laughs again. For a man who exudes the persona that his resolve is as hard as his body, he sure does laugh a lot. Still, his rugged smile and easy nature hint that he is extremely comfortable in his own skin.

"I suppose that is a bit of an exaggeration on my part."

I would hope so. "Good thing, or I would have begun to believe that the mess hall is something entirely different," I say.

Turning my attention mostly back to my ineffective filing. I catch him in my peripheral vision, shaking his head. "I see what you did there. With the word 'mess.'"

Yeah, my mama calls me a hot mess, too. "I'll be here all week."

"April, I hope this isn't presumptuous on my part…"

My stomach lurches. Please, Lord, don't let Mark ask me out. Besides awkward, that would be complicated in too many countless ways.

"How much would you charge to do my filing once Howard's and my business is up and running?"

Not the question I was anticipating.

Filing at a pizza joint? How desperate do I look today?

Sure, I know my hair is a frizzy mess right now. If I wasn't afraid of a repeat appearance from the freaky green severed-head lady in my mirror, I might've spent more than a few seconds checking my hair.

"Oh, that's sweet of you, Mark. But between working for Howard and my brother, I'm tapped out on time. If I can think of someone else, I'll let you know."

He clenches his teeth and pulls his lips back. "Oh no. I've offended you."

"No, you didn't." I wave the folder in my hand. "I appreciate the offer. A few months back, I might've jumped on it."

I cringed at the double entendre and feel my face flush when he grins.

"It's funny, I had a hundred and twenty-six soldiers working for me. You would think I wouldn't be the least bit nervous about all this. It has me saying the wrong thing occasionally."

"That's a mess of people."

"Yes, it is. Striking out into the private sector might be a little easier if my team were more like the general population. But basically, I have five very conscientious females and a hundred and twenty males with varying degrees of abilities and egos."

That rings true. Ever since I moved back to Guntersville, it seems like I have been swimming in a sea of testosterone.

After five months of intensive testosterone exposure, I regret to report I'm no closer to figuring out the male half of the species than when I was a party girl at Alabama.

"I know what you mean. I have this one case where even though they're half-brothers, they are nothing alike. One of them is incredibly smart and, at the same time, very deliberate in everything he does. The other brother—" *Let's try to be positive here, April.* "We'll just say his ASVAB score would be a little less than average. Still, he's incredibly loyal and fearless, almost to the point of recklessness."

Mark rests his chin in his hand. "Tell me about him."

Where do you start? "Well, he's a big young man and carries himself really well. From what I understand, he's incredible in both physics and chemistry."

Mark waves his hand at me. "No. The second brother. What else do you know about him?"

What do I know about Jayron? Other than he is destined to remove himself from the gene pool at the pace he is going. "Like I said, loyal, good with his hands from what I understand, likes to fish, hunt..."

"Is he a good shot?"

I'm drawing a blank if I ever heard anyone say. "I'd be shocked if he wasn't. Most of those types of boys can put a tight group together with a twenty-two."

"Did he finish high school?"

I realize why Mark is asking me a battery of questions. Jayron would make an excellent infantry soldier. My word, why didn't I think of this? "Yeah. He did. Who would he get in touch with to join the Army? Just the recruiting office?"

Mark makes a clicking sound with his tongue. "First things first. His legal troubles. Is it just a misdemeanor you're helping him with?"

Last I checked, terrorism was a felony. A *big* felony

"Why do you ask?"

He favors me with a knowing smile. "You'll need to do your job, then. The Army doesn't take felons."

Man, I'm sick of people telling me to do my job. With all my responsibility to other people, I'm starting to think my job has minimal upside.

Howard opens the front door as my attitude plummets. Thankfully he will take the distracting Colonel away so I won't have to be reminded that my young client's future is in my hands.

"I hope you're able to clear his name, April. If you do, let me know, and I'll give you a contact that will expedite the process for him."

I attempt to be polite and smile, but I'm sure it looks as fake as it feels. "Thank you for your help, Colonel Sullivan."

"Did the equipment shipment come in?" Howard asks as he gestures with his hand toward his office.

"All good there. But I have some other things I need to talk to you about."

They disappear into Howard's office.

As much as my curiosity is piqued, and as easy as it would be to listen to their conversation, I have my own fish fry to tend. I look up Deputy Gray's number and give her a call.

"Deputy Gray."

"Deputy. Hi, this is April Snow."

"Hi, April. What's up?"

"Nina Rodriguez."

"Congratulations on that lottery ticket."

Her sarcasm isn't lost on me. "Yeah, I guess I'll have to start living right."

She snorts. "Me too. Make sure to take copious notes just in case it works out for you. I know you didn't call so we could commiserate over our lousy day."

Yes, we don't exactly have the commiserating sort of relationship.

Growing up back in elementary school, we used to call Becky, Bucktooth Becky. Until I accidentally knocked her two front teeth out with a line drive during a softball game. Then we called her Bowl Cut Becky because of the Dorothy Hamill haircut her mother used to give her. Now that we are all older, and the hairstyle seems to fit, it is now more accurate to call her *Blunt* Becky.

"What can you tell me about her?"

"Shoplifter, liar, part-time housekeeper for people who aren't aware of her first two qualities."

Mostly what I thought. "Nina's given me a bizarre story about when you took her in. Can you elaborate on the arrest?"

"There's not a whole lot to tell. I responded to the call from dispatch, and when I got there, Nina told me she had been robbed. I knew it wasn't true, but I began to fill out a report anyway."

"How did you know she hadn't been robbed?"

Becky exhales. "Some of it is police officer intuition, but also there were drawers pulled out and emptied onto the floor, and a lot of furniture and lamps turned over."

"Sort of sounds like what I would imagine a robbery to look like."

"Sure, if things were broken. But as I looked around, I noticed that not a single light bulb, drawer, glass—I'm telling you *nothing* was broken. Overturned, disturbed, sure, but not broken. The whole thing had the look of being staged."

She isn't going to like this, but it needs to be said. "Becky, please take this the right way. You can't charge my client because you have an intuition that she committed a crime or because she has extremely careful robbers."

"You're absolutely right. But I can charge Ms. Rodriguez when she admits to *me* she is lying."

Why did I not already know this? "I did not hear she confessed."

"No, because in a moment of temporary insanity, I felt sorry for her. Filing a false report carries a maximum of thirty days. Intent to commit insurance fraud can be three to five years."

"Slowdown. Backup. You lost me somewhere," I say.

"Look, you need to figure out a way to convince her to plead out on the false report. I thought I was doing her a favor, but I think she believes she has me over a barrel now."

That's where Nina's attitude is coming from. What I mistook as contempt for me is actually her belief she has leverage on the arresting officer.

"Becky, I'll work with you, but you'll have to fill in all these blanks for me. My client's not helping, and you seem uncharacteristically vague, too."

"This falls under the classification of 'no good deed goes unpunished,'" she grouses.

I don't rush her. She is wrestling with some internal moral compass.

"Okay, the deal is that Nina didn't just file a false report. The whole thing was a setup to scam money from their insurance company. She and her cousin have renter's insurance on their apartment."

"How could you even know that they have insurance?" I ask.

"Because when I arrived, Nina was by herself. As I told you, I began filling in my report even though it felt wrong.

"Then Dominique shows up. They get into an argument and begin conversing in Spanish. It went on for a couple minutes, and they were done."

"And because they argued, you just figured that it was an insurance scam?"

"No." Her response is just below a yell. "It was an insurance scam because she told Dominique to keep her mouth shut about it and that she had it all worked out."

I have one of those moments where my brain shifts gear particularly hard, and I swear I can hear the gears grind in my head. I'm slow to the party, but I can be proud that I finally figured out the riddle. "You speak Spanish?"

"Yeah. My ex-fiancé is Latino."

I'm not sure what is more surprising: Becky is fluent in Spanish or that she was once engaged to someone of the opposite sex. Both are unexpected revelations.

"April, she just laid everything out when she told her cousin to shut up."

What am I supposed to do with this? Becky did Nina a favor by not reporting the full extent of the crime, and now Nina is taking advantage of that confidence.

"Why didn't you charge her with conspiracy to commit fraud?" I can't help but ask the obvious question.

"Great question. I wish I had an answer. But I assure you if I get out of this with my career this time, it will never happen again."

"All right. I'll talk to Nina in the morning and see if I can get her to understand that she doesn't have the influence she thinks she does."

"She's got to plead to that lesser charge, April."

The desperation in Becky's voice makes me uncomfortable. I hope to get Nina to see the light, and I will give it my best effort, but I'm not feeling incredibly confident about my prospects.

"I'll get her to understand." I hope that isn't an empty promise.

Chapter 13

I'm about to ask Howard if he wants me to run to Jerry's and pick us up a couple of sandwiches when Mama calls. This is unusual. I call her regularly, but she rarely calls me.

"Hey, Mama."

"Hey, doll. I just remembered that I forgot to tell you that Fabio has an appointment for shots today."

My dog that I named Puppy, everybody else in the family has a different name for him. Mama calls him Fabio. I suppose with his flowing hair and arrogant attitude, it's a fair name to select. However, it's my dog, my name.

"Like at the veterinarian?" I ask.

"Well, I don't think the pediatricians will want to see him, April."

Yeah, that was a stupid question. "What time?"

"It'll only take a few minutes, but his appointment is at one."

I steal a quick look at my phone. "That's only an hour away," I whine.

"Better hurry," Mama says.

I went from laid-back, cruise-control mode and thinking about a sandwich, to all-out panic and clampdown stomach. "Wait! What vet?"

"Doc Tanner's old place. Don't be late."

I could complain and tell her that there is no way I can make the appointment in time. But I would be complaining to air as she has already hung up.

Great. No lunch, and I must hustle home and back into town. "Howard, I've got to run an errand for a couple hours."

"Okay."

I gather up my purse and keys and jog out of the office.

I don't bother to take the T-tops off my car. For one, the temperature has crept up today and feels like an August day. More importantly, I do not trust Puppy to ride in the car with the T-tops off.

As I pull onto Gunter Street, it dawns on me that this will make for a long night. The plan was to go over Jayron's case today and practice a few contingencies that I might hear from the prosecutor or the judge regarding his arraignment. Now I'll have to do that work tonight.

What sort of shots does my dog need anyway? And why didn't I know that he required shots?

I pull onto my parents' driveway hot, my tires sliding as I slam on the brakes. A quick survey tells me that Daddy is the only one home.

Puppy likes to hang out with Daddy. Truthfully, Puppy likes to hang out with anybody available, but Daddy is high on his preference list.

The safe bet is, if I can locate Daddy, I'll find Puppy.

As I jog toward the glass kitchen door on the porch, I look down at the dock. They aren't there.

Checking my phone, I groan. I'm going to be late. I hate being late.

I enter the kitchen. No dog.

"Dad!" I trot down the hallway toward his laboratory.

I can see him working with a Bunsen burner on one of his counters through the pane of glass on his door. I knock twice and open the door. I'm greeted by a blast of AC/DC.

"Dad!" I yell as I move toward him.

His head jerks up. He smiles when he recognizes me. Lifting the remote, he presses a button, and the band goes mute.

"What's up?"

"Have you seen my dog?"

"Yeah, he's right—" Daddy walks around the counter to where Puppy's bed stays. "I just fed him lunch. I thought he was right there."

"I've got to get him to the vet."

The color drains from Daddy's face. "What's the matter with him?"

I shake my head as I check the other two dog beds in the lab. "Nothing's wrong with him. Mama just set up an appointment for his shots."

"Oh. You scared me."

I flap my arms as my voice turns into a childish whine. "I'm going to be late if I can't find that stupid dog."

Daddy laughs at me.

"What?"

He snaps his fingers at me as he walks out of the lab. "Let me show you something. You'll find this useful."

When Daddy says he's going to show you something useful, you'd better pay attention. But my anxiety level is peaking. "Dad, I'm in a hurry."

He doesn't answer me and continues toward the kitchen. "Haste makes waste."

"And late gets me a butt chewing by Mama."

Daddy closes the microwave, sets the "cook" button for fifteen seconds, and taps the start button.

"You didn't put anything in it," I say.

He raises a finger. "Patience."

I have been trying to develop patience for the last twenty years. If I don't have any yet, I doubt I'll miraculously manifest it today.

The microwave beeps, signaling it is done nuking the empty cavity.

Simultaneously, I hear what sounds like a hippo wearing tap shoes accelerating on the hardwood floor of the den. Seconds later, my forty-pound furball bursts around the corner so fast he does a Tokyo drift as he hits the kitchen tile floor.

"Modern-day Pavlov," my daddy declares triumphantly.

I start laughing. "My dog is broke."

"Nah. Bear just thinks he's alpha, and he thinks he's always hungry."

I go to pick Puppy up, and he squirms away from me.

"You'll have to give him a treat first," Daddy says.

"I don't have time to get a treat from my apartment."

Daddy opens the fridge and hands me the bag he pulled out. There are about six slices of cold fried bacon in the plastic bag.

"He'll follow you out to the car if you lead him with that. But don't give him more than a slice or two. It gives him horrible gas," Daddy warns.

I cringe and feel my lips roll back. "How do you know this?"

Daddy raises his eyebrows. "I can't use the Bunsen burner in my lab if we've had bacon for breakfast."

If I weren't running late and didn't believe getting Puppy in my car without the bacon treats would be equivalent to wrestling a furry pig, I would hand the bag back to my Daddy. But I am out of options and out of time.

I pull a strip of bacon out and hold it in front of Puppy's face. "Come on, boy. Follow me out to the car."

Puppy leaps at the bacon and steals half the piece before I can pull it back. "Good boy, come on." I back out of the glass door. "I'll see you tonight, Daddy."

"Good luck."

I don't need luck. I need a puppy whisperer.

The piece of bacon in my hand appears to be precariously close to my fingertips, so I toss the stub to Puppy and pull out a fresh, longer piece.

His interest does not wane. He is hypnotized by the cold bacon protruding from my hand. "Come on. That's it."

When we get to the passenger side of my car, I quickly open the door and toss the bacon onto the passenger seat. Puppy doesn't hesitate. He leaps up onto the passenger seat and devours the bacon strip.

I'm incredibly proud of myself as I walk around the car and get in on the driver's side. My daddy rocks. I now know how to summon my dog and get him to do whatever I need him to do. It is almost like magic.

My hands clench Puppy's thick mane. "So, Mommy has a new trick to get you to mind."

His tongue lolls out the side of his mouth, and he snorts at me.

I start my car and check the time, twenty minutes before our appointment. I do a three-point turn and fly down the drive onto the neighborhood street.

We turn onto Highway 79. Puppy has accepted defeat as he has his back turned to me. He doesn't appreciate being tricked.

I believe if he could talk, he would tell everyone he is more intelligent than me. He's not. He's just arrogant.

As we speed over Guntersville bridge, Puppy begins to howl and scratch at the passenger window. Within seconds, mucus imprints cover my window, and he begins to rabbit scratch on the door panel.

I pop him on his butt to get his attention. He either didn't feel it through all the padding, or he is ignoring me.

"I'm not rolling that window down, buddy. I don't trust you."

He turns and barks at me as if he is telling me off.

"No. You can complain all you want, but I am not letting that window down. You can just chill it, young man."

The stench rolls over me, triggering my gag reflex. "Oh, dear lord, what is that?" A second gag grips my body. I'm so thankful I haven't had lunch today.

Puppy lifts his snout to the air and turns back toward the window.

Bacon. Where is the leftover bacon? I know I put it in the center console.

A split plastic bag on the passenger floorboard catches my eye.

Bless it. My dog had eaten half a pound of bacon.

Puppy swipes at the window with his paw and whines. The sound of an air hose with a hole in it echoes in the cockpit of my car.

The noxious fog covers me, and my stomach turns. Oh, heavens, that is right disgusting.

I pull my tee-shirt up and breathe through it. That only puts a funky fabric softener twist to the putrid smell.

"For Pete's sake, you win, you nasty puppy." I hit the power windows, lowering both our windows. We simultaneously stick our heads out the windows for fresh air.

I arrive at the veterinarian's office fit to be tied. I swear I can still smell puppy air biscuit on my clothes, and I feel violated in too many ways to count and am in desperate need of a shower.

I stomp over to the passenger side of the car and motion for him to hop out. "Out, now."

He must understand I'm close to the edge. He hops out of the car and trots straight to the front door of the veterinarian's office. That just goes to show you the dog plays me. He knows exactly what I'm telling him.

I open the door for Puppy, and he strolls into the lobby as if he owns the joint. There is a cat in its owner's lap and a chihuahua that looks to be catching a cold it is shivering so hard.

"Can I help you?" an older woman behind the counter asks me.

"Yes, ma'am. Puppy Snow. He's here for his shots."

The woman makes a dramatic show of checking the appointment book before announcing. "No. No appointment for a Puppy Snow."

I begin to crack. If Mama got the day wrong and I just rode in the green fog of putrid death for no good reason, I'm not going to be pleased about it.

Wait. Mama made the appointment. "What about a Fabio Snow."

The woman makes another show of checking the appointment book and thumps her finger onto the book. "Yes. There he is." She looks up at the clock. "You're five minutes late."

Really? Because five seconds ago, we didn't even have an appointment. "Any chance you can still work us in?"

"I'm pretty sure we can." She pulls up a clipboard with what looks like a rather thick instruction manual. "Since he's a new patient, I will need you to fill out a brief information packet for our files."

I take a seat and begin to fill out the paperwork for Puppy. Between the dissertation I'm filling out and the residue I still feel on me, I'm wondering why in the world I have a dog.

There are still two pages left to fill in when we are called up. The receptionist opens the door for us and leads us to the first exam room on the left.

"The doctor will be with you in a minute," she says as she takes the clipboard from me.

"Thanks."

She lays a manilla folder on the exam table and leaves us in the room.

"I need the doctor to check your tummy while we're here. There's something wrong with you," I tell Puppy. He's too busy sniffing the corners to respond.

A woman with a full mane of brunette hair and wearing a white lab coat backs into the exam room. She is looking at a clipboard as she turns to Puppy and me.

Ice crystals form in my veins.

Her doe-like eyes grow in size as she recognizes me. "April."

"Hi, Jackie."

"What are you doing here?"

The shock only grows as I point toward Puppy. "My dog needs to be shot. I mean, get shots."

An amused smile creases her perfect face. I want to slap her.

Jackie Rains was my best friend from kindergarten all the way through our junior year in high school. For eleven years, she was the sister I never had, and we were inseparable.

Then she did the unthinkable. She stole my boyfriend, Randy Leath, right out from under me.

Well, technically, Randy and I were taking a break, but that doesn't make it any less traumatic that my best friend stabbed me in the back.

The worst of it is that our senior year, we were co-captains of the cheerleading squad. I'm still not sure how we got through the year without bloodshed.

I was certainly relieved to find out she was bound for Auburn, and I wouldn't have to deal with her in Tuscaloosa. Until a few months ago, I thought I would never have to see her again.

Jackie holds out her hand toward Puppy, and my traitorous dog licks her hand. Puppy has some severe loyalty issues.

As for Jackie, she acts as if nothing is wrong. "Randy told me you were back in town."

Randy was my boyfriend that she stole. They're actually engaged now. "I figured it wouldn't stay a secret forever."

She looks up momentarily. I think she is going to say something, but she turns her attention back to Puppy. "Well, we're going to give him his first parvo shot and a heartworm shot today. It's critical on the parvo that we continue for two more shots over the next two months. Elise..." Jackie motions over her shoulder. "You met her at the front desk. She'll set up the follow-up appointments and give you reminder cards."

I don't know why, but her acting like everything is good between us is really stoking my fire. I can feel my ears turning red as I watch her lips move. All those times we laughed and cut up together, and at this moment, the only thing I want to do is slap her.

My jaw falls open as she leans over and picks Puppy up, placing him on the exam table. He let her pick him up! He never allows me to do that.

"This is a beautiful Keeshond, April."

"Don't let him hear you. His head is big enough as it is." Did I just say that out loud?

Jackie laughs as she examines Puppy's teeth. "Male dogs can be that way sometimes."

All the anger I held against Jackie floats from me. I don't

want it to. I try to hold on to it. But no matter what sort of death grip I attempt to clutch it with, it slips away from me when I hear her laugh.

I miss my friend.

"I bumped into Randy. He told me y'all are getting married. Congratulations."

Jackie's cheeks blush. Her hands paused on Puppy.

She looks up, and our eyes meet. "Listen, April. I want you to know that Randy did ask me about the invitation. He wanted to send one to you." She shrugs. "I didn't send it because I didn't think you would come. It wasn't right. I should have sent it anyway. But if I did and you didn't come, it would be like re-living that mess all over again. By not sending it, I didn't have to worry about you rejecting the offer and be aware you still hadn't gotten over it."

I have no idea why tears prick my eyes. I have no clue what to say.

Jackie offers a quick nod of her head and exhales. She continues her examination of Puppy.

"Well, you can rest at ease. Your dog has an excellent constitution. He'll be keeping you company for a long time."

I hear Jackie speak, but I can't focus on what she is saying. My mind is lost, eight years back, replaying the events that ended our friendship.

Was I wrong? No. I didn't do anything wrong. None of it was my fault.

"Could you hold him while I get his shots ready?"

"Huh?" I shake the cobwebs of the past from my mind. "Oh, sure."

Jackie pulls a syringe from its wrapper and slides the needle into a vial. "Randy still thinks the world of you. I mean as a friend. I guess what I'm trying to say is, you don't have to feel awkward about talking to him if you two run into each other. It's not like I feel threatened by you."

It could just be an awkward statement by her, but it leaves me feeling slighted. "Good. I'm glad he was comfortable telling you we had a conversation."

Jackie pulls some of Puppy's skin up at his neck, slides the needle in under his skin, and looks up at me with a smirk on her face. "Of course. I know where his heart has always been."

Man, it is like a flashback to the cheerleading squad our senior year.

But you know what, this is the new April. The positive April. I'm not going to lower myself to some petty squabble from many years back. If Jackie wants to hold it over me, that's fine. But I'm an adult now.

"I hate to hear that you have to work with your uncle. I know that has to be tough when your dreams don't come to fruition."

Oh no she didn't! "At least I'm not stuck in some Pine-Sol smelling office shoving sticks up dogs' poop chutes all day."

Jackie narrows her eyes as she flushes red. "You've always been a mean, spiteful soul, and you're never going to change, April May Snow."

I step forward, and our noses nearly touch. "And you'll always be a lying, backstabbing traitor, Jackie Rains."

"Traitor! Is that what you think?"

"That's what I know!"

Jackie flicks the cotton ball in her hand, and it bounces off my forehead.

"I ought to kick your butt for that!" I scream at her.

"I'd like to see you try!"

As I seriously contemplate popping her one in the nose, she lets out a squeal and jumps to the side. We both look down at her starched white lab coat, and there is a growing yellow stain on the side pocket. My eyes follow the stream to Puppy on the exam table with his leg hiked.

Now I know why I have a dog.

Chapter 14

Yes, I took the T-tops off and rolled the windows down all the way home. I had to reward Puppy for hopping into the middle of the catfight before it turned bloody.

I can see my daddy cooking in my parents' kitchen when I pull up our drive. After parking, I slide the glass door back and pop my head in.

"What are you cooking?"

"Chicken Alfredo," he says as he continues to whisk the white sauce.

"Cool," I say as I let Puppy in and pull the door shut. My luck is definitely holding.

At this rate, Daddy will win favorite person of the week. Cooking chicken Alfredo for dinner, showing me the cool microwave trick to call my dog, and teaching me how to lead my dog anywhere with bacon. Okay, maybe the bacon idea shouldn't count for brownie points considering my dog has some seriously wrong gastrointestinal issues.

I look into the den and see my brothers at the dining room table. Dusty has a ballpoint pen behind one ear as he squints while reviewing a stack of papers.

Chase is leaned back in his chair with his feet propped up on the chair to his left. He appears to be playing a game on his tablet.

"Do you need any help, Daddy?"

"Thank you, but no. I'll have time to set the table as soon as this Alfredo sauce sets."

I move over to my brothers, curious to see what both of them are working on. I peek over Chase's shoulder and see what looks like a toad on his tablet.

"Are you eating bugs?"

"Most of them. You have to watch out for the scorpions and black widows. The poison will kill you if you eat them."

"Well, that seems like a stupid game," I say.

Chase glances over his left shoulder. "It's anything but a stupid game. This takes a lot of skill." His avatar eats two flies and a cricket in a matter of seconds. "What's your idea of a good game anyway?"

"Ms. Pac-Man."

Chase doesn't even bother to look at me this time and shakes his head. "It's the exact same game concept. You have an avatar running around eating stuff for points."

I open my mouth. Then I close it. I really hate it whenever Chase wins a conversation. In addition to that, it makes me unsure about my own mental faculties.

I walk over to Dusty's chair and examine the papers he is working on. The best I can tell, it looks like a collection of different paranormal venues with brief descriptions of what has been reported.

Dusty's books follow an anthology format. Each book is thirteen ghost stories, and it appears like he is deciding what thirteen to group together on the next book.

Odd, but for some reason, this makes me excited. It has been three months since I've been in the field with the paranormal team. For some reason, I'm itching to get back out there.

There's still a lot about the spiritual world that makes every hair on my body stand up. But at the same time, the adrenaline rush can't be bought.

Mama comes around the corner. "How did the veterinarian visit go, April?"

"You could've reminded me that Doc Tanner retired."

Mama wrinkles her face. "I think he's been gone a couple months."

"Exactly. At least I could've been prepared to see Jackie."

Mama waves a hand dismissively. "I would think that would be a bonus for you two to get caught up considering—oh my goodness. Are you and Jackie still having your little girl fight?"

"It's not a girl fight."

"Disagreement, argument, grudge match, whatever you want to call it. You know, Margaret and I talked about this. She said she was concerned that you girls still hadn't worked your way through this. I told her, of course you had. You both have bigger things to concern yourselves with these days."

"Yeah? Well, do us both a favor and don't make Puppy any more appointments there. It was too—awkward."

"Okay. But you'll have to drive all the way into Huntsville next time for his shot."

"Fine."

Mama rolls her eyes. "Are you still able to help set up Friday?"

Like I really have an option. "Yes, ma'am. Where is it going to be?"

Mama arches an eyebrow at me. "April May. I was born, but I wasn't born yesterday. I'll text you the address tomorrow about eleven o'clock."

Mama's been running the Halloween costume party since before she had Chase and Dusty. So, at least thirty-plus years.

Anyone who is on Mama's contact list is invited each year. The uniqueness of her party is that they are held at different historic homes in the Guntersville area.

All of the homes have been empty for over a year, and some for a decade or more. All have some haunting attached to them.

More times than not, Mama manages to move the property during or shortly after the annual Halloween party. Ghost stories are less scary if told during a party.

And that is the fun of the event. Each event house comes complete with a specter and a story about it. That is what

Halloween is all about anyway, isn't it? Sexy outfits, spooky houses, and friends.

Mama waits until noon the day of the party before announcing the location of the house selected for that year's event. This keeps the suspense level high the whole month of October.

"It sure would be helpful if you could tell me where it's at. At least I could make sure to be on the right side of town."

"We don't have that many decorations to put up this year. We can get it done in four or five hours. If you're still at work, you'll be close enough to the site."

I mentally check all the different vacant homes that would serve well for a haunted house near Snow and Associates. Honestly, I have no idea where we would be holding it this year. It seems like most of the spook houses have been inhabited the last few years.

"Y'all come fix your plates," Daddy hollers from the kitchen.

Dusty and Chase are slow to stand up. You snooze, you lose. I round the corner into the kitchen and pick up my bowl first. Puppy is right on my heels.

Chapter 15

There is no question that I have seriously hurt myself. After dinner, I spent a couple hours catching up with my family. It was delightful, but now as I open the door to my apartment, it is a little after ten, and I'm not even partially prepared for court tomorrow.

As I lock the door behind me, Puppy trots over to his bed and falls into it with a grunt. He has the right idea, but it will be a long time before I can do the same.

I shuffle over to my bed and, out of duty, pull the Jayron Freeman file out as I cross my legs on my bed. It is strictly out of desperation that I'm looking at the file. I still have no idea what I'm looking for, but I hope something will hop out as an excellent defense for the young man.

As I review the file, the words of Colonel Sullivan come back to me, pounding inside my head. If Jayron is to have an opportunity with the military, I must keep him free and clear of a felony.

"Do your job, April." It sounds simple enough. But I'm beginning to believe that possibly Jayron has the wrong attorney to help him with his situation.

The problem is that the court system routinely bends over backward for all sorts of extenuating circumstances. People are able to get reduced sentences all the time for consideration of their upbringing, socio-economic situations, and to a certain extent, if they were just out-and-out crazy.

The one thing the legal system absolutely abhors is stupidity. There is no adequate defense for stupidity. And as a rule, stupidity can add an average of five to ten years to any standard sentence.

Any self-respecting judge would deny this. Yet, I've seen it in action. The legal system does not tolerate stupidity.

After half an hour of reading the material that I'm highly familiar with, I make a disgusted sound and shove the folder back into my backpack. It appears I will be forced to rely on finding another impromptu golden moment. I don't want to leave Jayron's future to chance, but it's all I can come up with tonight.

Again, out of duty, I pull the Nina Rodriguez folder out. I make to open it, shake my head, and shove it back in my backpack. There is nothing in the folder that will help me with her case.

What I need in the Rodriguez case is the ability to talk sense into someone who has *way* overplayed their hand. Nina thinks that because she has a deputy in a half-truth, she wields leverage. The only thing she has going for her right now is my patience, and I've never had much.

I must get her to see the light. It is in her best interest and the deputy's.

I don't believe straight-out logic will do it. I'll need to find my own sources of leverage to play against her.

My eyes keep shutting for extended periods, and my head lolls from side to side. As much as I would like to think up something that might be able to persuade Nina, there is no way I'll do that as I'm falling asleep. Finally, I decide it's best to go to bed.

I strip down to my panties and bra and turn the light out as I slide between my sheets. My apartment is deliciously silent except for Puppy's steady snores. It's so dark I can't see anything. I close my eyes and draw in a deep breath.

I wake up out of breath and fighting for air. I clutch at the hands that are pressing down on my windpipe.

I bring my legs up violently, trying to dislodge my attacker. Still, they lean further forward and increase the pressure on my neck.

My eye pressure increases as if they will pop out of my skull. My lungs burn for precious oxygen as I feel every blood vessel in my head enlarge, threatening to burst. My arms and legs flail, scratching, kicking, and pulling, as I try to dislodge the hands of my attacker.

I no longer can move. I can see, but I'm paralyzed.

My attacker, a female, moves her knees from my chest. She jumps off—my bed? Then strides over to my kitchenette, where she lifts a butcher knife.

I didn't even know I had a butcher knife on the counter.

As she approaches, fear grips me as I realize her intent. The cool, sharp edge of the knife cuts into my neck as she begins to saw. I try to scream, but nothing comes out.

The pressure increases against my windpipe. Pain shoots throughout my body as my assailant leans her body weight onto the blade. I feel it cut further into my neck. The pain is ungodly.

Then it is dark. So very dark and quiet. I yell out, "Hello?" My voice echoes back to me four times.

Tentatively, I step forward. My heels click on the smooth, hard surface. *When did I put shoes on?*

I hear something growl. It sounds like a wolf to my left. Or is it on my right? I can't see anything.

No. There's a green glow up ahead. I move toward it, cautious not to trip over something unseen. My shoes still click on the floor that sounds like marble.

Again, I hear the low growl. It has to be a wolf. Behind me?

The glow is a flame. Green flames dance, jostled by the wind. Yet, I feel no breeze on my face.

I step closer toward the flame.

The flame floats in midair.

Where is the source? I can't see anything burning, just the green flame being disturbed by the nonexistent wind as it hangs suspended in the air.

Concern builds in my mind. That turns to anxiety and presses the air from my chest in a panic. Please, Lord, tell me I did not time travel. This feels like what Nana has described as the void.

She explained the void as the vast empty spaces in between time. Nana warned me that if I time travel without a clear destination in mind, I will end up in the void. With no possible way of ever finding my way back.

My panic builds to a crescendo. I'm hyperventilating as one of the many flames reaches toward me and, for a second, takes the form of a green human hand.

The low rumble of the wolf's growl begins again. I pirouette in a three-sixty. Still, I can't see the wolf.

I must find my way out. I can't stay here. I've only been here for a few seconds, and every fiber in my body is screaming that I'm in mortal danger.

As I twirl back to the flame, I spy a second tendril turning into a hand. Then the center flame develops shadows that look suspiciously like a human silhouette.

I back cautiously away from the flame, but my shoes now sink into the marble floor. As I pull my feet up, I lose my shoes in the muck below me.

The wolf lets out a more ominous growl followed by two sharp barks.

My eyes snap open. I'm in my bed, and Puppy is on it looking in the direction of the kitchenette.

Every hair on his back is standing straight up, giving Puppy an odd mohawk appearance. His lips are pulled back, exposing his canines. He lets out three more sharp barks. Each time the bed shakes.

I follow his stare to the kitchenette. Now I see the faint green outline of a woman holding a knife.

My stomach turns with repulsion. The ghost has no head.

This is not good. I have a specter in my apartment that has nothing to do with this property. Also, besides the painting Granny bought me, I haven't brought in any new items. Nothing that might be the essence of someone who has passed. This isn't making sense.

I watch cautiously. Afraid that if I say or do anything, the knife-wielding body might attack. After a few minutes, I know this must end.

"Leave me."

Nothing happens. I consider my options. Puppy and I can make a run for the door and spend the night at my parents'.

Still, that seems sort of lame. Plus, I'm not sure I want to turn my back to a ghost holding a knife.

I can try some magic. Maybe a warding bubble. But then again, I just painted. I don't want to mess up my walls.

Man, I've got court tomorrow. I don't need this. "Get out of my apartment!"

I'm startled when the knife falls; the blade sticks in my wood floor. The female body turns into a flame that subsequently turns into a loosely organized green orb and floats toward my mirror.

Touching the mirror, it transforms into a green, gaseous mass. As the last of the green smoke slides into the mirror, I jump up and throw my comforter over the mirror. I'm not sure if that will work, but it sure does make me feel better.

I lie back down in bed and coerce Puppy to snuggle up against me. I doubt I will be able to fall back asleep.

Chapter 16

I turn my alarm off just before it is set to sound off. I feel like I've been chewed up and spit out. My nerves are shot, too.

It was bad enough when I had the random head on my dash screaming at me. But hindsight being twenty-twenty, that is nothing compared to last night. Seriously, what's a severed head going to do? Bite you?

This headless body thing in my apartment cutting my head off? I just can't. It's too many levels of wrong.

I don't understand what the head or the headless body thing is about, or why they have attached themselves to me. I do feel a great solution would be for the two of them to pair up and get the devil out of my life. I don't have time for this creepy nonsense.

The worst is while I'm brushing my teeth, I kept imagining I see something green in the bathroom mirror. But there is nothing there.

My skin is pale and gray, and my eyes are bloodshot red. Awesome. I yank my hair back into a bun and apply a layer of makeup ineffectively.

I'm going to look *fabulous* for court today.

I trudge out of the bathroom and note that Puppy had already bounced. Probably headed to the big house for breakfast with my brother Chase if I were to venture a guess. That sounds pleasant, but I have some details I want to check on at the office before I meet with Nina.

I begin to lift my comforter off my full-length mirror and think better of it. I'll wait until I can discuss my unique visitor with Nana. She might be able to help me identify the issue at hand.

I suppose I should be thankful I did not wind up lost in the void. The thought of it gives me the chills.

Still, rather than grateful, I'm feeling agitated. I didn't ask for this haunting. If this was a ghost that had attached itself to me because I worked on one of Dusty's research projects, that would be fair. This ghost is connecting to me strictly because it senses I am a conduit to the living world.

Just because I'm a conduit to this side of the veil doesn't mean I'm free access. Verizon doesn't let you use their cell towers for free just because you need to make a phone call.

Nana will help me fix it. If not, Puppy and I will be sleeping in my parents' den tonight.

Nina Rodriguez has lived in Guntersville for four months.

Going on the principle none of us have too many original ideas, and when we do, we tend to repeat them until they no longer work, it does not take me long to find Nina Rodriguez in Arizona and Texas, who has also been charged with insurance fraud. In both instances, the case ended in a hung jury. The DAs had decided not to retry. Interesting.

In my world, I call this sort of information leverage. This will be my stick to convince Nina to take the deal she cut with Becky if the carrot of a lesser charge won't move her to be true to her word.

I continue digging and find another case of her handiwork in Mississippi. It seems she has slowly worked her way across the southeast, into Kentucky, and down the Carolina coast.

Perhaps it's time somebody puts an end to her little game. I feel like the right girl for the job.

Howard comes through the front door at five to eight. He is carrying a white paper sack with a grease blotch on the bottom.

"Jasper is cooking at his mom's today."

I accept the bag from my uncle. "On a Thursday?"

"He had a breakfast event for the football team. They play Albertville tomorrow night," my uncle informs me as he walks to his office.

"That'll be a good game. I hope it doesn't affect Mama's turnout too bad."

"Just might have some later arrivals, is all."

I unwrap the biscuit, and a strange fragrance wafts in the air. I pull the top off the biscuit and finger the meat. Something doesn't look quite right. "Is this tenderloin?"

"No, he wasn't cooking tenderloin today."

I lift the biscuit and sniff the meat. I can't identify it to save my life. "What is it?"

There is a long silence that does not put me at ease.

"Rabbit," Howard calls from his office.

"Like bunny?"

"It tastes pretty good to me."

Heck no. I wrap my biscuit back up and scoot it to the edge of my desk. "I'm not eating Peter Cottontail."

"What are you talking about? Your ancestors used to eat rabbit, squirrels, and opossum all the time."

"Sure, and forty used to be really old because they all died in their thirties."

I hear Howard chuckling in his office.

"What? You know it's true."

"You might have a point. I suppose I never thought about it," Howard says.

I glare at the biscuit, mocking me at the end of my desk. "So, do you want this? I'm not going to need it."

"No. It's too gamey for my taste. I could only get one bite of mine down," Howard says.

What the heck? Then why bring me one?

I suppose the silver lining is that I lost any appetite for breakfast. All I can visualize is sweet furry little rabbits.

At eight thirty, I load my backpack and grab my purse. "I got to go handle that Nina Rodriguez thing."

"Do you need backup?"

"No. Nina doesn't scare me. But she better watch out, or I'm going to show her my crazy, and she'll wish she had been more cooperative."

"Play nice now."

I ignore that comment. "At ten, I've got the Freeman bail hearing."

"Did you pull Judge Rossi or Phillips?"

"Rossi."

"Tell her hi for me."

"I will." I close the office door behind me.

The morning's mild temperatures linger. I sling my backpack over my shoulder and decide to walk to the County Annex.

No breakfast *and* exercise; it looks like I'll fit into my Halloween outfit after all.

Being so close to death's door last night, or at least an endless dark night in purgatory, has changed me. Despite getting zero sleep last night, all my senses are hyperactive.

The colors of the flowers along the walkway, grass, trees, and cars all pop with unusual vividness. For the first time in a long time, I'm able to discern different smells in the air, and I can hear the birds and cicadas readily over the light traffic in town.

I would never want to relive last night again. Still, I must say, it has made me more appreciative of my life today.

It takes every ounce of my discipline to push the memory of the void into a mental box so I don't dwell on the sensation. I do find it odd. I would think experiencing someone choking me to death and then attempting to saw my head off would be the worst thing I could ever experience.

As frightening as the apparition's attack was, it doesn't come close to the prospect of being stranded, fully conscious, in the void for all eternity.

Per Nana's instructions, I'd taken great care not to accidentally put myself in a situation where I might time travel. I had always viewed this phenomenon as a temporary affliction.

I believed that as the control of my "gifts" under Nana's tutelage improved, I would naturally begin to be able to control the time travel, too. Possibly enough to try it again someday.

Last night showed me the risk is much higher than the reward. How many dinners with famous historical figures would it take to balance out eternity alone in the dark?

Yeah, I just don't think there's anything worth risking that consequence.

I enter the Police Annex building and turn into room twelve, where we had agreed to meet. Go figure, Nina isn't there. I pull out my notebook, find her number, and text her.

Where are you? I am at the Annex like we agreed.

While I wait for her response, I flip through some of the headlines on my news feed. I become bored with the news, pull up my favorite book-buying site, and check if my brother's book has gotten any more reviews.

His last novel has attracted another hundred reviews in the previous week, I can't help but smile. Not only did I help with the story investigations, but I also did most of the original draft of this latest book.

It is a source of immense pride for me. For the first time in my life, I feel like I have participated in something that has long-standing value. I like the feeling.

I wonder if there might ever be something I could write about. Something that keeps people's interest and makes them smile when they read it.

It wouldn't be paranormal; it gives me the heebie-jeebies. Besides, that is my brother's shtick.

I could do a cookbook. I'd have to learn how to cook first.

Then again, that seems like a lot of work.

Nina enters through the open door, rolls her eyes, and falls into a chair in front of me. "The traffic is really heavy this early in the morning."

This girl is as windy as a sack full of farts. "When you get a real job, you'll get used to it."

Nina bows up on me as she narrows her eyes into slits. "What is that supposed to mean?"

"It means I have been doing some investigating and have learned that your idea of work is what a lot of other people consider a crime."

Nina's eyes hood over as if she is bored. "I don't know what you're talking about. I'm a hard-working taxpayer just like everybody else."

"No, you're a grifter."

"What did you call me?"

I lean forward. "A grifter. You run the same tired, sad scam over and over. The only difference is that this time you ran into somebody who's on to you."

"This is so messed up. I'm the victim here. It was my apartment that was robbed." Nina stands and points at her chest. "I've got rights. I don't have to sit here and listen to you accusing me of stuff I've got no idea about."

"Well, okay." I point at her chair. "Sit down, and I'll explain everything to you. Then you can tell me your side of it. Perhaps I am wrong."

Nina eyes me suspiciously. She sits as I asked.

"I'll admit I haven't done full due diligence yet. But I'll make you a deal. When I get back to my office, I'll call the DA in Phoenix, the DA in Laredo, and the DA in Biloxi. I'll request they send me the booking pictures of the Nina Rodriguez they tried for insurance fraud."

Nina's facial expression collapses. She sucks in a breath and regains her composure with a stern expression set on her face.

I must give her credit. The girl is as tough as a pine knot.

"You can call whoever you want, but it ain't got nothing do

with me," she insists.

"We'll see."

Nina leaps up from her chair and leans over me. "You think I care what you believe, lawyer girl? I mess up spoiled little girls like you for fun."

Instinctively, I push up from my chair. Something smacks into the top of my head.

As I finish standing up, I see Nina holding her hands over her nose. Blood is gushing between her fingers. The raging anger I had felt just seconds earlier dissipates into confusion as the blood traces down her forearms and trickles off her elbows.

"You hit me? What sort of crazy lawyer are you? You can't hit me!"

"I did *not* hit you."

Nina removes her hands from her nose. Blood pours out from her nostrils.

The girl really shouldn't be so ready to fight if she can't take a tap on the nose better than that. She bleeds like a stuck pig. "You better put some ice on that," I say as I hand her a couple of Kleenexes from my purse, careful to avoid the puddle appearing between us on the faux marble floor.

Nina tilts her head back, pinching her nose. It is ineffective. The blood now trickles down her neck. "I'm going to put you on ice!" she screams.

"Did you just threaten me?" I pull the tissues back.

Nina glares at me sideways, keeping her nose elevated. "Oh yeah, lawyer girl."

There are two correct responses when someone threatens your life. You can be scared, which is certainly an understandable emotion. You can also be outraged and threaten them with like retribution.

Instead, I giggle. I mean, the situation is just ignorant. My giggling leads into a full-out gut laugh by me.

I know it is inappropriate and illogical, but Nina is standing in front of me with a broken nose. She's already lost probably half a pint of blood. And still, she's threatening *me*? Her street cred is in serious doubt.

"So now you're gonna laugh at me?"

I regain my composure and tuck the unaccepted tissues into my purse. "No, Nina. Now I'm going to ask to be recused from your case. Then report all of your past scams to the DA. After I confirm them, of course."

"I am so going to kill you," she snarls.

"I heard you the first time, Nina. Unlike Deputy Brown, who tried to help you by giving you a lesser crime to plead, I won't cut you any slack. I'm also going to request that the DA looks into you for threatening a counselor of the law." I plaster the sweetest smile I can on my face. "But I really hope everything turns around for you, dear."

She raises a clenched fist in a threatening gesture.

I waggle my fingers at her. "You have a blessed day now."

There is something profoundly satisfying about walking out of the Annex office, knowing she is staring holes in my back. I've won arguments in a drop the mic fashion before, but I can't say I've ever won a fight without throwing a punch. I checked off a bucket list item I didn't even know I harbored.

Chapter 17

The argument with Nina took longer than I expected. I have to jog to the courtroom where Jayron's hearing is to make it on time. Discussing the Nina issue with Lane must wait until after the hearing.

I hit the right side of the courtroom's double door. The door flies open so hard it strikes the interior wall and vibrates back toward me. I freeze in horror and scan the room to see if anyone noticed.

Everyone in the courtroom, most notably Judge Rossi, is staring in my direction. I grin like a fool.

Judge Rossi raises her eyebrows as she adjusts her wireframe glasses. "I'm pleased you could make it to our little meeting today, Counselor Snow."

I struggle to get my arms free of my backpack straps as I make my walk of shame up the gallery aisle to the table where Jayron sits. He is decked out in a crisp, bright orange jumpsuit. "Yes, Your Honor. I'm terribly sorry for the delay. Please accept my apologies."

"No need to apologize, Counselor Snow. As long as the extra preparation time shines through during the defense of your client."

No pressure there. It is doubtful I shine today, given I still am without the brilliant defense epiphany I had hoped would come under pressure.

I pull my folders out of my backpack as I take a quick look to my right. When it rains, it pours.

Lane is not present at the prosecutor's table. Warden Swain is as expected, but the very fit man in a dark blue suit in his late fifties or early sixties beside him does not strike me as a good omen for my client.

The stranger's neat, compact salt-and-pepper hair is beginning to recede. I've never met the man before, but I surmise this is our FBI agent from Gadsden.

"I was worried you had given up on me," Jayron whispered.

With the turn of events, including the FBI now, I'm not sure Jayron wouldn't fare better if I had given up on him. He might stand a better chance if someone else were defending him. "What, and miss all this fun?"

Judge Rossi leans back in her tall, winged chair and crosses her arms. "Agent Taggart, since you have so adeptly wrestled control away from our local officials, you may have the first say in the matter.

Agent Taggart stands, refastening the button on his suit coat. His eyes are grim and dark. Selfishly, I'm glad he is glaring at Jayron and not me.

"Since the Oklahoma City bombing in 1995, the interior of this great country has been under siege by the worst sort of terrorist imaginable."

Agent Taggart is in the wrong occupation. He is wasting his talent as an FBI agent. His voice, so clear and commanding, makes me sit up straight and on the edge of my seat.

If anyone is taking a survey for the voice of God, this man definitely gets my vote.

"Domestic. These treacherous traitors lie in wait in our sleepy hamlets, biding their time. Always vigilant for the most opportune time to strike at the soft underbelly of our civilization and to wreak havoc and mayhem on our citizens. These cowards have but one goal, the complete and utter destruction of our way of life. They wish to hold our very dreams, hopes, and aspirations hostage to their violence."

Agent Taggart points a condemning finger at Jayron. "In this very courtroom is one of the individuals who seek to bring down the very system of justice that has allowed our democracy to flourish. The prosecution intends to protect the American citizenry from such a vile threat and show beyond a shadow of a doubt that the only place for such evil is in a cell deep in the bowels of a maximum-security institution."

Judge Rossi stares at agent Taggart.

The silence feels awkward and uncomfortable.

She raises her eyebrows. "And then?"

"Ma'am?"

"Where's the beef, agent. I mean, don't get me wrong. You give a beautiful speech." She favors him a shoulder shiver. "You have my attention. I half expected to see Timothy McVeigh sitting over there. But no, it's still Jayron Freeman. So please continue."

"Yes, Your Honor."

Agent Taggart undoes the button of his jacket. I wonder if that is like his pompous control button. Button fastened, pompous. Unfastened, not pompous.

"From the written documentation provided by Warden Swain, it must be understood that Jayron Freeman meant to wreak maximum havoc on the God-loving population of Guntersville with his actions."

Nope. The button has nothing to do with his pompous factor.

"When you contrast the heinous terrorist attack Mr. Freeman sought to complete against the unsuspecting citizens of Guntersville against the low-key, amiable nature he projected over the last two decades, you understand he is the most devious and deceitful mastermind that could befall your all-American town."

Jayron Freeman is a mastermind. Who knew?

Judge Rossi raises a hand. "Agent. I almost enjoy listening to you speak as much as you do. However, I have a hectic schedule today, so please quit going around your butt to get to your elbow."

"Ma'am?" The agent's brow wrinkles.

"Cut to the chase." Judge Rossi makes a circular motion with her finger. "Just the facts, sir."

Agent Taggart raises his chin, signaling comprehension. "Ah. Yes."

He fastens his jacket button again.

"On the morning of October twenty-fifth, Warden Swain observed Jayron Freeman dropping explosive devices into the water next to the Guntersville Dam. We have checked with the Army Corps of Engineers and have determined that the Guntersville dam was at risk. Such detonations at the proper distance could, in theory, cause a fissure that would ultimately lead to the rupturing of the dam. Subsequently, this event would flood the Guntersville Lake community. We believe this was the goal of Jayron Freeman."

Judge Rossi leans forward. "His motive, Agent?"

Taggart shifts his weight. "Well, it's obvious he's part of a terrorist organization."

"Humor me, Agent. It's not quite so obvious to me. Which terrorist organization?"

"From his MO, our analysts are in the belief that it would be Isis- or Al Qaeda-related."

Judge Rossi looks pointedly at Jayron. A slight grin accentuates the laugh lines on her left cheek. "Really?"

Taggart appears to understand the source of Rossi's incredulous tone. "Not all jihadists are of Middle Eastern ancestry, Judge."

"No. I know that to be true. But your original speech was about homegrown terrorists, and now you're conflating that with some sort of jihad. It just all sort of has a feel like a reach to me. As if you're trying to cover all bases at the same time."

"The quality of our analytics is beyond reproach."

"Maybe so, Agent. Still, unless you can show me documentation of Mr. Freeman being online communicating with terrorist organizations, domestic or international, and researching bomb-making, I must believe your analyst is wrong. Regardless of their track record."

"We searched the Freeman property late last night."

That revelation makes me so dizzy I almost fall out of my chair. All I can think about is what they may have found at the Freeman property. Kenny's laboratory, where he manufactured the pipe bombs, will end up putting Jayron in jail for life.

"And?" Judge Rossi rolls her hands palms up.

"We found some fertilizer on site."

"How much?"

"About ten pounds," Taggart mumbles.

I see an opening, and I leap on it. "Your Honor, the Freemans have a garden. Ten pounds is hardly excessive for anyone growing a garden."

Taggart swings on me. "We're showing opportunity here, Counselor Snow. The question is, *did* Mr. Freeman have the material available? He did. End of story."

"In this instance, I believe size does matter, Agent. I would be surprised if you didn't find at least ten pounds of fertilizer at most homes in Guntersville. Unless you're ready to charge the entire town with terrorism"—Rossi lifts her hands side-by-side above her desktop—"including me, that's not very compelling."

"Yes, Your Honor," Taggart says.

"What did you find on his Internet usage?" Rossi asks.

Taggart attempts to look shocked, but it comes across as comical. "He's been in custody since we became aware of his intents. You know we wouldn't have a warrant to collect anything before that."

"Agent Taggart, you and I both know you could tell me what soup recipe I perused online this morning."

"Oh no, Your Honor. The FBI does not collect data on citizens without a warrant."

Judge Rossi pulls off her wireframe glasses and makes to clean them with a tissue. A discomforting silence ensues.

"As you would have me understand it, Agent. We have a terrorist mastermind in our midst that is so proficient our Federal Bureau of Investigation cannot identify what terrorist organization he belongs to, where or how he receives the information to build multiple pipe bombs you claim could destroy our dam, and he plans to do this with an amount of fertilizer that could blow the glovebox of a compact car to smithereens."

"I wouldn't exactly put it that way, Your Honor."

"I understand, Agent. You would've used more half-dollar words and flowery phrases in a much deeper voice. If you don't mind, sit down so I can talk to Warden Swain."

Judge Rossi, still my idol.

Still, I can't say my confidence level of success is any higher now than at the start. But I'm giving thanks for having drawn Judge Rossi rather than Judge Phillips.

Rossi is a complete BS destroyer. The woman's common sense is incredible, and her level of fairness is beyond reproach. I can only hope someday I might be like her.

"Warden Swain, you were the arresting officer. I've read your report, but I'd appreciate you retelling it in your own words."

Swain's color looks off to me as I watch him stand. He has bags under his eyes, and his leathery skin appears to hang on his face today. I would guess he has not slept since we met at Jester's.

"Your Honor, on the morning of the twenty-fifth at approximately six thirty in the morning, I was making the first run by the dam. I like to go early in the morning and make sure any catfish lines strung the night before have been picked up.

As I was doing so, I saw a small, flat-bottom boat sixty feet out from the dam. At first, I didn't think anything about it. I thought it was most likely somebody picking up their lines from the night before, albeit a little bit on the late side.

Then I felt a tremor in the water, and a two-foot wake rolled out from around the base of the flat-bottom boat.

I changed my direction to investigate the boat. I continued toward the suspect at idle speed, and as I neared at a hundred yards, Mr. Freeman dropped something into the water. Seconds later, I felt another tremor in the water followed shortly by another wake."

Warden Swain cuts his eyes toward Jayron and continues, "Mr. Freeman's back was to me. As I pulled my boat within fifty feet, he lifted a two-foot-long section of two-inch diameter pipe in the air and held it out over the edge of the boat.

"I realized he held an explosive device, and I gave him an order to stop. Which he did. It was then I tied to his boat, and we discussed the infractions and that I would be arresting him." Swain looks back to Jayron. "He cooperated, and I made the arrest."

"There's a whole mess of catfish over by the dam, Wayne," Judge Rossi comments. "Some big ones down toward the bottom. Big enough a family of three could have a fish fry for—what would you say—a week or more?"

Swain looks down at his hands. "Yes, ma'am."

"I'm not second-guessing you. But I got to wonder why you immediately thought Mr. Freeman was trying to blow up the dam rather than catch catfish through an illegal method."

Swain shrugs his shoulders. "Just a judgment call."

"Just a judgment call," Rossi repeats. "Illegal fishing method is two hundred hours community service and confiscation of the fishing boat. An attempted terrorist attack, ten to thirty years. That's an awfully significant difference from a judgment call, wouldn't you say, Wayne?"

"Yes."

"It seems if I was faced with that sort of *judgment call*, I would want to take my time and gather all the evidence."

"Now wait just a minute, Maggie. It's not like that. I had already caught Jayron dropping those pipe bombs in the lake on three other occasions. It's just the explosions were so close to the dam. This time it concerned me that if I didn't put an end to it once and for all, the Freeman boys would end up hurting themselves or somebody else. I would have just felt awful about that."

I pop out of my seat like a jack in the box. "I object. Past incidences shouldn't influence this event. Besides, Jayron wasn't even charged with those other events."

Judge Rossi waves her hand at me. "Sit down, Counselor Snow. There is no jury in here, just me."

She redirects her attention to Swain. "Is this your twisted version of 'scared straight,' Wayne?"

Swain rubs the stubble on his cheek vigorously, refusing to make direct eye contact with Judge Rossi. "I just charge them, judge. It's up to the court to try them."

"Good thing, too, Warden. It's a mighty good thing." Rossi scribbles notes on her folder. "We'll set a trial date for November sixteenth, and I'm setting bail at five thousand dollars."

It's Agent Taggart's turn to pop up like a Jack-in-the-Box. "Your Honor, please reconsider. Mr. Freeman has been charged with a serious crime, which makes him a high flight risk."

"Agent, I have made my ruling, and you will respect it." Rossi's eyes narrow. "Not that I need to explain myself to you, but that young man over there has no family outside of Guntersville. He has no passport, no mode of transportation, and is too poor to pay attention or buy himself dinner tonight."

She stabs a long, bony finger toward the double doors of the courtroom. "You could tell him to run right now, and he would end up coming right back here because it's the only place he knows. So, no, sir! I vehemently disagree with you that Mr. Freeman is a flight risk."

Judge Rossi lifts her gavel, slamming it down so hard the sounding block bounces into the air, lands on its side, and rolls across her desk. "Court adjourned."

It requires a few seconds for me to realize we have our victory. I don't even need that brilliant, last-minute defense epiphany I was counting on. Instead, Judge Rossi, in her infinite wisdom, steered the proceeding to a rational conclusion.

It doesn't hurt my feelings in the least that I did next to nothing for our little win today. As Chase likes to say, "I'd rather be lucky than good."

"What does that mean? Can I go home?" Jayron asks at my side.

I turn to face him and grin. "It most certainly does."

Motion in my left peripheral vision catches my attention. Lane stands at the back of the courtroom gesturing to me. He lips something at me.

From a distance, it's difficult to tell, but it looks like "I need to see you now." That can't be good. I lift a finger in the air, signaling I will be with him as soon as I'm done with Jayron.

While I'm distracted, Hal Joiner, the bailiff, has made his way to Jayron and puts his hand around Jayron's elbow. Hal's immense size is in stark contrast to Jayron's emaciated frame.

Jayron's eyes open wide with fright. "No! I'm going home!"

Hal and I know each other through my brother Dusty. I place my hand on his arm. "Hal, can you give me two minutes with Jayron to save me a trip back over to the jail?"

A light rose color appears on Hal's massive white cheeks. "Sure, April. Whatever you need."

"Over to the jail?" Jayron's voice pitches high.

"Listen. Calm down." I put the palm of my hand on Jayron's bony chest. "I'm gonna call your mama and work with her, so she knows how to post bail for you. Then you will be out until your trial."

"That's what they're talking about when Judge said five thousand dollars?"

Given his family's circumstances, I understand why the thought of five thousand dollars would cause his voice to crack. "We don't have to put up the full five thousand. Your mama will just have to put up ten percent, which is five hundred. Then offer something worth five thousand dollars in value as collateral if you don't show up for your court date." I poke him lightly in the chest. "But you will show up for your court date, so that's not going to be a problem."

Jayron's gaze falls to the floor as he mumbles, "I'm never getting out of jail. The judge might as well have set my bail at five million."

"Listen to me, your mama will work out a bail bond and get you out. You just have to go back to your cell while we get the paperwork done."

He fixes me with his bloodshot stare. "April, you just don't get it. My family doesn't have five hundred dollars. And Mama doesn't have anything worth five thousand dollars. She hawked the trailer back in late August to pay for Kenny's tech school tuition the grants and scholarships didn't cover. That's why the only groceries at the house are what Kenny and I grow or catch. Mama's money is going toward the payday loan and electricity." Jayron slaps his hands together in frustration. "Haven't you been listening to me?"

Well, I thought I had. But it's dawning on me that perhaps I did not fully appreciate the desperation of the family's situation.

"Why do you think I was out on that lake dropping pipe bombs into the water. I was scared to death I was gonna blow a hand off or blow a hole in my boat and drown, or worse, be sucked into the dam's intake."

He taps his head. "Messing with explosives will make you start thinking about all kinds of weird ways you might die. It ain't for the faint of heart," he adds with a shrug. "But going out with a bang gots to be better than starving to death."

I manage to shut my mouth, which I realize has fallen open during his explanation. For some odd reason, I feel shame even though I have done nothing in this situation except try to help keep Jayron out of jail. I know his family's situation is their own making and has nothing to do with my fortunate circumstances.

That knowledge doesn't make me feel any better.

Swallowing hard, I attempt to clear the tightness in my throat. "Jayron, you're going to have to trust me. I will get you out of jail no later than tomorrow. Can you do that for me?"

His lips disappear as his face tightens. He favors me with a single nod of his head.

"Thank you." I point to where Hal is standing at the front of the courtroom. "Now, if you will, please go over to Bailiff Joiner and let him know you're ready to leave with him."

He gives another nod, turns, and slow shuffles toward Hal. His sluggish march to confinement is breaking my heart.

Pulling it together, I raise my hand towards Hal. "Thank you, Hal."

"No worries, April. Let Dusty know I said hi."

I force a smile and nearly choke on my answer. "Will do."

Slinging my backpack over my right shoulder, I start back toward Lane. Everything about his posture and facial expression reads controlled rage. I really don't need any more drama at the moment, given my present emotional state.

Unfortunately, being a professional doesn't allow for "tender feelings" timeouts.

Being a professional often requires I act like an unfeeling machine and allow nothing to bother me. I'm required to keep everything on an even keel while taking nothing personally.

I'm sure my exterior appears unflappable and in control as I near Lane. Never mind that inside I want to find a dark corner, curl up into a fetal position, and feel sorry for myself.

"Are you aware of what a bar review is?" Lane closes the last of the gap between us and towers over me.

"Hello, Lane. How has your morning been?" I manage a sarcastic smile, which is excellent considering my face wants to pull into a snarl.

"How's my morning been? My morning has been a complete nightmare. A crap show I owe to my usually competent contracted defense attorney."

"Thank you for the compliment, I think. But I can't take credit for your nightmare."

"You broke your client's nose. What were you thinking?"

"I really don't think it's broken. I think Nina's just a free bleeder."

Lane's face flushes red with fury. "April, this isn't funny. This is a serious business."

"I'm not laughing, Lane. Look, so far, you've got the criminal client's side of the story. I'm a bit disappointed you're not seeking your defense attorney's take on the facts before you jump all over April."

"Don't do that," Lane says.

"Do what?"

"Talk about yourself in the third person. It's irritating."

"Seriously?" I slam my fists onto my hips. "You're gonna come in here all big and blustery threatening a bar review and then have the nerve to critique my speech patterns?"

Lane regains most of his usual composure. He is a professional, like me, after all. The difference being I *really* need to hide out somewhere quiet, while he looks like he wants to go to the gym and pummel a punching bag until his fists bleed.

"I apologize. You're correct. I definitely want to hear your side of the story first," he says.

Remaining angry with a contrite Lane is impossible. I feel my body relax, and I can finally breathe again. "Just to get it out of the way, yes, I did cause her nose to bleed. But I did not strike her. She was standing over me attempting to intimidate me, and when I stood up, the top of my head must've caught her in the nose."

Lane's eyebrows knit. "Why was she standing over you?"

"As I recall, she was threatening to 'mess me up.' But after I accidentally bloodied her nose, that threat quickly escalated up to killing me."

Horror flashed across Lane's face. "She threatened to kill you? Are you positive, April?"

A short burst of laughter escapes me unexpectedly. "Oh, yeah. She made it quite clear more than once."

"Why?"

"Simple. I researched and found out that Nina Rodriguez is a scam artist working her way across the country. She's been tried in three other states for insurance fraud. That's what she was up to this time.

"We were having the meeting so I could convince her she needs to accept the plea, and she refused. When I then brought up the information of her past trials—well, let's say she didn't like it very much."

"I'm confused. This was a simple plea bargain situation for a simple false report. Where did you get the information on Rodriguez?"

I shrug. "It should've been a simple plea bargain. The problem being Nina didn't realize she was getting a great deal."

"Then let her have her stupid day in court, Counselor. You can lead a horse to water..."

This horse could use a drink about now. I can't explain to Lane why I don't want the case to go to court without revealing that Deputy Brown cut Nina slack. If I announce that fact to Lane, I might as well let the case go to court and allow Nina to blab about Becky not charging her correctly.

Given her past myopic actions, I believe Nina is foolish enough to rat on Becky, not realizing it will hurt her as much as Becky.

"You don't have a problem with Nina, do you?" Lane asks pointedly.

Oh, I definitely have a problem with Nina. But I understand Lane is really inquiring if I have a problem of a different sort. I must admit, it ticks me off. "Why would you ask that?"

"You went through a lot of trouble to dig up these past cases on her. I'm asking what would have motivated you to go to all these extra steps." Lane exhales loudly. "I know you don't want to hear this, but I must ask. Was there profiling involved here?"

Wow! There it is. "Yeah, actually, there was. I've found that people that come across with a smart-mouthed, disinterested attitude have a higher propensity to be a liar and often a criminal."

Lane considers what I said before he responds. "Okay. That's good enough for me."

"That's it?"

"Well, I have to remove you from her defense."

"Man, I'm heartbroken," I say.

"A simple thank you would've been more appropriate."

He is right, but a smart comment was so much more fulfilling.

"All right then, I have to go find a defense attorney for Miss Rodriguez," Lane says.

My mind snaps back into gear. "Lane, one last thing. With those other three cases, I would think you have to consider her a flight risk."

"The other three cases are inadmissible, April. Unless the next defense attorney is dumb enough to introduce the information into the trial. Digging up old dirt on your client isn't typically the way to develop a strong *defense* case."

"Point taken. Still, I'm warning you there won't be a trial unless you get her picked up as soon as possible."

Lane walks away from me. "Not your problem now, Counselor."

I make to object, but he slips through the double doors and is gone. Something in my gut tells me Nina might be gone by the end of the day, too.

Lane is correct. It isn't my problem. Still, for some reason, the idea of Nina Rodriguez escaping justice once again really makes my butt itch.

I push through the double doors in a foul mood. There is a particular injustice about Jayron sitting in jail and maybe staying there until his trial while Nina Rodriguez plans her escape. Nina has been tried on three prior occasions for crimes, and Jayron has not.

But then again, according to Warden Swain, Jayron probably should've been brought up on charges three prior times. Plus, Jayron's crime could cause injury or death to innocent bystanders. Nina's case is just financial. Other than stockholders' pocketbooks, nobody really gets hurt.

The truth of the matter is I just don't like Nina. I don't like her attitude toward me, and I don't like the fact she wants to use Sheriff Brown's decision to lessen her charges as leverage.

I still am not sure how she can use that information to her advantage, but it is apparent she feels it will keep her out of jail.

Forget about it, April. It's not your problem now.

That isn't a hundred percent true. I still need to call Sheriff Brown and fill her in on what had transpired to be prepared if Nina smokes her out.

If I'm going to spin my wheels about something, I would be better served to figure out how to get Jayron's bail posted. It is discouraging to ponder the troubles caused in people's lives by the lack of money.

Blast it. Lack of money is at the root of Nina's issue, too, if I'm going to be fair. I can't reasonably empathize with Jayron's case and not empathize with Nina's situation as well. The problem being I'm not feeling very reasonable at the moment.

Chapter 18

I let the office door of Snow and Associates slam behind me. I shove my purse into the bottom drawer and collapse dramatically onto my chair.

It is high time I spend some quality time figuring out how I'll escape the madness of this town. This town is making me nuts, and I'm no longer sure I'll be able to make it to after Christmas, per my last life plan revision.

Dusty has always said you have to keep your plans fluid and ready to change at a moment's notice. That's where I am. There is no waiting. I must restart my job search in earnest.

I jotted down a few firms in Boston, New York, and San Francisco a couple months back. Rather than search on the enormous job board, I want to go into each firm's personal websites and see if they have any positions available.

The additional research has to give me a leg up.

The notepad I wrote the firms' names on has been in my top drawer, but now I can't find it. I continue to rifle through the rest of my drawers. Still, I see no white legal pad.

I can visualize the pad clearly in my mind. It's a white legal pad with each city ranked and color-coded by firm size and number of firms.

"Are you all right?"

Startled, I look up to see Howard's head and shoulders

wrapped around his doorway. Oddly, I feel chagrinned. "Yes, sir. I seem to have misplaced a notepad."

"Okay. I was curious if a troop of orangutans had broken loose from the zoo and was assaulting your files."

I guess I was louder than I intended to be. "No, sir, it's just me."

He steps out of his office and leans against a file cabinet. "I see that. Do you need to talk?"

"No, sir." I suck in a breath, suddenly fighting to keep my tears at bay. "Yes— I— don't know."

He crosses the office and sits down in the nearest chair. "Sometimes it helps to think it through by saying it out loud."

I know my uncle is attempting to help, but the last thing I want to do is rehash what took place this morning. The only thing I want to do is get into bed and sleep.

When I look up, he is still there, sitting patiently. I look away.

Everybody wants to talk, talk, talk, but it never fixes anything. My life is one tough decision followed by another, and talking has never made the decisions easier or more correct.

I check my peripheral vision. He hasn't moved. Crud. He's not going to leave until I tell him something. If I don't, he's liable to sit there like a bump on a log the rest of the day.

"Nina Rodriguez is a serial felon. I confronted her about it and accidentally broke her nose. She reported me to Lane.

"The FBI showed up and took Jayron's prosecution from Lane. Judge Rossi did a better job defending Jayron than I did and set the bail at only five thousand dollars. His family doesn't even have five *hundred* dollars for his bail.

"Lane called me out for breaking Nina's nose and then removed me from her case.

"Jayron's gonna rot in jail until his court date while Nina's going to jump town tonight. So, as you can see, I've had an incredibly dreadful morning, and now I can't even find my..."

I freeze. I swallow hard as my mind whirls to say something witty to break the silence.

"Find your what? Maybe I have seen it?" he says helpfully.

I hope not. It's not any secret that I intend to leave Guntersville for another firm someday. But there is no need to be ungrateful and flaunt it in Howard's face.

"With days like today, I feel like I can't find my mind at times?"

"Over those minor setbacks?" he asks.

I can't help but snort a laugh. "Minor?"

He stands and pulls out his billfold. "Regarding Nina, it's not really your concern. But if you feel the need, call Jacob and tell him your suspicions. He'll keep her from running."

That is excellent advice. Just giving Jacob a heads-up will probably take care of that concern. If I'd been thinking, I would've already thought of that.

Howard pulls a card from his billfold. "As far as Jayron, call this number here and ask for Amy Copeland. She's the bondswoman I refer some of our clients to."

"But you don't understand, Jayron's family…"

Howard tucks five hundred-dollar bills next to the card and extends them to me. "Give this to Amy. She'll take care of the paperwork."

I hesitate in accepting the money. "But what if Jayron doesn't show up for his trial?"

Howard shrugs his shoulders. "Then I owe Amy five grand, and you are a poor judge of character."

I pick the card out from the cash. "If I'm going to do this, my client, my risk."

"It doesn't work like that, April. Amy and I go way back. She'd require collateral from you that can bring in five thousand on a short sell."

"I'll figure it out."

Howard is still frowning as he tucks the hundred-dollar bills back into his wallet. "April, it's one of the few benefits of not being a partner. The firm should take that risk. Are you certain?"

"I've got this, Uncle Howard."

The only thing I own worth five thousand dollars is a cherry vintage IROC Z-28 I earned a month ago. Easy come, easy go, I guess.

"Since you're going to be broke for quite some time, at least let me buy you pizza at Torino's for lunch."

The correct answer is no. I need to somehow get myself into a Tinker Bell outfit tomorrow night that I'm not prepared to admit is two sizes too small—yet. But free Torino's? Folks will have to just deal with it if Tinker Bell's curves aren't fully covered tomorrow night.

Chapter 19

The fragrant smell of freshly baked bread slathered in garlic butter envelops me as we enter Torino's. My mouth immediately waters, and I feel my thighs gaining weight just from the aroma.

Howard leans in conspiratorially. "I bet you're wondering why I'm coming here when I'm buying nine pizza joints."

Honestly, it never crossed my mind. I was only conscious of my incredibly traumatic morning, and somebody was offering one of my favorite comfort foods, for free no less.

Now that he mentions it, though, my curiosity is piqued.

"Just scoping out the competition. You have to know what you're up against," he says.

I can advise him of that comparative intel without the reconnaissance. With the texture of cardboard smeared with ketchup, his pizza crust does not pose any competition to Torino's. Their pizza makes you pause after each bite as your brain fires a dump truck load of dopamine into your system.

While both products claim the name of pizza, the name is where their similarities end.

Torino's is already packed. The hostess informs us there will be a fifteen-minute wait.

"See, that's one advantage my stores will have. We'll be able to seat customers faster."

Yep. You can definitely seat people quicker when there are no other customers in the restaurant. "Uh-huh."

"I wonder where they got those nice tablecloths," he says.

I examine the plastic red-checked tablecloths he is admiring. "I'm sure I saw those at the dollar store."

Howard's eyes widen. "Really now. See, right off the bat, I'll be able to save money. I bet they ordered those from some expensive food service company."

This reminds me of whenever a friend would be totally gaga for a guy, and I just couldn't see the attraction. A case where she would be so in love she didn't notice he was six inches shorter than her, needed a shower, or just, in general, was a loser.

Howard is giving off the exact same vibe. And it concerns me.

It's terrible since, like the girlfriend's blind love, I have to be oh so careful about what I say. Not vocalizing the obvious flaws is not my stronger suit. My struggle is real.

Our hostess leads us back toward our table. Howard stops so abruptly I bump into him.

"Frank Crowder!" Howard exclaims.

The wiry old man smiles broadly as he stands and shakes Howard's hand as if they were arm wrestling. "Howie, where have you been?"

"Always tied up at the office, busy, busy, busy."

"Is your office still out there on the thirteenth hole of Cedar Pines?"

"Oh, listen to you." Howard does a double-take to his right. "Tootie Hurley?"

A classy, silver-haired lady with mischievous blue eyes winks at Howard. "How are you, Howie."

Howard looks from Frank back to Tootie. "How am I? Heartbroken. I'm obviously too late."

"Oh, Howie. You always were all talk," Tootie says.

So, I'm like in an alternate universe right now. First, the last thing I ever would've thought my uncle to be is a flirt. I obviously missed there.

Second, Frank Crowder is more commonly known as Doc Crowder, the local medical examiner for our county. He must be in his early seventies and looks like he's in his early eighties. However, despite him weighing in at a hundred and thirty-five pounds, I have personally witnessed him sling a two-hundred-and-forty-pound dead man onto a stretcher like the body was a bag of taters.

Third, the attractive elderly lady has the last name of Hurley. There are only so many Hurleys in this county, and one of them happens to be my best friend, Jacob Hurley. The woman with the unfortunate nickname must be his paternal grandmother.

I check to make sure my mouth isn't hanging open.

"Have things been dead at your place lately?" Howard asks.

I cringe at his morgue humor. If he's not embarrassed, I'll be embarrassed for him.

"Actually, we've been quite busy," Doc answered. "Which is good given I have the intern from Atlanta visiting next month."

"Intern? When did you start taking on interns?" Howard asks.

Doc grins, exposing his smoke-yellowed teeth, "Since Tootie and I decided we want to travel."

"You're leaving us?"

"We'll see. First, I need to decide if the young man from Atlanta takes to the environment. Country living is not for everybody, but I have a feeling he might like it. Besides, it's not like I'm getting any younger."

"True. I have to admit I'll miss you. But if it's what you want, I hope it all works out," Howard says.

"Thank you, Howie."

I feel a warm hand around my wrist. Tootie is looking at me, her face full of humor.

"These boys have never had any manners, dear. I'm Tootie Hurley. What's your name?"

"April Snow, ma'am."

The older woman's face brightens as if she has just received the best of news. "As in April May Snow, Vivian and Ralph Snow's daughter?"

"Yes," I answer hesitantly.

Tootie pops up and gives me a hug, then holds me at arms' distance. "My grandson Jacob has always told me what a great friend you are to him. That little scoundrel never let on to how beautiful you are, too."

It's embarrassing, and I struggle a thank you. It is suddenly hot in Torino's, and I begin sweating like a sinner at church.

"Obviously, he's not as smart of a boy as I thought if he hasn't tried to be more than friends with you after all these years."

Nervously, I rub at the back of my neck. Wet. Yuck. "Yes, ma'am. You know what they say about not wanting to mess up a good friendship."

Her brow creases. "No, I can't say that I do. Although I've heard that couples who start out as friends have a much better love life."

"Now, Tootie," Howard interjects on my behalf. "Us old folks know better than to insert ourselves into young folks' business."

"Come now, Howard. You have to admit they would have beautiful babies."

I'm feeling faint. This is not happening.

Why is it so blessed hot in here?

"True as that is, it wouldn't work out. April is leaving Guntersville to start her career elsewhere next year."

Tootie stares at Howard. She cuts her glance to me. "Is that true?"

"Yes, ma'am. I'm hoping so."

"Oh." She sits and straightens her napkin back into her lap. "Yes. You are right, Howard. That would never do. I want my darling grandbabies close to me."

Jacob and I are *not* an item. We are incredibly close friends with personalities that lean to the flirtatious, but just friends nonetheless. This is why I don't understand that it hurt my feelings when Jacob's granny dismissed me once she knew I intend to move out of town.

Suppose I had designs on Jacob, which I don't. Would my wanting to better my career in a larger city automatically disqualify me as a suitable bride? That doesn't make sense to me.

Maybe a bigger mystery is, since I have no intentions of moving Jacob's and my relationship up a notch, why do I even care? I'm not sure I really want to investigate that enigma.

Howard must understand it hurt my feelings since he offers to get us a bottle of wine with our pizza. He is always charitable with meals but rarely offers alcohol as part of the deal.

"We sort of talked Jacob up, or at least his granny," Howard teases.

I find my way back from the fog in my mind. "How do you mean?"

"You need to call Jacob about Nina since you think she'll jump town."

I'm going to have to start carrying a notebook with a to-do list. I had already forgotten I need to make that call. "Yeah, I suppose you're right."

We enjoy our meal and wine in companionable silence. The pizza isn't the best I've had from Torino's. I guess we all have our "off" days.

"What do you think Doc Crowder's intern from Atlanta is going to be like?" he asks.

I couldn't care less right now. "I guess if we're going to start an office pool on it, I want my money on a young version of Doc Crowder."

Howard laughs. "Freakishly strong little dude with glow-in-the-dark white skin?"

"Actually, I meant small and nerdy with a thoughtful streak," I say.

"That wouldn't be all too bad." Howard pushes his plate away and twists his paper napkin into tiny knots.

"What's up?" I ask, noticing his fidgeting.

He looks up from the napkin he is mutilating and grins. "What makes you think something's up?"

I point at his napkin. "You're mutilating your napkin again."

He discards the napkin onto his plate. "I don't know if this is a good time to tell you. I'm only gonna tell you because you were asking earlier this week. About Vander."

"What about Vander?" My stomach tightens, and the pizza becomes a giant dough bowling ball.

"I got to thinking, after you mentioned it, it has been an awfully long time since I heard from him. I have some folks I can check in with at least to find out that he's okay." He huffs. "They won't tell me where he is or what he's up to, but that's not what I would want to know anyway."

This is the first time Howard has let on there is an opportunity to find out about Vander. I eagerly lean forward in my chair. "And?"

Howard looks me directly in the eye and shakes his head. "He's gone dark."

"Dark? Was does that even mean?"

"Nobody's heard from him in the last sixty days. Him or his crew."

"Sixty days? That's a long time. Is that normal?" I ask.

"No." Howard looks away from me.

Anxiety tightens into a knot in my chest. I don't understand any of this. "So, what does this mean?"

"It just means we don't know," he replies.

"Then why tell me?"

Howard clasps his hands on the tabletop. "I'm sorry. I just thought you would want to know."

I understand Howard is tight with Vander, and he probably needs to share his concern with someone about his disappearance. Still, I don't think I'm the right person. If he cannot tell me Vander is alright, I would prefer he keep his misgivings to himself.

He rises and tosses a ten-dollar tip onto the table. "I'm sorry I upset you."

"It's okay. I mean, it's Vander. He's indestructible, right?" I say it more for my uncle's benefit as I know all too well that nobody is indestructible.

If someone does approach superhero status, it's Vander. He must be alright. I won't let any other thought take root in my mind.

"Sure." The smile his lips form does not reach his eyes. "Don't forget to get by Amy's for Freeman's bail, and if you change your mind and want help, just say the word. I'm there for you."

Man, I almost forgot that, too. "Thank you."

"Do you think you will be back around three?"

Three o'clock. Why does that sound familiar. "I'm sorry. I forgot to ask if it was okay if I left early today to get my nails done. Mama's party is tomorrow night," I explain.

Howard laughs. "I buy you lunch, and then you play hooky the rest of the day."

"It's the last time I can fit it in before the party," I whine.

"Shh. I'm just pulling your chain. You probably could use some time at a salon after the day you've had."

Howard leans forward and kisses me on the forehead. I can't ever remember him doing that before. "I'll see you in the morning, and call me if you need any help."

Stunned, I sit and watch my uncle make his way out of Torino's.

Chapter 20

I call Jacob from my car as I drive to Boaz Bond Buddies. He picks up on the first ring. "Hey, hot stuff, you want a tip?"

"Don't roll the condom on before you have a full erection?" he asks.

"No fair, you already knew!"

"Experience is the best teacher, Snow." He rolls into a deep laugh that makes me tingle.

"What's up? I know you didn't call to reminisce about health education class with me."

That brings back memories, some funny and a number quite awkward. Jacob and I met in first grade and were in the same class until middle school. After that, we always had a few classes together each year, and health education in our eighth-grade year was one of the more memorable.

There is nothing quite like a bunch of pubescent kids learning sexual anatomical correctness in a coed setting while amusing each other with silly double entendre. The struggle to keep a straight face during class each day was profound.

"I actually do have a tip for my favorite police officer," I say.

"What's that?"

"Do you know who Nina Rodriguez is?"

There is a pause before he answers. "I know her cousin Dominique."

That comes out of left field. "How do you know her?"

"Mind your beeswax, Snow."

"I am. How do you know her?" I feel my temper flaring.

He grunts. "I wrote her a ticket a couple of months ago for an expired tag when she moved here from Missouri."

"Mississippi. She was coming from Mississippi, not Missouri."

"Maybe."

"Why do you sound funny?"

"I don't sound funny." His voice takes on the nasally quality it always does when he is lying.

"What are you hiding? You're not dating her, are you, Jacob Hurley?"

"What's it to you?"

I huff. "I'm your friend, and I'm trying to protect you."

"Man, if you think I need protection from a five-foot-two, one-hundred-and-ten-pound woman, I need to get back in the gym."

If Dominique is half as mean as her cousin, muscles won't help him. She'd just cut his stupid throat while he slept. "I was calling about her cousin Nina. I don't care about your stupid love life."

"What about her?"

"She has another court date next week, and she's going to skip town."

"So, call her bondsman."

I love Jacob, but sometimes, especially if he has turned defensive, he becomes so obtuse it drives me crazy. "She's out on her own recognizance."

I hear him take a deep breath. "I don't know what you expect me to do about that. Even if Nina left town tonight, she might be coming back for the trial."

"What if her car is packed?"

"Spending the night at her parents," he counters.

"Dominique is the only family anyone knows about."

"Boyfriend, then."

"Darn it, Jacob, why can't you just keep tabs on her?"

"I don't know. Maybe because I'm busy doing my job, and I don't have time to be a babysitter."

That must be nice. Most days, I feel like a glorified babysitter.

"Why are you so concerned anyway? If she blows her court date, it's her butt that will be in hot on water, not yours," he says.

"She threatened me today, Jacob." I know it is slightly manipulative, but hey, don't judge. Sometimes I need to insert a little drama to get Jacob moving in the right direction.

"Threatened you? How?"

"She got in my face and said she was going to kill me."

"Kill you? Why are you just telling me now? This is serious, April."

"I wanted to keep it low-key. Maybe Nina was just blowing off some steam." Or ticked off about her nose being broken.

"But if she threatened you," he says.

"Can you just check on her? Maybe drive by her apartment a couple times tonight?"

"I ought to bring her in for questioning," Jacob mumbles.

"Low-key."

He exhales loudly. "Yeah, I can go by their place a couple times this evening."

"Thank you." I hope that if she is packing to leave, the sight of a Guntersville Police cruiser idling down her road like a huge green shark might make Nina think twice.

"No worries. Now, if you're done, I have some policing to do."

I almost forgot the fun stuff. "Hey, did you know your Granny is dating Doc Crowder?"

"Uh-huh."

"What do you think about that?"

"Kids, what are you going to do?" He drawled.

"It would be so much easier if we could get them to listen to reason," I joke. "What, are they both, like, in their seventies?"

"Sure. But I figure let the lovebirds make their own mistakes. Besides, if it's a screw-up that lasts the rest of their lives, how long is that anyway?"

"You're morbid." I can't contain my laughter.

"It's true! They're the lucky ones. They only have to deal with it for a decade at tops if it doesn't work out. You or I pick a bad partner, and it could easily be a fifty-year mistake."

The rate I'm going it will be fifty years before I need to worry about it. I change the subject. "Are you coming to Mama's party?"

"I wouldn't miss it."

"What are you going as?" I ask.

"A lost boy from Neverland."

"That's apropos."

"Uh-huh."

I can tell he was expecting a different response from me. I'm getting wise to the game. Howard must have pulled Jacob in on the "make April uncomfortable about being Tinker Bell" game. I won't give them any satisfaction.

"Well, show up early if you can. We can always use the extra help getting ready."

"I'll try."

I think of Jacob as my closest friend. Yet he has been seeing the cousin of a crazy woman for the last two months while his Granny hooked up with the medical examiner, and what did I hear from him? Crickets. He hasn't said a thing about either.

I try to remember the last time I called him just to talk. Not to ask for a favor.

The fact that nothing comes to mind makes me wince. Am I a terrible friend? Oh Lord, I am. I am *that* friend. The one you never hear from unless they need something from you.

When did this happen? I don't want to be the user friend.

It isn't my fault. My current lifestyle sucks all my leisure time away, and all I have time for is work and work conversations.

Something has to give. Maybe that's why I'm anticipating Mama's party so much.

Chapter 21

Boaz, where the bail bondsman is located, is only fifteen minutes outside of Guntersville. But given the schedule I'm keeping today, I wish Howard's favorite bond company were located in Guntersville. Because, I don't know, our office is in Guntersville?

I'm not sure what I'm getting into as I pull up. The building is a three-store strip mall. Left to right is a seedy-looking pawn shop, a check-cashing store with a counter and a single desk in the center of the store, and then Boaz Bail Buddies. I know it is a bail company by the cartoon silhouette of a curvaceous woman bending over while placing an antique key into a pad-lock. Classy.

I step inside and immediately struggle for my breath. The low-hanging cigarette smoke mimics a house fire. A burning house with a considerable amount of plastic furnishings. I fight the urge to drop to my knees and crawl back out before I asphyxiate.

"Can I help you, doll?" I cannot identify the gravelly voice that greets me as a man or a woman.

"Yes. My Uncle, Howard Snow, sent me." I move toward the counter, searching for the source of the voice.

A short woman with leathery skin and thinning hair the consistency of cotton candy rises from behind the counter. She takes a long drag on the unfiltered cigarette in her left hand then hollers over her shoulder. "Amy!"

An angry voice responds. "What?"

"You got a customer."

The sound of something being shoved against a wall is followed by a door slamming. "I swear, Mama, it wouldn't hurt you to learn how to fill out the forms."

"That's not my job. That was always your daddy's job."

Amy comes around the corner, and the likeness is uncanny. She is the same height as her mama, same round face, and her skin is the same leathered texture. The most significant difference being that Amy still has a full head of bleached blonde hair and is smoking Salem longs. Filtered.

"He's been dead for eight years; it seems like you might be able to learn a few more things about the business." She directs her attention to me. "Hi, I'm Amy Calloway. How can I help you?"

"I need to buy a bond to bail out one of my clients."

Amy looks me over from head to toe and takes a long drag on her cigarette. "Is this what the world has come to? Girls are expected to bail out their Johns, too, nowadays?"

"I'm his defense attorney."

A smirk appears on Amy's face. "And that's not any odder."

"My uncle, Howard Snow, said you would be able to help."

The name drop works because Amy's body language changes immediately. "Sure, what's the bail amount you're working with?"

"Five thousand," I say.

Amy pulls out a worksheet and begins jotting information down. "Your client's name?"

"Jayron Freeman."

"And what is he charged with?"

I feel like if I tell Amy he is charged with terrorism, it might be a quick and unprofitable conversation. Since she probably wouldn't accept that he is being accused of stupidity, I finally tell her he's been charged with the unsafe handling of explosive materials.

"Okay, now the way this works is the bond will be ten percent of the bail amount plus the seventy-five-dollar paperwork charge. Neither of those is refundable."

Seventy-five dollars for filling out an application seemed sort of pricey, and I'm a lawyer.

"But we'll need some sort of collateral for the other forty-five hundred dollars in case your client does not show up for court. What were you planning on putting up for collateral?" Amy asks.

"I have a reconditioned 1985 IROC."

"Is the title clear?"

"Yes." Jayron better show up for court. If I lose the IROC over this, Dusty and Chase might kneecap Jayron and never speak to me again.

Thirty minutes later, I'm officially Jayron's benefactor. For good or ill, we are attached at the hip now. Specifically, the wallet.

When I get back into my car, I try not to remember that Boaz Bond Buddies now holds my vehicle's title in their safe. Some things are best not to think about.

I check the time on my phone. If I'm going to make my three o'clock appointment at the beauty college, I'm going to have to put the pedal to the metal.

For the last four months, I have been doing my own manicures and trying to ignore my toenails. I'm broke, but I'm not cheap. Usually, I like to get both my fingernails and toenails done professionally.

When I initially moved back to Guntersville, I was elated to find a manicurist named Tiffany Bates, who runs the local beauty academy. She did excellent work at a reasonable price, and as a bonus, I liked her.

That was until she decided to date Patrick McCabe.

I'm still not sure if I've ever been in love. Don't get me wrong, I've been in lust a lot of times. But I'm still not sure exactly how love feels. But I may have been close with Patrick McCabe.

I don't understand why Patrick was different, but *everything* felt different with Patrick. I was always—euphoric. I was saying and agreeing to things I usually wouldn't, just because I wanted to be around him regardless of the situation. It had gotten so bad I even decided that maybe I would settle down with a respectable law firm in Huntsville, Alabama, and marry Patrick.

That all ended when I found out Patrick already had a young son. I like kids. As a general rule, I also find boys before they are teens to be a complete hoot.

But I'm not ready to be a mom. I screw up my own life enough. I don't want the responsibility of not messing up a kid's, too.

In short, I sort of freaked. As soon as I met Patrick's son, I excused myself and left their house, and then failed to take any of Patrick's calls that night.

Eventually, I became an adult again. Well, Mama shamed me into acting like an adult.

I called Patrick, apologized, and did my best to explain my odd and unacceptable behavior.

There may have been a small part of me that hoped Patrick could forgive me and we could remain in the friend-circling pattern. Just in case I became used to the idea and decided I wouldn't mind being a mom sooner than I anticipated.

But things had been altered for both of us. Even if I ever did change my mind, it would never be the same.

Then unexpectedly, Tiffany tells me Patrick has asked her out, and she wants to know if I'm okay with it. Honestly? How does anybody expect you to answer that?

No, I'm not going to date him anymore, and I'm not going to marry him because I'm not ready to be a mom.

But that doesn't mean I want my friends or my manicurist

dating him. Why does everybody have to shop at the same man store?

I'm not sure if I was holding a grudge the last four months because Tiffany was dating Patrick or if I'm embarrassed to see her because I know what a great guy he is. There's no way I can explain to her why I let him go. Bless it, for the first month, I had a hard time explaining to myself why I set him free.

But my nails are skanky, and the biggest party of the season is tomorrow. So, I will have to swallow my pride so that my nails are not a source of embarrassment tomorrow night. This is truly a "suck it up buttercup" moment.

I hesitate with my hand on the front door to the beauty salon. I pull on it and enter the salon.

Tiffany is writing something into the appointment book at the front counter. Her eyes lock onto mine, and her face lights up with a genuine smile.

"My word. I was starting to worry that you were dead," she teases as she comes around the counter.

"My schedule is trying to kill me."

"Tell me about it. We usually slow down this time of year, but we're still going strong." Tiffany lifts both of my hands to inspect my nails. "Your nails look like you might have died. Maybe buried alive?"

Instinctively I curl my nails into my palms. "I haven't hardly had time to even paint them."

She grabs my hand and pulls me toward the back of the academy. "We'll get you fixed up right."

"Good. Mama's Halloween party is tomorrow night."

"I know it sounds like a lot of fun," Tiffany says.

"Are you coming?"

Tiffany frowns as she starts work on my nails. "No. I'm not invited. I think my parents might be going."

"You don't need an invite. I'll just tell Mama you're coming if you want me to."

"I probably should get out some more. It's tough to meet guys if you're staying at home watching crime shows and drinking wine."

Tiffany's comment short-circuits my thought pattern. "What happened to Patrick?

"Well," Tiffany says with an eye roll.

Her partner, Glenda, leans into our conversation. "That boy is a freak."

Tiffany shrugs her shoulders. "He's incredibly hot and loaded, but even with that, it's hard to get over his weirdness."

Loaded? Patrick? He is a blue-collar HVAC repairman. I also don't find him to be odd in the least.

Glenda clicks her tongue. "Of course, if a boy's loaded like that, I might make some exceptions for his weirdness."

"Oh, hush your mouth. You know anything other than that, you would."

Glenda's lips thin as she nods agreement. "Hmm-hmm."

"We must not be talking about the same Patrick. Unless he won the state lottery last month. He's not exactly hurting, but he's just an HVAC tech."

"I thought you dated." Tiffany wrinkles her nose. "Did y'all ever even talk?"

"Of course, we did." My voice cracks.

Tiffany stares at me sideways as she works on my other hand. "He's not just a technician, April. Patrick owns Cool Breeze HVAC service, and it makes bank. He started it from scratch when he was twenty. Right about the same time, he found out he had a son on the way."

I am desperately searching my memory. I'm hoping to re-member a conversation where I asked Patrick about his career. Maybe I inquired, and he concealed he was an entrepreneur.

In retrospect, I honestly don't think I ever asked him. I knew I wanted him, and the rest was just white noise.

"Yep, but you got the right of it," Glenda says with a fierce nod. "All the money in the world is not going to make a woman happy if she's not getting what she needs out of a relationship."

It is still like they are talking about someone else or talking in code. Patrick is kind, considerate, and generous with his time and humor. What in the world wouldn't a woman be getting that she needed from that relationship?

Tiffany leans in, and Glenda follows suit. "I went out with that boy for four whole weeks. Four weeks!" She waves a finger in the air. "And he never laid a hand on me not once."

"Didn't try to kiss her, neither," Glenda adds.

Tiffany purses her lips, accompanied by an eye roll. "I think that boy's batting for the other team."

"He has a son." I object as if I have a dog in the hunt.

"That don't mean nothing. There's a lot of those men who try to make a marriage work first."

"It sure would explain a lot." Tiffany picks up an emery board. "You had to notice that the boy is a better talker than any girlfriend you ever had."

"He's not—he likes women." Why am I defending him? Why do I even care?

"A woman has her needs," Glenda says.

"This woman does, at least," Tiffany says.

Patrick is straight as any heterosexual man I have been around my entire life. I know this for a fact because the whole time we dated each other, we nearly spontaneously combusted just from being near one another. If Tiffany wasn't feeling those same vibes the four weeks she dated Patrick, their chemistry might not be a good mix.

Patrick and I had fabulous chemistry from the start. At least, if you consider nitroglycerin a good thing.

The only thing that blew up our relationship was his oversight to fill me in on a minor detail about his domestic situation. I'm not saying I would have changed my mind, but it would have saved both of us some embarrassment.

This is all hashing up things I don't need to think about. Look, I came into Tiffany's today. I couldn't have done that if I hadn't mostly put the Patrick fail behind me. Now she's just stirring up a bunch of new thoughts.

Like the fact Patrick owns his own company rather than works for the service company. That'll take a while to sink in.

On some small level, I'm embarrassed I assumed his socio-economic status from the start.

But hey, it isn't my fault he wore worn-out blue jeans, scarred steel toe work boots, and was so polite and humble all the time. Who would've thought somebody like that ran a profitable company?

And it never mattered to me anyway.

I do like the thought of Patrick being successful. His being successful makes me believe the good guys can and do win occasionally.

Would it have changed things if I had known he had a thriving business? I can't see how it would. I've never been a "let a man take care of me" kinda girl. Besides, before our last supper and the revealing of his son, I don't know what could make me any more committed to our relationship.

It wouldn't have changed my reaction to the surprise son he introduced me to that night. The two minutes I saw him, he seemed like a nice enough and well-behaved young man, but he isn't the issue. I am.

I'm not ready to be a mom, and I felt like Patrick had cornered me on his turf.

Even the next day, after I had run away from Patrick and his son, I tried to rationalize in my mind it wouldn't be terrible to raise a kid.

Still, in those daydreams, I always ended up the wicked stepmother at the end of the script. I don't want to be anybody's evil stepmother.

Chapter 22

At four thirty, I walk out of the beauty academy feeling like a model. Well, models don't wear pinstriped pantsuits, but I'm feeling pretty for the first time in a couple of months.

I'm not due at Nana's for another two hours. I could go home and let Puppy out, but who am I kidding. Ever since Daddy put the doggy door in my apartment, Puppy lets himself out. Besides, everyone else in the village is raising him, which is precisely how he likes it. He really doesn't need me anymore.

I start my now-hocked IROC and drive out toward Nana's.

The ride is just what I need to clear my mind. I wouldn't be exaggerating if I said I am getting Jayron, Nina, and Patrick overload. It's making me break out in hives.

How wonderfully comfortable it must be for married people. Where they don't have to worry about relationships, and they just wake up and have someone in their bed without all the drama of having to date. That must be incredibly satisfying.

The sun lights up the sky with salmon and bruise-purple ribbons as I approach the old covered Willoughby bridge. She is waiting for me.

Water trickles down her gray face from the long bangs hanging lank across her dark eyes. The back of her tangled rat's nest hair matches the hair on the doll she clutches by one foot.

She sets her face in a wild grin that sends a shiver up my spine. I take my foot off the brake of the IROC and begin to roll forward toward the bridge. I swear I can hear every chunk of gravel protesting the weight of the wheels.

My eyes never leave her face. I know she can't be trusted.

Willoughby bridge has a captive spirit of a twelve-year-old girl. Her wet clothes are circa the late nineteenth century. It is apparent she drowned. She carries a doll that has an eerie resemblance to her.

She also hates my guts for some unknown reason.

That's cool. I'm not particularly fond of her, either.

I continue to edge my car closer to the entrance of the covered bridge. I hold out some slim hope that as I approach, she will step aside, although I know from past experience, it is doubtful.

When I'm within ten feet of her, she moves directly in front of my car. Her smile cracks open to reveal her fangs. I know it must be an optical illusion, but they seem to telescope longer and thicker from her gums. I don't realize that my foot has slid back to the brake as I watch her show in horror.

I'm mesmerized as her teeth continue to grow in length and girth until they seem in proportion to the fangs on a rattlesnake. There are many things that wig me out. Rattlesnakes are comfortably in the top three.

The drowned girl shifts her bottom jaw left to right as if attempting to make her jaw pop. Her bottom jaw separates and pulls apart from the rest of her head, and my stomach turns. Her jaw continues to stretch open in an anaconda manner until her bottom lip has passed her chest. She could easily shove my head into her mouth.

Which suddenly dawns on me that might actually be her plan.

I slam my right foot onto the accelerator, and my IROC spews gravel before it grips asphalt and lurches forward. First, she's standing in front of me with her jaw approaching her waistline. The next second, she vaporizes as the front of the car passes through her.

Fear grips me as I am convinced she will reappear inside of my car. If I look in the rearview mirror and she's sitting back there with her mouth open, she won't have to kill me. I'll just fall over in the front seat and die.

Despite the fear ripping at my mind, I decide it will be better to know than allow her to swallow me whole from the backseat. I reach up and adjust my rearview mirror as my car takes the slick planks of the old bridge too quickly, and I feel the vehicle skate to the left.

I'm elated the drowned girl is not in my backseat. Instead, she's behind my car as if she never moved and I passed through her.

That is fine by me, too. Never one to miss out on an opportunity to celebrate, I shoot drowned girl the bird in the rearview mirror. That should fix her.

Focusing on regaining control of my car, I ease off the accelerator until the sliding sensation stops. The wooden blinds of the bridge are designed to keep wooden wagons from falling through the sides, not two-thousand-pound automobiles.

I'm almost out of the bridge when I steal another look in my rearview mirror. That is odd. The drowned girl raises her arms outward toward the sky, palms up. She doubles over, flexing her arms to her side like a bodybuilder striking the perfect pose to show off his pectoral muscles.

Flexing her arms against her sides, her lower jaw comes unhinged, forming a cavernous "O." One hundred overgrown black tadpoles blow out her mouth like a human howitzer. I stand on my accelerator.

The IROC's tires spin ineffectively on the bridge planks as the inside of my car begins to sound like I'm caught in a hail storm. The tires grip and the rear of my car fishtails hard to the left.

The left bumper taps the side of the bridge, and I hear a snapping noise as the rear of the car swings to the right now. As I fly out of the bridge, the rear tires bite hard, slamming my head hard against the headrest.

Keeping my car at maximum speed for the next few miles, I nearly miss the turnoff to Nana's trailer.

I don't dare look in the rearview mirror again. If the drowned girl follows me, I might accidentally crash my car into a tree, giving her a chance to eat me alive. I don't want her to eat me.

Passing all of the charms and spirit catchers hung along Nana's gravel driveway, I begin to feel better. Surely drowned girl won't follow me in here. Would she?

I back into the dirt patch Nana and I use for parking and leave the motor running. I need to see what she spewed at me. There is also the need to get out of here quickly if it is something more than what I'm prepared to deal with tonight.

Exiting the IROC, I swing wide from the side of the car as I move toward the back. Those black tadpoles had flown at least a hundred feet. I have visions of something stuck on the car's trunk, jumping off the vehicle, and landing on my face, where it proceeds to suck all the juice out of my body.

Folks might consider that an overimaginative mind on my part. I would submit to them that I just had a dead girl spew black creatures at me.

There are over twenty black lumps stuck to the pristine red paint of my car. It's odd what came to my mind. I'm really hoping whatever they are, their guts aren't as acidic as bug guts.

My paint job is brand new, and I don't want it ruined.

The longer I look at the black lumps, the more I become convinced that their flying days are over. I move in for a closer look and am still unable to positively identify them. I lean over for an even closer look. Finally, I pick up a foot-long stick and try to pry one of the lumps free from my car.

At first, it will not move. When it finally slides from the stick's pressure, it makes a suction cup sound and leaves a transparent mucous film on my car.

Great. The little suckers are going to ruin my paint job.

Having still not identified the black lump, I move toward

Nana's screen door holding the stick at arm's length.

I rap on the screen door. "Nana? Nana, can you come out here?"

"Just a minute, April."

"Can you sort of hurry?"

Nana comes out of the kitchen, wiping her hands on a towel. "Honestly, April. I wish your mama had named you Patience."

I do a double-take of Nana. Something is off since the last time I saw her. Not in a good way like, "Hey, you sure have lost a lot of weight," but more like, "What the heck is wrong with your face?"

I realize what has changed. "Why did you shave your eyebrows off, Nana?"

She covers her forehead with the back of her right wrist. "I didn't."

Alright, then who stole your eyebrows? As interesting as that is, I need to identify the black blob that resembles a burnt marshmallow on the end of the stick I'm holding first.

I lift the stick out to her. "What's this?"

If she had eyebrows, they would have come together when her brow furrowed. Instead, there is an odd collection of wrinkles coming together over the bridge of her nose. "That's the biggest darn leach I have ever seen. It would have had to be feeding on a big animal. Was it on a cow?"

"No, a little girl?"

"Oh, how awful. Did you help get the leeches off of her?"

"Actually, they came out of her."

Nana squints. "You must be thinking of tapeworms. Leaches don't come out of you."

"Came out of the drowned girl."

"April, I'm not so sure you should get that close to the bridge spirit."

"I didn't. The drowned girl spewed these at me."

Nana slams her hands onto her hips. "Why in the world do you have to antagonize that ghost?"

I point at my chest. "Me? I didn't start this."

"Well, she's zeroing in on some sort of negative issue you two are having."

Yeah. I have plenty of negative issues in my life, but I haven't shared any of them with the drowned girl. Wait, had I? Oh my gosh, when I thought about how scared I am of rattlesnakes, that was the next thing she did. Open her mouth wide as if she was about to devour me.

"Honestly, April, you must have done something to animate her. She's only been seen a few times in the past fifty years, and you can't seem to go past the bridge without waking her up."

"I didn't do anything," I complain.

"Well, she has a lot of animosity toward you."

Yeah? Well, I don't like her much, either. My love for her will be even less if she is drawn to me because I can read people's mental visions. That idea spooks me so badly I must distract myself from pondering it any further. Luckily, I only have to look at Nana's eyebrow-less face to distract myself.

I fight back a laugh and point at her forehead. "So, what happened there?"

Her hand covers her brow again. "Don't."

"I'm not making fun. I'm just curious."

Nana huffs as she motions for me to follow her into the kitchen. I start toward the kitchen and look at the black blob on the end of the stick I'm carrying. "Let me get rid of this first."

I lean out the front door and toss the stick toward the woods to the right of the trailer. As I shut the front door, two dim, yellow lights at the entrance to Nana's property catch my eye through the bushes, charms, and demon wards.

A chill runs up my spine as the lights blink out for a brief second and then reignite. My suspicions are confirmed when the lights move in unison to the left and then blink again. The drowned girl is stalking me.

It is comforting to be able to shut the door behind me as I reenter the trailer. I believe that I'm safe, surrounded by all the magic precautions my Nana has on her property.

I had been so focused on identifying the black blobs attached to the back of my car I had not noticed the delicious scents coming out of the kitchen. "It smells like you went all out for dinner tonight?"

Nana turns and smiles. I'm almost getting used to the sleek new look of her face. Sort of. "Of course, I'm going to go all out, cooking dinner when my baby girl is coming over. I have some greens, black-eyed peas, and skillet corn."

"Wow, that sounds fantastic," I say.

"How are your practice sessions going?"

"Pretty good. I'm doing really well at the controlling movement of small objects, but the fire is a little less certain."

Nana nods her head as she stirs the greens. "Fire can be unpredictable in real life. Understandably, it's the same in magic."

That makes sense. Nana is good like that; she can distill things down to their basics.

"Are you going to tell me what caused the mishap with your eyebrows?" I ask.

Nana rolls her eyes, which looks particularly comical without eyebrows, and I have to stifle a laugh.

"You know I expanded my business from the newspaper articles. About three weeks ago, I started advertising on social media."

I wasn't even aware Nana had a social media page. "No, you didn't mention that."

She waves her hand at me. "Well, it's all experimental, so I wasn't thinking much about it. But the fact is that my products have really taken off."

I begin to get an uneasy feeling. "Would you mind describing *really taking off*?"

Nana shrugs. "I used to sell maybe twenty potions a month. The last three weeks, I've been selling about a hundred a day."

"A day?"

Nana smirks. "I know crazy, right?"

I'm not sure crazy is how I would describe it. Dangerous is more apt. Nana has been selling her potions for as long as I can remember. The most common one that she sells through classified ads in the newspaper is a love potion. Even though Nana can work some magic, my family's consensus is that her love potions are no more reliable than two frozen margaritas.

The family has been concerned somebody may accuse Nana of being a snake oil dealer, which would be accurate, and get their money back forcibly. But over time, we came to view her entrepreneurial ventures as mostly harmless. She wasn't selling many, and the price was too low for someone to get violent over. Also, who's going to admit to their friends they were desperate enough to try some witch's home-brewed potion?

But if she is now selling a hundred potions a day, the probability of selling one of her worthless concoctions to a maniac is significantly increased. And these people aren't local. They won't necessarily be shamed by the fact they thought the product would actually work.

"Nana, I don't know if that's necessarily a good thing."

She teeters her hand side to side in front of her face. "Yeah, it made me realize that I need to up my game. Selling a novelty item to people who are desperate for love, that's one thing. But it only takes a click of a key for someone to give you a bad review on social media. That could kill all your sales, so I decided it was time to enhance my product offering."

"Actually make a love potion that works?" I ask incredulously.

The skin on her forehead wrinkles upward. I don't think I'm ever going to get used to this no-eyebrow look.

"Heavens, no. Love potions, by their very nature, are risky. I can make ones that work, but what about consent?"

I'm confused. "What do you mean consent?"

She waves her hands wildly in front of me. "Consent, April. Think about it. If somebody found you attractive and wanted to be with you, you wouldn't need a stupid potion to make him love you. Love potions are just a step above a roofie. The only difference is you don't pass out. You're conscious but are not actively thinking."

That is the second time Nana made sense tonight. That in

and of itself has me wondering about my own mental health. Also, it is disconcerting to realize all these years, Nana had purposefully been making potions that would not work. Here I thought she just wasn't very good at potion-making.

"But I like the idea of this social media advertising." She holds her hands up and makes a euphoric expression. "I mean, the money is incredible. For the first time in my life, I actually have money. But I can't be selling a product that I know doesn't work."

"Then why have you been doing it all these years?"

"Those were people I knew for the most part. They were desperate to have somebody love them, and I just wanted to help them feel like they were doing something to make it happen. Besides, it serves a secondary purpose when the potions don't work. It confirmed to people in this town that I was just odd and not an actual witch.

"Then why would they continue to pay you for potions that they didn't expect to work?"

"If there was a guy who you really thought was destined to be the love of your life and he wasn't giving you the time a day, you wouldn't try a ten-dollar potion?"

I start to say no and bite my tongue. You're not supposed to lie to your elders. I know deep in my heart, if I came across the right guy, the guy I wanted to spend the rest of my life with, there wouldn't be anything I wouldn't do to jumpstart the relationship. "I guess."

"That's right." Nana begins to make our plates.

"That still doesn't answer what happened to your eyebrows."

"That's an accident. You see, if I'm going to sell products on social media, they have to work. This means it has to be something people want that doesn't compromise anyone else. So, what does everybody want?"

"More money?"

"There are some ethical issues there as well, plus you wouldn't use a potion for that."

"Clear skin."

Nana hands me a plate full of vegetables. "There are already hundreds of products to clear up blemishes."

I tire of this game, and I'm ready to shovel some vegetables into my mouth. "I don't know, just tell me."

"Hair. Thicker, stronger hair."

"You can do that?"

"Sure, I can—well, in theory, I can." She points at her hairless brow. "As you can see, the original potion has some devastating side effects."

"That was from your hair growth product?" I begin to giggle.

"I obviously reversed something."

"Obviously." If that is what she was planning on selling, she should stick to the fake love potions. I think the customers would be a lot more forgiving about a love potion not working than waking up and not having any hair on their heads.

"As you can see, I've got some more work to do."

"But you believe you'll be able to get it to work?"

"Oh, your Nana has got serious game. I'll get it to work. I probably wasn't paying attention the first time."

The vegetable plate is delicious. Everything Nana cooks is always delicious.

I am probably pushing my luck when I go for seconds. But hey, it's vegetables, right? Vegetables aren't going to keep me out of my Tinker Bell outfit.

As I sit, Nana asks without looking up from her plate. "I can tell that you have some confusion and anxiety in your aura today. What has you troubled?"

That's the thing about living with my family. Everyone is so perceptive it's hard to hide anything. "I've just had a few odd things going on lately."

She moves the last of her corn around on her plate absently. "Odd? Like how?"

All week I thought about asking Nana about the ghost in the mirror. Now it is suddenly more difficult to talk about than I expected. I realize that deep down inside, I'm genuinely terri-fied about the event.

Despite my fears, I begin to relay the events from the last few days. I start with the message scrolled on the police annex mirror, the head appearing on my car dashboard, the headless ghost's attempt to chop off my head, and end with me being lost in the void if not for Puppy's growling.

The stories rush from me quickly, and I feel my blood pres-sure rise commensurately with my voice, with each sentence of the story. Finally, I finish and suck in a breath of air to steady my nerves and keep me from bursting into tears.

Nana pauses before answering. "You do not recognize the ghost?"

"The head or the body?"

Nana lets a short bark of laughter escape her. I'm not sure what she finds humorous.

"I suppose the face. I'm going to go out on a limb here and guess that the head belongs to the headless body."

That makes sense. "No, ma'am. I don't recognize the face at all. Why?"

"Just trying to determine a timeline."

"It all happened this week."

Nana shakes her head. "No. The timeline for the spirit. You should know now that spirits have no set time. Time is mean-ingless on the other side of the veil."

Yes, I know that, and it still gives me a chill when she says it aloud.

"You are drawn to the infinity for some reason. As if the spirit is hoping you will cross through the veil."

"But you said that I should never alter history," I complain.

Nana's face pinches together. "I was considering if it could possibly be a spirit from the future."

My mouth falls open. It is a bombshell that I don't need to hear, and I hope I misheard. "Future?"

"It's just the 'Help me.'" It could be that a spirit is asking you to intervene in the past, but I get more of a feel of the case of a fate exposed."

I hold up a hand. "Ghosts from the future can reveal themselves to me? As in live people?"

"Fates exposed can be altered without side effects. I think that's correct," she says.

"Nana! How can somebody that is not dead yet haunt me?"

"Honestly, April. You're too smart to not catch on to this. If time is meaningless on the other side of the veil, there is no future, past, or present for spirits. There's just one time all rolled up into one big ball."

You know I hear that, but I don't think my head's entirely around it yet.

"You know what really doesn't make sense," she says.

"Everything?"

She ignores my sarcasm. "That the spirit is asking you for help, but then you say the headless body tried to cut your head off. That makes no sense to me."

It doesn't make any sense to me either, then or now. Killing someone is not exactly the best way to get them to help you. I think it's one of the reasons I never married the head to the headless body.

The vision of the woman sitting on my chest holding the blade against my throat flashes back into my mind. This time it is more lucid. This time I do not focus on the feel of the sharp edge pressed against my tender flesh, the weight of her knees on my elbows, or the feeling of her long hair brushing my cheeks as she leaned over me.

Hair? Wait, she had her head. Her head was still attached! Oh my gosh, it was a different woman. The woman on my chest was shorter and more compact than the headless body holding the knife by the kitchen sink when I returned from the infinity by following Puppy's growls.

"There are two separate women," I announce.

"Good. That makes more sense. Now we might be getting somewhere. Did you recognize the woman who tried to kill you in your dream?"

Her face was heavily shadowed by the darkness. She did look vaguely familiar, but I can't place her. "No. Not exactly."

Nana shrugs. "Well, at least it makes more sense now."

"But what do I do about it?" I whine.

"Nothing," Nana says as if it is obvious. "How are you going to affect anything if you can't identify who's needing help?"

This stinks. I thought we were getting somewhere.

Nana picks up her plate and walks toward the kitchen. "However, that does dovetail nicely into our lesson tonight."

As much as I now enjoy my Thursday night lessons with Nana, the drowned girl picking a fight with me and the re-hashing of the mirror ghost have quelled my enthusiasm. I feel more like going home and cowering under my blankets.

"The lesson for tonight is how to use an object for ex-tended views." She reappears from the kitchen holding a size-able amber sphere I know to be her version of a crystal ball. "It's possible that by concentrating on the faces of these two women, you might be able to see where they are currently. If you can do that and identify the women, you might have the answers you need."

Now we are getting somewhere. *This* is the heavy-duty magic stuff I was hoping Nana would reveal to me when we first started our Thursday lessons.

Nana sets up the opaque, honey-colored ball on her tiny kit-chen table. Cupping her hands around the orb, she closes her eyes close and appears to hold her breath.

I wait.

My breathing sounds abnormally loud. I scan the kitchen, noticing Nana has a new pattern of dish towels draped over the oven's handle.

Having lost patience, I begin to ask her if I'm supposed to do something, too. The honey color of the sphere marbleizes to a milky white. Blue-gray streaks, appearing like veins, grow and twist within the orb, transforming into small cloud banks.

Leaning closer to get a better look, I see small, clear openings forming within the moving clouds. All the original honey-colored amber has disappeared. The grey clouds churn and dissipate until her crystal ball is clear, save for a few smatterings of swirling white clouds.

The view is as if I were standing on my parents' porch, looking down at the lake. I can see the back of two people sitting at the edge of the dock. It seems like Mama and Daddy.

The moment I identify them, the point of view changes abruptly, and I'm standing directly in front of them. The fact this would mean I'd be standing on the water has no ill effect.

The two of them are sharing a moment over a bottle of wine. My parents are watching the sunset together, which I have seen them often do during my childhood. Puppy is lying on the dock next to Daddy.

What I don't anticipate is that I can hear parts of their conversation. I can't make out their words precisely. It is more low-droning noises. When they laugh together, the sound is as clear as if I were sitting with them on the dock.

I know I'm probably supposed to be quiet, but I can't help but whisper, "Is this now."

Nana, whose eyes have opened while I was watching the scene, replies, "Possibly. It could have been earlier."

"How did you make it happen?"

"I wanted to see my daughter happy. So, I focus on that desire. The crystal revealed the most recent event where she was happy."

It makes me grin. It may be odd, but it is a source of pride that my parents still enjoy each other's company the way they do. "It seems sort of voyeuristic."

Nana shakes her hands on the side of the now-transparent sphere, and the cloud bank rolls in as the ball flashes its original honey-colored amber. "There's no 'sort of' about it. It's highly voyeuristic."

Yeah, but think about all the cool things you could know. No more guessing about how people really feel or what they did. Pull out the crystal ball and just check it out for yourself. It is like the best research tool ever made. "When do I get one?"

Nana laughs. "Slow your roll, April. This is a continuation of the control theme that all your lessons have strengthened. I have no doubt you will be able to read crystals. The key is, do you have enough focus and discipline to use them correctly?"

"I'm highly focused." At least I want to be.

Nana ignores me. "The key to reading crystals is a clear picture of what you want to view and the discipline to focus your mind *only* on that one pinpoint idea. If you are undisciplined, unfocused, or just let your mind wander in general, you could be seeing any timeline in the past or future.

"We were discussing this earlier. All times run concurrently on the same parallel tracks. Jumping the track is easy if you're unfocused, and the information you receive will only confuse you because you do not know whether it's in the past or future."

"Okay," I say eagerly. I'm hoping Nana will let me try out her crystal ball now. Or maybe she even got me one of my own.

"The other thing about extended views is you only do them under extreme circumstances."

I feel my spirits fall. Here we go again with more restrictions on the few cool things about my "gifts." "Why is that?"

"First, it is highly intrusive on people. You have to consider, when is it appropriate for me to watch someone without their knowledge—and never abuse the use."

I understand her point. I really don't care about morality right now; I just want to try out a few views that have been niggling at me.

"Most importantly, these viewings are highly addictive. And they drain considerable amounts of energy from their viewer. I have known many talented individuals to wither away because they cannot break their binge-watching of other people's lives.

For some, living vicariously through others is more rewarding than living their own life."

"That doesn't make any sense. That wouldn't be me," I promise her.

Nana's smile tells me she doesn't believe me. "Everybody

says that, April. But understand, if this skill were misused, it would be the kind of addiction that you can never break away from. It will eat your soul."

Eat my soul—that gets my attention.

Nana reaches into her apron and retrieves a milky white crystal the size of a golf ball. "This is your practice crystal," she announces.

I must admit, it is underwhelming. I'll need a magnifying glass to see anything in that little rock. "That's it?"

"Size really has no bearing in this manner, April. Just your level of focus and clarity of thoughts. The other thing is, the smaller size will help curb your desire to binge-watch until you become used to the practice and also does not drain the same level of life force from you."

She hands the crystal to me. At first cold, it immediately warms in my hand. I like the feel of it and clasp my fingers around its smooth surface. It's difficult to explain, but it's as if the crystal is claiming me, melding our energies, as if it knew it always was destined to be mine.

"This first lesson, I want you to concentrate on the face of the woman who attacked you in your vision. If your focus is strong enough, you should be able to pull in a vision of her that may give us a clue who she is. Even if you don't recognize her face, it might show us where she works or some other detail about her identity."

I run my thumb over the warm, smooth contour of my crystal. The heat from it increases, and I swear I can feel tingles of electrical charges emanating from it into my hands and traveling up to my elbow.

"Hold it out and look at it while you focus. Remember, you must hold your focus tightly," Nana encourages me.

Suddenly all I can think about is Vander. Our last meeting at the restaurant when he talked in riddles to me. I think, deep down, I knew then that he was off to do something dangerous. Something that might make it where I never saw him again.

In my mind's eye, his hair and eyes are the same dark coloring and his skin the same light olive tone, but the clarity of his features is fading. That makes me profoundly sad. The knowledge that slowly but surely, over time, my memory of him will erode into nothingness.

"April, are you focusing on the ghost's face?"

Nana's voice draws me back to the present. Bless it. I thought I was going to be good at this too.

I steal a quick look at my crystal, fully expecting to be embarrassed by seeing Vander in the sphere rather than the face of the ghost. The opaque ball has a slight glow emanating from it. As if it has a small fire on the inside. But there is no clearing to view through. Certainly no visual of a ghost—or Vander.

"It might be difficult the first time, April," Nana coaches. "You'll need to really focus on any detail you can remember and clear all else from your mind."

Forget that. I'm not even positive I can focus on the female ghost. Her features were so heavily shadowed during the attack. I only recently realized she had *her* head because I remembered feeling her hair on my skin.

What's happened to Vander is something that is of overwhelming concern to me now.

I draw as much of Vander to me as humanly possible. Things I remember about him from high school, our first dealings together when I came back to Guntersville, and even the smell of his cologne.

Focusing as hard as possible, I pull it all into me and push out with my energies—in the same manner I use my "gifts" to read people. Surely the energy required to fire up the sphere must be similar to how I summon other magical powers.

Eagerly I look down at the sphere in my hand. It immediately turns pitch black, and the crystal turns so cold it stings my palm. I drop it on the table and rub my hand.

I have a red circle in the middle of my right palm.

Nana gasps. "That's odd."

Feeling chagrined for having strayed from the lesson, I grab a napkin, wrapping it around the crystal before lifting it with my left hand. "Is it broken?"

Nana hesitates. "I've never seen that before. It's as if you were blocked. Chalk it up as another first."

Saying I'm disappointed is a significant understatement. "What do I do to make it work?"

Nana shakes her head. "I'm sorry, April. I assumed it would be in your skillset. Maybe extended views are not something you will be able to do."

But I want to. "Why not?"

"Everybody doesn't get the same skills. You're powerful in many areas I barely have any power in."

"But I can work on it and get better. Right?"

"Maybe—but you need at least a spark of talent to build on the skill. If you don't have it, building on zero is still zero. I've never seen a crystal react in that manner, April."

"This bites," I grouse.

"You can still continue trying off and on. You never know. It might be something that comes in late for you."

I drop the sphere into my pocket. I can tell by Nana's tone she isn't very optimistic things will change for me.

The crystal immediately warms in my pocket. What a tease. It acts like it wants to work, but...

A new fear grips me.

If I don't have the skill, it would make more sense for my sphere to stay the same cataract white. It was only after I focused on Vander it turned black and subzero cold. Gnawing anxiety creeps in as my concern for Vander grows.

Dark and cold is not what I want for Vander. It would explain why no one has heard from him.

I wish I never thought to use the crystal to check in on him.

"Do you want me to show you how to make this hair potion?" Nana says. First, I need to throw out this batch that will make your head as smooth as a baby's butt."

Through my sorrow for Vander, an idea clicks in my head. "Nana, that's your new product."

She stares at me as if I've lost my mind and laughs. She notices I'm serious, and her mirth transforms into concern. "No. I don't believe the no-eyebrows thing will ever catch on as a fashion statement."

"No. But—" I make air quotes with my fingers. "'No Shave 'Em body smoother will be a huge hit."

Nana squints at the menacingly large stockpot over her right shoulder. "You know what? That is an excellent idea. That means that as soon as I get the hair growth going in the right direction, I won't have one but two products to sell online."

"You can mail my royalty checks to my apartment," I joke.

"Absolutely, I will."

Nana is quite serious. She is also, by the upward stare of her eyes as her mouth mumbles multiplication tables, calculating her newfound fortune.

"I'm going to gather up my stuff and head on home. Thank you again for dinner and the lesson."

Nana breaks briefly from her calculations and gives me a quick hug. "I want you to be really careful this upcoming week about any time you feel like you're close to the veil. You must stay away from it until we get a better handle on this. Okay?"

"Yes, ma'am. Believe me, I will try."

"Good. I love you."

"I love you too, Nana."

I scan the woods for the yellow eyes stalking me earlier as I get into my vehicle. I'm getting sadder about Vander by the second, and I'm agitated about not being able to identify the ghost that has been haunting my dreams. I'm not in the mood for any more of drowned girl's silliness tonight.

Surprisingly, she is not waiting to ambush me once I leave Nana's property. I don't even see her when I drive over the bridge on my way home.

Maybe things can still improve, and my crystal will reveal the information I need to put an end to this recent haunting. Perhaps Vander is okay.

Chapter 23

I have a dreamless night's sleep, waking five minutes before five, which allows me to beat my alarm to the punch.

My golf-ball-sized crystal ball rests on my nightstand. It's still cataract white as I lift it.

I intend to try a quick scan on the ghost that tried to kill me, but Vander pops into my mind again. When the stone turns to a ruddy brown and begins to cool, I quickly set it back down on my nightstand.

Stop doing that, April.

This is supposed to be a happy day. The Halloween party has always been one of the highlights of my year. Still, my concerns for Vander, whether real or imagined, are putting a damper on my spirits.

Puppy is snoring, blissfully unaware, at the end of my bed with all four paws suspended in the air. I watch him for a few moments as his right front paw keeps stretching out as if punching at something in a dream.

I have to find out. Nana said that it will take a spark, and then possibly I can get better. I'll just have to throw everything I have at the crystal and see if I can get a reading on Vander.

I pick the crystal up again, but this time, rather than hold it just in my right hand, I keep it in both hands, holding it as tightly as I can against my chest. I focus all my energy on the ball. Momentarily, I forget what I'm searching for. I'm so focused on producing energy that my mind wanders from what I desire to see.

The crystal produces immense heat, and I open my cupped hands and see a swirling, half-opaque and half-clear surface.

Suddenly, in a flash of light, it becomes completely transparent. I lean forward and peer into the tiny ball, eager to see a vision.

Please let it be Vander. Please let him be okay.

I'm shocked to see Nina Rodriguez. A rather unwelcome site at any time, but especially when I'm searching for Vander. I'm about to set the sphere back on my dresser when I notice Nina has something in her hand. I draw the sphere closer until it is inches from my nose to get a better view.

Nina has a gun in her right hand as she walks into a gas station.

My body jolts involuntarily. Quickly, I put the crystal sphere back on my nightstand and pick up my phone instead. I immediately hit Jacob's number on speed dial.

"April?" he answers, before I can say hello.

"Jacob, I've got to tell you something."

"Hold up just a minute. I meant to call you this morning, but there's been a flood of activity since last night. Like you said, Nina skipped town last night. I talked to her cousin Dominique, and she told me that she left at about three this morning in her car. Dominique said she didn't like the way she was acting. She told Dominique to have a great life."

My gut clenches as I realize my vision might be real. "Jacob, I think she is armed and that she may be about to rob a gas station."

"April, how in the heck could you know that?"

I wasn't about to tell my best friend that a smooth rock has shown me the vision of Nina robbing a gas station. "I guess it's just a premonition, like how I knew she might skip town."

"Premonition?" His question is higher pitched. Silence ensues.

He sighs. "Okay. Never mind. I'll let all responding cars know that she should be treated as armed and dangerous."

"Thank you, Jacob."

"For what?"

"For just rolling with it."

He makes an odd sound I take to be a laugh. "Half of police work is a premonition. I'll call you as soon as I know something."

"Okay, thank you, Jacob." He's already disconnected our call.

I sit on my bed, holding my phone. I think I'm one more bad piece of news away from having a total breakdown.

Seriously. How much is one girl supposed to be able to handle before she cracks? I really don't think I'm a wimp. I've just been pulled in too many different directions, into too many life-and-death situations recently. Nobody should have this much stress on them.

Yeah, that's it. I've made up my mind. Going down memory lane with Halloween parties, football games, and Christmas is a nice thought, but I have to get out of this town. My sanity is more important than any fun activities with my family and friends.

At this rate, my family and friends will be visiting me at Bryce Mental Hospital very shortly.

Chapter 24

When I unlock Snow and Associates at a little before seven, I'm the only person in the office. I don't like using company assets or time to search for a job, but given Nina has eaten up my early-morning hours, I really feel it's more of a trade-off of time for the day.

I fire up my laptop and begin searching the legal job boards. Right off the bat, I find an opening in Houston that looks to be tailor-made for my skillset. I begin to send them a résumé and then think better of it.

Guntersville can be hot, but I've heard Houston on some days can be so humid that you never dry off from your morning shower. Yeah, I don't want to work at a law office with swamp butt the rest of my life.

It must be a Texas banner day as there is also an opening for a junior defense attorney in Austin. That sounds promising. No, it's not New York or LA, but I've heard many nice things about Austin.

Besides, I like cowgirl boots.

I do a cursory review of my most current résumé and send a copy to the Austin firm. Austin must be better than Guntersville. There's no way the people in Austin are as crazy as my hometown. Right?

Leaning back, I take a deep breath and close my eyes.

Get a hold of yourself, April. Just get a hold of yourself.

The front door unlatches, and my eyes open to Howard's welcoming smile. He walks over to me with a grin and sets a greasy white paper bag on the top of my desk.

"Surprise," he says.

I poke at the bag. "That's not another Little Bunny Foo Foo biscuit, is it?"

"No. Tenderloin."

"You're the best."

"I know."

Howard turns without any further conversation and walks toward his office. I eagerly open the bag and peer in. It is still taking me a little bit of time to shake the treachery of the rabbit biscuit.

Cautiously I unwrap the biscuit, and happiness washes over me all over again as the scent of spicy tenderloin wafts into my nostrils. I wonder what tenderloin biscuits smell like in Austin?

Mama calls at ten thirty and finally lets the cat out of the bag. The location for the party is 412 Birch Street. The address does not ring a bell.

She asks me to be there within the hour and tells me she has sandwiches scheduled for delivery at eleven.

Turning onto Birch Street, I realize the address is old widow Motlow's house. The Motlows were some of the oldest of old money in the area.

During the Civil War, one of their ancestors had been a blockade runner at the Port of Mobile. The family continued the tradition of bringing needed supplies to the masses during prohibition with the illegal transportation of fine Canadian whiskey. The fortune made was steadily invested in the stock market on margins. The only cash splurge for the family was a beautiful ten-thousand-square-foot home constructed on an estate-sized lot overlooking the lake and downtown Guntersville.

The house is one of only three homes on Birch Street. Smaller homes of well-to-do merchants, bankers, and politicians are further down the hill. These three homes at the intersection of Fourth and Birch sat like crown jewels above Guntersville. They were our "castles" of the early twentieth century.

The Motlow house is an odd blend of Mediterranean and antebellum. It is not in general disrepair, but it is going to seed and will need some profound love.

It is a perfect house for the Halloween party. It has the old, lived-in feel that gives way to the imaginative ghost story. It is a home that needs the eyes of many potential buyers to see it in as festive a setting as possible to stir the imagination of what it *might be*. The event should help it sell and at top dollar.

I lock my car and stroll up the pebbled driveway toward the home. As soon as my left foot touches the first step, I become dizzy and must extend my arms to keep my balance.

I withdraw my foot from the porch, gawking at the house while I get my bearings. You would think with all the experience I have I would get used to this and start being more prepared. Is it really all that crazy to believe that I'll feel something in a house this full of history?

Once I've taken the time to raise the mental buffers in my mind, I step back onto the porch.

All good now. No dizziness, and not a peep from any voices.

Voices are the worst. There's nothing like trying to have a good time while multiple dead people decide to share their needs and wants with you. It's sort of a downer.

I hear feminine voices down the wood floor hallway. I'm

nearly at the back of the house when, through the opening on the right, I see Mama, Wanda Neil, and Diane Rains standing with Granny around a granite island."

"Am I late?" I ask.

Mama turns her attention to me. "Just in time. Jerry's just delivered the sandwiches."

Well, if I'd known it was Jerry's sandwiches, I would have been early. "Cool."

I move over to the island and lift one of the sandwiches off the colorful orange-and-green serving platter they are displayed on.

Mama makes everything a show. Even simple things.

"I'm surprised you can spare any time from your busy schedule," Wanda Neil snipes.

Wanda Neil and Diane Rains are my mama's two best friends outside of Daddy. Since high school, they have known each other and have always been thicker than thieves, from what Nana has told me. Unfortunately, their strong positive feelings do not pass down to the next generation.

Wanda, the director of nursing at the Boaz medical clinic, works with my mother every other weekend at the women's shelter. She is habitually recruiting me to help out, but I just haven't worked it into my schedule yet.

Wanda is a busy woman herself. Therefore, a busy schedule is not an acceptable excuse for shirking your civic duty. I avoid her at all costs. One, because she is a passive-aggressive bully who doesn't take no for an answer. Two, she could've easily lined up as the right offensive guard for the University of North Alabama's football squad.

"Oh, don't you just look cute as a button." Diane Rains lays a delicate hand on my forearm. "I'm surprised Howard will let you dress casually on Fridays. He's so old-fashioned."

Diane Rains is the mother of my former best friend, now nemesis, and I suppose Puppy's veterinarian, Jackie Rains. Diane is what you would call well-preserved. From a distance of fifty feet, I'm sure you would mistake her and her daughter as sisters. Her perfectly dyed auburn hair never has a single strand out of place, and I don't know that I have ever seen the woman sweat.

"He doesn't normally, but he knew I was coming over to help Mama. As he always says, 'Viv gets what she wants.'"

"Smart man. He knows how to keep the ladies happy." Diane smirks.

Right. That's why Howard is pushing sixty and still not married.

"When did old widow Motlow move out?" I say before biting into my chicken salad croissant.

"They sort of moved her out about a month ago," Mama answers.

"They put her into a home? I didn't even know she had family left."

Mama squints so hard her eyes nearly shut. Diane barks a quick laugh as she covers her mouth with her fist.

"She died, April," Wanda hisses. "If you would read the obituaries occasionally, you would know these things."

Why in the world would I want to read which one of my old neighbors kicked the bucket this week?

Something that feels like cold fingers rake up the back of my scalp, making me duck and turn quickly. I catch the slightest frosting of my breath when I turn.

Then it is gone.

Fudge nut. This house is active!

"Are you okay? Mama asks. "You're acting like you just saw a ghost."

Felt one. Didn't see it. "Yeah, I just got a bit of déjà vu." I try to sound nonchalant.

"I told Vivian she outdid herself this year. The ghost tales session is going to be wild this year." When Diane says the word "wild," she extends it.

Her phoniness makes me ill.

"As long as we keep everybody to the three-drink coupon we agreed on, we won't be creating any new ghosts," Wanda adds, devoid of all humor.

I shake my goosebumps away with a shoulder shiver. "So, what do you have me on, Mama?"

"As soon as you finish your sandwich, I want you to make some more of those crêpe paper chains you make." She turns and produces a cardboard box, sliding it toward me.

I peer inside to find thirty rolls of black crêpe paper. My idea of purgatory is sitting, hour upon hour, folding rolls of crêpe paper back and forth four inches at a time to create a crêpe paper chain. It must be the most mind-numbing activity ever created.

"Mama, can we just skip that this year?" I ask.

"No! It's perfect. And you always do such a wonderful job," Granny adds in unhelpfully.

"It just wouldn't be a Halloween party without the black crêpe paper chains." Mama refuses to relent.

Whatever. I know better than to argue with Granny or Mama. It's just a waste of breath. Besides, the crêpe paper chain project would allow me to keep out of "picking on distance" of Mama's best friends, Beauty and the Beast.

I pick up the box of paper and march off to the living room.

Chapter 25

Two hours later, my eyes are crossed, my shoulders are elevated higher than my ears, and my hands ache. I hadn't used all of the rolls of crêpe paper entirely, but really, how many hundreds of feet of the chain do we need for one party?

Besides, I'll need some of the rolls to decorate the exterior columns and probably a couple other decorations.

I walk back toward the kitchen and hear Wanda's voice booming down the hallway. "No. Nobody has seen Faith since Wednesday. Chelsie said she left a little bit before she did on Wednesday."

"That has to be just a little bit after April and I visited them. I was looking for a new trunk," I hear Granny say.

"The last thing you need is another trunk," Mama says.

I take the right-hand turn into the kitchen and am surprised by its transformation. Six eight-foot tables have been decked out in Halloween decorations and now hold twenty Crockpots, five cakes, ten pies, and four trays of cookies.

One thing's for sure, Mama doesn't do anything halfway.

"Looks good, Mama."

She beams. "Thank you, baby. Do you have the chains ready?"

I motion over my shoulder. "Yes, ma'am. They're in the living room."

Mama starts toward the living room. Wanda and Diane fall in line behind her. Granny continues to busy herself in the kitchen.

I fall into the living room-bound procession. I'd rather help in the kitchen.

"We'll need to set up the bar. I want to set it up separate from the food this year, so we're going to put it in over there," Mama says, pointing.

That's typically Daddy and Howard's responsibility, so I give a disinterested shrug. "Okay."

"Can you put the yard decorations up for me?" Mama asks.

It's been so long I forgot the best part of the setup.

Next to going door-to-door trick-or-treating, before I turned sixteen, my all-time favorite activity of Halloween was the outdoor decorations. I love figuring out the best place to stake Frankenstein or Dracula into the yard. It was preferably slightly concealed by a bush or tree so the unsuspecting guest would not see them from the road. Nothing is better than someone seeing a six-foot-tall Dracula appear out of the shadows from behind a tree only inches away from them.

"On it," I say as I hustle to the front door before she changes my task.

All the wonderful decorations are waiting for me on the left-hand side of the front porch. I must've missed them on my way in due to the brief dizzy spell I had to fight back.

In a moment, I'm twelve years old again. I'm making fake spider webs over the doorbell button, poking skeleton hands in the remains of the flower bed, and setting up the motion-activated jack-in-the-box.

The jack-in-the-box is one of my all-time favorites and never fails to give me the heebie-jeebies. Daddy built it for Mama twenty years ago. It has a motion sensor that activates the spring inside, opening the top of the three-foot by three-foot colorfully painted lid.

Even people who have seen Daddy's jack-in-the-box years prior are caught off guard. When they get within four feet of the decoration, a seven-foot-tall clown leaps out of the box and swings side to side as its momentum subsides.

I'm not sure if jack-in-the-box is what we should call it. The clown Daddy loaded into the box makes Pennywise look like a clown you would hire for a six-year-old child's birthday party.

True story, the first year after he made it, I had nightmares about the clown for three straight weeks. It still creeps its way into an occasional nightmare.

What Wanda said about Faith bothers me. It also concerns me Granny and I are two of the last people to see her.

It's not like I really know Faith. I had seen her around town growing up, and I know who she is. I mean, it isn't really my issue she is missing. People go missing all the time.

Maybe she has a hot younger boyfriend on the side, and she finally decided to run off with him. Then there are always drugs. People get caught in the web of narcotics. It's out there. Just because nobody is comfortable naming it as a possible reason doesn't make it any less plausible

Still, there's no telling what is going on with that situation. In all likelihood, in true small-town form, we're all making much ado about nothing. If I had to lay a bet right now, I'd bet Faith shows up before the end of the weekend, and it will be mystery solved.

"Baby, don't you need to get dressed?"

Mama is standing on the porch. Her expression is full of concern.

I pull my phone out of my back pocket and check the time. Oh my! I have been at the outdoor decorations for four hours now. Time has gotten away from me.

"Yes, ma'am."

She surveys the front yard as I come to the steps. "You really have a flair for decorating, April."

I don't want you to think that my mama is an unkind woman. Because she's not. The comments of praise from my mama are like special-occasion candies wrapped in the expensive foiled paper. They are handed out sparingly and are something to be cherished. "Thank you, Mama."

"Thank you for your help. The entrance decorations set the tone for the party." She gestures toward my car. "Did you bring your outfit with you, or do you need to go home and get it?"

"I intended to run home and freshen up when we got done decorating."

She gives a single nod. "Okay. Go on home and hurry back."

I was worried I might break a sweat during the decorating and need a quick shower, but the temperature is relatively mild today. Still, I'm glad I'll be able to change into my outfit in the privacy of my apartment. I'm still concerned about whether I will be able to get into my Tinker Bell outfit.

Not that safety pins and fabric tape wouldn't hold me all in if it doesn't fit.

Sure, a logical person would've tried the costume to see if all my critical areas were sufficiently covered. But Granny always talks about the power of positive thoughts. What can be a more positive action than assuming it will miraculously fit like a glove?

The only trouble with the manifestation through positive thinking method is the moments of doubt creeping in around the corners. I'm concerned they may sabotage my manifestation in the end.

I have even gone so far as to think up backup outfits if the Tinker Bell outfit does not fit. That, as Granny would tell you, is a severe hex on the positive-thinking juju.

Puppy lifts his head briefly from his bed when I burst into my apartment in a frenzy. He stands, turns a one-eighty, and lays back down with his butt toward me. I suppose he doesn't care to witness the ensuing drama. Smart dog.

Having *now* broken a light sweat thinking about the fitting on the way home, I take a quick wash-off shower anyway. Besides, if there is an extra layer of dirt on me, I might need those few microns of space to pull the outfit into place.

Calm down, April.

It is just a stupid costume and only a fun work party my

mama is putting on. There is entirely no reason to be getting all worked up. I know all these people. They're the same people I've been seeing over and over again for the last six months.

Standing naked in front of my full-length mirror, I take several deep breaths as the last of the moisture dries from my skin.

Okay. I've got this.

With controlled purpose, I slip on silk panties. Next, I fasten the one push-up bra I own. Given my natural endowment, this bra is only worn for these sorts of occasions.

I pause to control my breathing and think small thoughts.

"Please, please, please," I whisper as I step into the darling seafoam green outfit and delicately pull it up my legs. I slide both arms into the outfit while holding my breath. Gingerly, I pull the zipper up the right side.

The zipper does not catch or break as I pull it closed. That is a good sign.

Almost confident now, I stand straight and rotate my shoulders back. I don't hear a single seam rip. I want to do a little victory dance, but I know better than to push my luck.

I rotate in front of the mirror to see how the back looks. The wings are still flat against my back. I reach into the back neckline, finding the ring I was searching for. When I pull the ring, a cord tightens, and the wings spring to life.

"Oh, now that is just too cute," I whisper.

I might not be confident enough to do a victory dance, but I twirl side to side, enjoying the magic of the outfit. I have just been transformed into Tinker Bell in a matter of minutes. And let me just say, it's good to be Tink.

There is a snort from my right. Puppy must've decided the all-clear was given on the drama alert, and he is watching me intently.

"You like the wings?"

In response, he stretches, steps out of his bed, and pads over to the mirror. In Puppy language, that's, "Heck yeah. You look awesome, Mom!"

To complete the outfit, I slip on a pair of seafoam ballet slippers I ordered separately. Forget about how cute they are. The slippers are so comfortable I'm left wondering if I can get away with wearing them in court instead of heels on Monday.

I step back a little further from the mirror to get the full view, including my legs and slippers.

Being objective, my girls are almost overflowing out of the minuscule cups right below the deep scalloped neckline. Plus, the triangle-shaped runners from the waistline that are designed to partially conceal my fanny do not do an adequate job of covering their target. Consequently, the sheer mesh bloomers below leave very little to the imagination of what my tush looks like.

Yep, a little slutty like I planned. I am one hot Tink.

Fundamentally I know it is wrong to crave this affirmation. It had been ages since I felt the need to dress up in such a provocative manner.

Since the senior year of undergrad school at my sorority, to be exact. But honestly, I have had a significantly long run of bad luck or no luck in the sexual arena lately.

My self-confidence during this dry spell has been more than bruised. Yes, I understand my value in this world is not derived from my level of beauty or sexuality. But tonight, I just need confirmation that the problem is the shallow, small lake I have been fishing in and not the bait.

Satisfied I'll rock the evening with my outfit, I reach for the ring behind me at the bottom of the bodice and lower my wings. When they close, I have a moment of sadness overcome me.

How long am I going to live this way? Is this it? The new April? Lord, what happened to you, girl? You had everything going in your direction. Now, what are you doing? Teasing a bunch of young country boys, most of them whom you've known all your life and think of more as brothers, and making a few old men have to slip a glycerin tablet under their tongue. It's just sad.

I'm so deep into my own self-admonishment, I don't notice

the wonky vibration. Puppy stands and begins to growl. I see the first green tendril of smoke escaping from the full-length mirror.

"Dang it!" I quickly pull the comforter off my bed and toss it over the mirror.

I stare at the comforter over the mirror for several minutes. I can feel Puppy's hair against my right leg as he stands next to me, continuing to growl.

Reaching down, I grip his fur in my right hand. As I clench and release, clench and release his fur, I feel my heartbeat slow.

Puppy finally stops his growling.

"Thank you, buddy." I rub his ears roughly. He likes it like that. "Let's get outta here."

Chapter 26

As I hustle back to the widow Motlow's house, I think about how many paranormal experiences I've had in just the past week. Since I've been back home, especially since working with Dusty, I have become less alarmed by the events.

No, I am not numb to them, and I would never consider them normal. However, the encounters don't seem to give me the long-lasting heebie-jeebies that would mess up an entire day like they used to.

But this week is unusual, even for me. There seems to be some electric charge in the air that brings out all the freaky spirits.

Sure, it's Halloween. I get it. Spirits are supposed to roam, but they don't all have to come to me.

Speaking of coming to me, what's with this headless mirror ghost? If it really wants to contact me, why didn't it just appear in my crystal this morning instead of letting Nina Rodriguez take its place?

I park in the small alley behind the Motlow house. There are only a few cars in the lane, and even fewer up front when I had passed by.

It is only seven, and the real party doesn't start until eight thirty. This gives parents with young children a chance to go trick-or-treating before they leave their children with the babysitter and come to the party.

Walking up the back path, I see my brother Dusty. He is dressed as Frodo, complete with huge feet. Chase is next to him, dressed as Gandalf, complete with a white beard, laughing in front of three fifty-five-gallon drum barbecue smokers. Each brother has a beer in their left hand and a pair of tongs in their right.

"You need a hairnet around that grill, Gandalf," I quip.

They look over their left shoulders in complete synchronization. They both flash the same mischievous smile.

"Try her."

"No. She'll get mad." Chase snorts.

I'm right in front of them, and they talk as if I'm not here. This is not entirely unusual behavior by my twin brothers, but it is annoying. "Try what?"

"She'll think it's funny," Dusty coaxes.

"No, she won't."

"I'll think what's funny?" I ask.

As if to do it quickly before he loses his nerve, Chase holds out his right index finger to me. "Quick, pull it."

"I'm not pulling your finger and falling for that stupid fart joke." Such is life with my brothers. There are a lot of positives. One of the significant drawbacks is dealing with their frequently sophomoric idiotic idea of comedy relief.

"Aww, come on, April. Don't be a spoilsport. Just give a quick pull," Chase continues.

"Yeah, pull it, April," Dusty chimes in.

Sometimes to be the perfect sister, you must take the good with the bad. I roll my eyes and shake my head as I reach out and take hold of Chase's finger. "Whatever." To complete the joke, I give a quick tug. Oddly my elbow bumps against my side.

Chase's eyes widen, and he begins to holler in pain, "Oh, it hurts! It hurts so bad!" He lifts his hand, and three spurts of blood shoot into the air.

I look down at my hand, and I'm holding a finger. I drop it, taking three steps back on the patio in horror.

I'm still looking down at the finger when I hear both my brothers burst into laughter.

"Oh man, did you see her face right before she dropped it?"

"I knew we should've filmed it," Chase complains.

It is a short trip from my revulsion to anger. Another trait you master as the only sister of two knuckleheads. "You two are the worst!"

"Aw, come on, April. It was funny," Dusty whines.

"No, it's not funny to scare people!" I shake my finger at them like a ticked-off schoolmarm.

"But it's Halloween. You're supposed to scare folks. Isn't that like the whole trick-or-treat thing?" Chase asks.

I hate it when Chase wins a conversation. He is right, of course, but I'm still angry that they tricked me. "Yeah, but you're supposed to ask first. It's trick or treat, not *just* I tricked you because I want to."

The smile evaporates from Chase's face. "Oh. I didn't think about that."

"Yeah, well, there are rules to things. So, since you didn't ask, now you have to give me a treat."

"You hungry? These butts are done. That would be a make a good treat."

"She looks hungry," Dusty interjects. "With that whole starving ballerina look."

Now I can't tell if they are trying to be overly nice or making fun of me. I decide they are teasing me. "I'm Tinker Bell, Fred Flintstone."

"He's Frodo," Chase says.

"Where are your wings?" Dusty asks.

I reach between my shoulder blades and pull the ring that pops open my wings. Both of my brothers give an appreciative smile.

"That's pretty cool," Dusty says with an admiring tone.

Chase produces a ceramic plate with about half a pound of pulled pork on it. "Here, try this and tell me if you like it."

I don't have to try it to know I like it. The tangy scent in the air tells me that the grill masters still possess all their magic. But, to be sure, and since they asked me to, I pluck a piece off with my fingers and taste it.

Oh my gosh, that is divine. I nod my head. "Excellent."

Chase smiles. He shrugs his shoulders, looking down at the patio. "Sorry if I spooked you."

"It's okay. It's funny *now*. You did a great job of making it lifelike."

"Thanks."

I can tell he is genuinely pleased. Gesturing over my shoulder, I say, "I'm gonna go inside and see what task Mama assigned me. You two stay out of trouble."

Not only did I get an apology, but I also got a fresh plate of pulled pork and the forgiving sister award. Why can't all male relations be as easy as the men in my family? It is a total mystery to me.

Granny Snow stirs one of the Crockpots containing baked beans as I walk into the kitchen. She is dressed as the wicked witch from Snow White and doing a pretty good job of pulling it off.

"Hey, Granny. Don't take offense, but if any of those pies are apple, I'm not touching them."

"Aren't you just the cutest thing."

"You like?" I twirl for full effect.

"Oh yes. I don't know that I've ever seen anyone dress as a pole dancer before tonight."

"I'm Tinker Bell," I correct her as my ears turn red.

She chuckles as she stirs another Crockpot. "Of course, you are, dear. But I do believe Tinker Bell didn't have quite as many feminine curves to conceal as you do."

I'm not sure if she means that as a compliment or a cut. My ego is soaring too high to be dinged. "Thank you. I thought for a moment you might have a problem with it."

"Lord, no. The way I see it, the church was able to hijack every other pagan holiday. They were bound to have one they couldn't convert fully."

You learn to avoid religious origin conversations with Granny at all costs. "Can you spare any of those beans and potato salad? The boys gave me some pork, but I'd like some fixings with it."

Granny inspects the plate in my hand. "Is the pork done?"

"I think they're just getting ready to take it off the smoker."

Granny takes my plate from me and dishes out a little taste from the different Crockpots for me. "I was getting concerned. Those boys seem more interested in drinking beer and horseplay than getting the pork done."

It's probably best not to mention Chase's amputated finger trick at this point. That's right, I'm the little sister who doesn't rat you out.

I take my plate back from Granny. There is twice what I need, but there's no point in worrying about it now. "Thank you, Granny."

She motions toward the kitchen exit. "Now run along up front. Your mama was looking for you a few minutes ago."

Great. If Mama is looking for me, I'm late by her standard.

I wolf down bites from my plate as I travel the hallway, now complete with my crêpe paper chains. As I enter the living room, I spot mama, dressed as a stunningly beautiful Olive Oyl. Daddy, by her side, makes for a less-than-impressive Popeye while Howard rocks his Wimpy outfit.

They are to the right side of the room, where the bar is set up.

"Are you looking for me, Mama?"

"There you are." She takes a quick scan of me from head to toe. With the notable exception of her eyebrows coming together, she manages to conceal her disapproval. "You're going to be working the bar with your daddy and uncle."

This strikes me as odd. Mainly because I don't know how to mix a single drink other than a margarita and a bullfrog.

Then again, after seven years of higher education, I probably have more experience with drunks than anybody else in the room. This qualifies me to be one of the barkeeps.

"Now, the important thing is that each guest will be given three drink coupons. Nobody gets a drink without a coupon," Mama insists.

"What if they want a bottle of water?" I shovel another piece of pork in my mouth.

Mama's eyes narrow. "Alcoholic beverages."

That question is for not approving of my outfit. But with Mama's present high level of stress, it's best not to poke mama bear anymore.

"Now I'm serious. If you think anybody is collecting tickets from people who aren't drinking *alcoholic drinks*—" She cuts her eyes to me. "Cut them off."

Daddy and Howard salute Mama, which clears them.

Her expectant stare catches me with my mouth full. "Yes, ma'am," I mumble.

"Ralph, come with me to make sure the boys have the meat off the grill on time."

Howard and I watch them make their way down the hallway. "What happened to the Captain Hook outfit?"

"Oh, you know," Howard says.

"No, I don't."

"I just got to thinking about what a pain it would be if I had to take a leak with that hook. It just seems like a health hazard," Howard says with a deadpan look.

"Uh-huh." I know with those outfits, you just hold the hook in your hand, and you can let go of it at any time. Still, I'm relieved nobody is trampling my Peter Pan theme.

"I have to admit, you're looking a little exposed tonight." Howard raises his eyebrows.

"Just showing it while I have it."

"I see. Fortunate you caught a break, and Halloween is warmer this year than usual. If it were colder, you would run the risk of catching pneumonia."

I shoot him a disdainful look. "With any luck, maybe I'll catch a guy's eye tonight."

"Oh, you'll catch some guy's eye. With any luck, that is all you will catch."

He can be so stupid at times. I want to hold it in but laugh anyway. "All right. Since you're going to pick on me, I'm going to go out on the porch, finish my dinner, and greet our guests."

"Let me know if you want to borrow my coat." Howard hollers at my back.

I take the rocker at the far end of the porch and sit with my dinner in my lap. From my vantage point, I'm able to survey the entire front yard as dusk starts to give way to night.

Mama is right. I did do a splendid job with the decorations.

She did a good job, too. The old Motlow house is perfect for this event, and I'm sure she'll have a couple of offers on it by the end of the week.

Finishing my plate, I set it on the porch and begin to rock the chair. I'm happy. My family is here, and everyone is in a jovial mood. I'm full of delicious comfort food, and the weather is just right for a party.

Looking out and up from the porch, I watch a navy-blue cloud skirt in front of the three-quarters-full moon. The edge of the cloud lights up as if it is hemmed in silver. I grin. That must've been where that silver lining cloud thing came from.

Icy cold fingers comb up through my hair from the base of my neck. I leap from the rocking chair, nearly knocking it over.

I stand facing the chair for a full minute. I half expect the rocking chair to begin moving on its own.

It stops naturally. There is nothing there, but I know what I felt.

I lean forward and retrieve my plate without taking my eyes from the rocking chair. There is something in the air tonight. Something that portends trouble.

Chapter 27

The party gets rolling at eight thirty. By nine, the revelers that have kids have arrived in a steady stream. By nine thirty, the feeding frenzy has died down, and by ten thirty, the bar has died as almost everyone had spent their three drink vouchers.

I'm about to ask Daddy and Howard if they care if I mingle with the guests when I see him approach the bar. He isn't tall, just under six feet. His eyes are dark, almost black. His hair is equally dark, long by today's standards, and wavy. His slim, muscular build is attractive, but it's his full lips that my eyes rest on.

"Tinker Bell was my first crush," he says as he rests his hands on the bar.

"Maybe she will be your last." Where did that come from?

He laughs.

I like his laugh—a lot.

"You may be right. Justin Lakes." He extends his hand to me.

I accept it lightly. "April Snow."

He smiles, and it lights his dark eyes. "Viv's daughter?"

Viv? The familiarity he uses with my mama's name tweaks me a bit. "Yes."

His eyes settle lazily on my face. "Wow. She mentioned she had a daughter, but she never said you were a model."

I know that's just a silly line. Whoever heard of a five-foot-nine model anyway? Still, it feels good. "Thanks. How does my mama know you?"

"I'm one of the developers she works with."

"You build homes, Justin?"

He rocks his hand side to side. "Sometimes. Not as much as I used to. I spend most of my time developing subdivisions and then selling the lots to builders."

Truthfully, I wouldn't have cared if he was a dog catcher explaining how best to capture a dog. I just like looking at him and want him to keep talking in that smooth, deep voice of his.

He suddenly holds out two blue drink vouchers. "Hey, I have these two drink tickets but can't stay long. Would you care to split them?"

"I guess. What are you drinking?"

He grins as if he knows something I don't. "I'll have whatever you want."

"Frozen margarita?"

Justin laughs again. I think my knees are going to unhinge. "Well, I would like to keep my man card and have it on the rocks, but what the heck." He hands me the two tickets. "Two frozen margaritas, please."

I go to work with the blender. It's good to have something to do. If I didn't have something to keep my hands busy, I'm afraid all I would do is stare at Justin.

He isn't the most attractive man I have ever seen. Still, the sensuality seems to float off him like tiny electrical currents, and my body responds to him in kind.

I hand him his frozen margarita as I wipe the overflow from the side of mine. Intently, I watch his lips touch the salted rim.

As he lowers the glass, there is a bit of salt on his mouth. I barely keep myself from leaning forward and kissing his lip clean.

His eyes and mouth open wide. "Wow. Your margaritas will make your hair stand up."

Is that a double entendre, or is my mind in high-lust mode? "I wanted to give you your money's worth. Besides, given the number of calories in a margarita, you need to get all your alcohol in one take."

He leans against the bar. "You do not look like you need to count calories."

"Is that how you sweet talk all the girls?"

"Only the ones who make me free drinks." Justin looks over to Howard before returning his gaze to me. "Are you on duty the whole night?"

I look over at Howard. He's trying hard to appear like he is inventorying how many bottles we have left to get us through the night. "Uncle Howard..."

He turns and waves his hand. "You two go ahead. I'm sure the rush is over."

I'm not going to wait for him to change his mind. "Thank you," I say as I slip to the other side of the bar.

We step toward the center of the room. "So, is Mama working with you on a project now?"

"We've got one subdivision just about ready to open, and I'm about to start dirt work on a separate one."

Another couple bumps into Justin's back. He nearly spills his drink. I reach out for his arm and think better of it. "Hey, you want to step outside and get some air?"

"Yes. These are pretty close quarters in here."

"It'll thin out considerably over the next hour," I say as I lead him out the front door.

I walk down the brick steps and sit on the short column at the base. Justin takes a seat on the brick base opposite me.

"Now you're Viv's daughter, who is the lawyer, correct?"

"Well, actually, I'm her only daughter. But yes, I'm an attorney."

"What is your specialty?"

"Everything, and nothing." I bark an unladylike laugh.

He leans forward. "That sounds intriguing. Explain."

I roll my eyes and look to the sky. "Right now, I'm working for my uncle. I say most of what I do is public defense work. But I also do contracts, wills, divorce papers, anything you need to be done by an attorney."

"Sort of like a general practitioner doctor."

I laugh again and wish I could stop doing that. "I think you're making it sound better than it actually is."

"I don't know. It seems like it would take an exceptionally resourceful person to be able to do all those different facets of law."

Man, even when I think he's not trying to sweet talk me, it makes me feel good. I wonder what it would be like to be with a man who built you up all the time like this. "I didn't say I have a handle on it every day."

"I bet you do. I think you're probably just modest," he says as he takes a sip of his margarita.

I don't know what is going on, but it's like the entire essence of my being is leaning toward him. As if he is some vast, irresistible human magnet, and my core is made of iron. If I have ever been this attracted to someone at the first meeting, I cannot remember.

"Have you ever thought about real estate law?"

"Not really." I considered it. Still, if I specialized in real estate law, it would be too easy for Mama to talk me into setting up shop in Guntersville to work with her.

"You should. I swear my attorney makes more off my deals than I do."

"Really?"

"No, but it feels like it. It is second only to the IRS. You should really come up to Huntsville and talk to Jonah. My attorney"

"I don't know. I sort of already have something cooking in Texas."

"Texas? Why in the heck would you want to move to Texas?"

I just realized I don't want to move to Texas. Truth be known, some days I don't know what I want anymore.

"Travel to Huntsville Monday, and let me buy you and Jonah lunch. Let him tell you what his job consists of, and if it sounds interesting, you can come back and shadow him for a few hours."

"I don't know, Justin. I don't even know what my schedule is Monday."

"It's just lunch. You have to eat."

"Not in Huntsville."

He rolls his head backward. "You're killing me here, April. Are you always this stubborn?"

"I prefer to call it certain."

"Okay, certain." He falls quiet, but his sexy eyes continue to implore me to make the trip to Huntsville Monday.

I let out an exasperated breath. "Fine. I'll go to lunch with you and your lawyer friend."

"Jonah."

"Right, Jonah in the whale."

"Ha-ha!" He laughs with a triumphant tone. "I knew I would get you to come. This is going to be life-altering for you. It will blow your mind."

My mind must be in the gutter. Nobody uses as many double entendre in a row.

Justin reaches for his back pocket. "I'll send you an invite in Outlook, as well as Jonah."

I guess once you have an official invite through Outlook, there's no way to cancel. Too bad for me if I regret this decision over the weekend.

Justin does a double-take at his phone. "Is it really already eleven thirty?"

I don't bother to check my phone. I can tell his question is strictly rhetorical.

"I really have to get going. I was just planning on stopping by. Of course, I wasn't expecting to meet someone so easy to talk to."

His stare is so impassioned, my gut tightens involuntarily, and a small giggle escapes me. Good Lord, I sound like an eight-year-old.

He moves toward me in a single fluid motion, standing only inches in front of my knees as he looks down into my eyes.

"Can I ask you a favor?"

Oh boy, here it is. I can't wait to find out if Justin kisses as good as he looks. "Anything."

He lifts his margarita glass. "Can you take this in for me? I'm afraid if I go in, I might have to talk to some folks I don't care to and lose time that I don't have to give."

That isn't the favor I was expecting. "Sure." I reach for his cup, and our fingers touch.

Vivid Technicolor visions explode to life in my brain. It is like a five-second blip from a porno movie starring Justin and me.

He is on his back, and I'm straddling him. Most of my Tinker Bell outfit is gathered around my waist as I ride him with almost comical gusto in the cowgirl position.

I freeze and clench tightly in fear. It isn't necessary since Justin doesn't know that I saw his thoughts.

"It was a pleasure to meet you, April Snow. I'm looking forward to having lunch with you on Monday."

I think I say goodbye. But I'm not entirely sure.

The five-second mind's eye porno has short-circuited my brain. I watch Justin retreat down the sidewalk while I admire his well-muscled backside.

I'm waiting for my adrenaline to calm down. It is stuck in a high position.

Never ever have I felt this level of raw animal magnetism with a man. What would it be like to be in a relationship that hot? I'm not sure I could survive it, but I'd like to try it.

There has to be some truth to that saying about it being better to die happy. Right?

Chapter 28

I check in at the bar, and Jacob, Chase, Daddy, and Howard are playing poker.

The party typically stays packed until the witching hour. But it's already almost just family members.

A flash of pain shoots up the back of my neck, and I swear I see white lights blinking in front of my eyes. "Oh. Not now." Of all the times to get a migraine.

I need to find Mama. I forgot to bring any medicine. Maybe she has some with her.

"Hey, Snow!"

Jacob is crooking his finger at me while he holds his cards in the other hand. I gesture for him to come to me instead.

"Heck no. I already had to wait an hour because I didn't want to interrupt you and your swarthy date."

"He wasn't my date, and he wasn't swarthy."

"Okay, then short," Jacob says.

"Jealous?"

"Of my time. Shift's over, Snow, and I'm tired. I just came to fill you in like a good friend."

I shake off another migraine stab just below my left eyebrow and move toward the makeshift poker table. I'm trying not to show that I'm in pain, but I'm not sure if I'm succeeding.

"You okay?" Jacob asks.

"I thought you were in a hurry."

He throws three black chips onto the table. "Y'all better fold while you still can," he says to the men in my family. "You got a gun?"

I look over my shoulder and then point at my chest. "Are you talking to me, Jacob?"

"Yes, I'm talking to you, Snow."

"Yeah—"

Jacob squints his eyes. "Is it loaded?"

"Maybe. Why are you asking?"

"Nina Rodriguez robbed a gas station this morning, just like you predicted."

Tiny shockwaves reverberate through my body. "Oh my gosh. Please tell me nobody got hurt."

"Everybody will survive. But Nina pistol-whipped the cashier and put him in the hospital. Then on her way out of the gas station, she shot one of the responding police officers twice in the chest."

I had a feeling Nina Rodriguez was evil from the get-go. But I really did not think she was a complete sociopath.

"Both rounds struck the officer in his body armor. Knocked him to the ground, but he was still able to return fire. Nina ran around the corner and smacked into the police cruiser coming to the front of the building. They tell me it knocked her six feet into the air."

"Did it kill her?" My voice sounds a little too hopeful. It must be the alcohol talking.

"No, the officer said she hopped up and took off running without any visible injuries. She was into the woods and disappeared like a puff of smoke. They have a team of dogs out there trying to track her now. But nothing so far."

"It's a shame she didn't roll under the cruiser at high speed." I let it slip.

"What's the rub between you two anyway?"

"I don't know. I didn't like Nina from the start."

"She doesn't like you, either. Of course, after this, you have the entire police community in agreement with you."

"Well, I would rather they just catch her. Nobody is safe until she is in jail."

"True, but that goes double for you. Word on the street is that she's already taken out a hit on you."

"A hit? Why on earth would she hire a hit on me?"

"I'm guessing she just doesn't like you much."

"So, what? I'm supposed to stay home with my doors locked?"

"No. I'm just telling you so you will keep your eyes peeled for anything out of the ordinary. Don't take any chances. If you see someone hanging around your parents', give the police a call."

"Maybe I'll shoot them instead," I say.

Jacob throws another chip on the pile. "Makes my job easier. If you do shoot her outside your apartment, make sure to scar up your door's lock and drag her body inside."

"Seriously?" I'm horrified.

"Well, yeah. It's what I would do."

The migraine headache I experienced earlier was a gentle prelude to what I feel now. Little white fireworks are exploding behind my eyeballs, and someone keeps jabbing an ice pick into the back of my neck. I have to find Mama now.

I cruise through the kitchen, now a total wreck from the festivities. Mama is across the kitchen, close to the back door. I squeeze in between folks and eventually reach her.

"Mama, I don't feel so good. And I don't think I can drive home."

She swivels toward me. Immediately she lays the back of her hand against my forehead. "You don't feel hot, baby."

"No, ma'am. It's migraines again."

"Oh, baby. I'm sorry. You need to lie down. Go upstairs to the second room on the left. There's still a bed in there, and that'll allow you to rest until they pass. I'll come to check on you in a bit, and if I need to, I'll have the boys take you home."

"Okay."

I do as she says and work my way back through the crowd to

the stairs.

When I reach the top of the stairs, I notice jackets to the right. The room must be serving as the coat closet.

I open the door to the left and immediately feel ghost bumps.

That's goosebumps caused by spiritual electricity. The room is full of electrical memories.

I'm sure I don't want any part of the paranormal aspect of this home. It became pretty apparent during the decorating phase today that something or someone is trying to reach me. Which, if I had to guess, will turn out to be a ghost who doesn't have a head, or a head without a body. Either way, it is becoming disconcerting.

Another flash of pain changes my mind on bailing—just yet. I need to take Mama's advice and lie down until the pains subside.

The room has its own fireplace on the far wall with an ornate marble mantelpiece. The room is furnished with an antique wrought-iron bed, a delicate small writing desk, and a sizeable rose-colored vanity complete with side cupboards and an armoire. The furniture is era perfect for the age of the home.

I open the armoire door out of curiosity. Nothing is inside. The degree of furnishing in this one room is far more significant than in all the other rooms put together.

I sit on the edge of the mattress and stare into the dormant fireplace. I'm thinking about the trite saying about things happening for a reason. Could Justin be the reason that April's version of the forty years in the wilderness is taking place? If he is the reason, how would I know if I moved to Austin?

What? I'm just thinking things through.

As many good things as I've heard about Austin, a great career isn't everything. Is an excellent position worth missing out on the sort of sizzle that is between Justin and me?

The smell of vanilla bean and gardenia overwhelms me as the air turns cold. I cross my arms instinctively to maintain some of my body heat.

An indentation appears on the mattress two feet to my left side. The sound of the mattress support springs stretching has my breath catching in my throat.

My left side grows noticeably cooler than my right. I can sense her. Yes, the spirit is definitely female.

She materializes to my left. Short, black bobbed hair, white teeth crowded to the point that they turn sideways, and full lips that carry some sort of concern. She leaps up from the mattress and vacillates between the desk and the armoire.

I'm genuinely surprised when I hear her voice. "Where did I put it?"

Standing, I look through her left shoulder. She is rifling her hand through the top center drawer of the desk. It is as if she is shuffling through years of collected ballpoint pens that don't work, coupons, and old bank statements. There is nothing there. The drawer is utterly empty.

She slams it shut. "He'll want me to wear the pearls he bought me." The ghost continues talking to herself.

She opens the armoire and tears through its empty contents. Again, she slams it shut.

The young lady I'm watching is dressed in 1920s fashion. She looks ready for a night out on the town and would be comfortable in any speakeasy.

"A girl must do what a girl must do." She reaches into the empty armoire again. This time a bright red paisley scarf materializes in her hand. She wraps the scarf around her neck and checks her nonexistent reflection in the mirror.

"There." She pats the scarf tail against her chest. "He'll never know if I have the pearls on or not."

I'm mesmerized as I watch the roaring twenties flapper. The migraine headache I felt earlier is a distant thought now.

Watching her stomp through her room in such an agitated state, it is exciting that I can hear her speaking.

I consider touching her hand while she is still unaware of my presence to see if I might glean information from her that would tell me who she was in her living days. But I'm concerned if I touch her, I might see things that living people are not meant to see.

I can read her. I know I can because I have done it accidentally with spirits in the past. With the training I've had, I'll be in control.

I do want to know why she is so agitated. Who is waiting for her? My curiosity is tearing at my mind.

Still, I remember what happened the other night when I touched the spirit attacking me, and I was thrown into the void on the other side of the veil. I still recall the cool darkness and the utter loneliness and despair. I don't care to ever feel that again.

My curiosity continues to chew up my reservations. As I overcome my fear and reach for the young woman's shoulder, she bolts through the bedroom door.

I open the door to give chase, but she is gone. All that remains is the scent of gardenia and vanilla.

Dusty needs to know about this. That's all I can think about.

It's not every day you come across a fully formed, eighty-percent-solidified spirit. This sort of haunting can provide spectacular photos, or spooktacular, as Dusty likes to call them. That makes books jump off the shelf into people's baskets and drives a book up the bestseller list.

I take the stairs two at a time. Dusty is still playing cards at the bar, and I rush to his side.

I whisper in his ear. "I need to talk to you outside."

He studies my face, then examines his cards before tossing them down. "I'm out, guys." He places his hand on my elbow as we walk toward the front door.

"A garbage hand anyway," he mumbles.

"Well, I think your luck has changed," I say as we step onto the porch.

"How so?"

"Oh, I don't know. How about the ghost that will give you your next book cover?"

"Okay, I'll bite."

I gather my frayed nerves. The adrenaline is still pouring through my body like it always does after an encounter. "What do you know about this house?"

He shoves his hands in his pockets. "Nothing really. As far as I know, there are no paranormal events recorded here."

"There's a bedroom upstairs that is decked out from the 1920s. Before the crash. Everything is in pristine order."

A smile flickers across Dusty's face. "And then you found a twenty-dollar bill?"

"No, smarty. Then I found a frustrated twenty-something flapper getting ready for a hot date."

"You're serious?"

I lock eyes with my brother and nod my head.

Dusty scans the front porch as if he is looking at it in a whole new light. "If you have your period right. That's a long time for anyone to keep a ghost secret. It sure as heck shouldn't stay dormant that long."

"Unless the house is owned by the same family the whole time," I say in a conspiratorial tone.

Dusty's lips tighten. "Yeah. You've got a point there."

"Do you think Miles might be able to find out something on it?" Miles Trufant is my brother's researcher. He's excellent at digging up information that never makes it into the mainstream. He is one of the reasons my brother has been able to find new hauntings to write about. In contrast, his contemporaries write about the same hauntings over and over.

"It won't hurt to ask. I'll give Miles a call in the morning and see if he can do some research on the family that lived here."

"Not family, just females. Specifically younger females in the 1920s."

"Right, I'll have him start narrow, but if he doesn't find anything, have him broaden the search." Dusty crosses his arms. "Is it good quality?"

"Better use a soft-filter lens, or everyone's gonna think you faked it. The clarity is incredible," I assure him.

The edges of his lips turn up in a smile. "Nice."

Chapter 29

I hate to leave everyone to clean up the party afterward. But Mama had understood that I was going with Lane to Tuscaloosa in the morning. Besides, I helped her decorate that afternoon. The guys can help her break it all down and clean up.

When I get home, Puppy is sitting in front of my apartment door. This is not a good sign because Puppy has a doggie door, and he can go into the apartment anytime he wants. It is almost one in the morning, and Puppy goes to bed at eleven like clockwork. If he isn't lying in his bed, something is wrong inside my apartment.

Only one thing comes to mind—the mirror.

"Hey, buddy." I rub him behind his ears as I rummage for my house key.

"Why are you sitting out here?" He doesn't answer me.

When I open my door, I see the issue. The comforter I put over the full-length mirror has fallen to the floor.

Presently there isn't anything scrolled on the mirror and no green smoke. But given the day's activity and that it is Halloween, I can understand if Puppy might not care to stay in the room with the mirror uncovered.

I'm not going to even contemplate how the comforter fell off the mirror.

The plan is pretty simple. Puppy and I are not going to

sleep in our apartment tonight. But I do have to get back in there and get my clothes for an early trip to Tuscaloosa in the morning.

There is no way I'm gonna let whatever bad juju is coming out of that mirror have the run of my apartment tonight. Besides I don't want the spirit sneaking out the doggie door and coming to visit me on my parents' sofa.

I run into my apartment, scoop up the comforter, and throw it over the mirror. I take just enough time to make sure it is secure, and then I lock the doggie door and pull the apartment door closed, locking it behind me.

Puppy lets out one short growl, turns, and marches to my parents' sliding glass door. He's smart like that.

My parents' sofa needed to be replaced a few years back. It's okay for watching a thirty-minute sitcom. After that, all your body parts sink to the wooden frame, and it's like sitting on two-by-fours. Consequently, I wake up and feel like somebody has beaten the tar out of me.

Checking my phone, I notice it is four fifty-five. Five minutes before I'm due to get up. If I kept this up, I won't have to set my alarm again for the rest of my life.

I need to shower, grab the dress I plan to wear today, and get ready.

Lane is due to pick me up in an hour and a half.

My Tinker Bell outfit lays abandoned on the floor at the head of the sofa. Since I slept in my bra and panties, I wrap the sheet I had around me, retrieve my costume, and pad to the glass door.

I turn around to check. Puppy hasn't followed me. "You're going to let me go by myself?"

He stands up, turns a one-eighty, and lays back down. I'm unsure if he is unconcerned or scared.

"Fine. Some protector you are."

Honestly, I'm not expecting anything odd when I open my apartment door. So, the fact the comforter has fallen off of the mirror again is slightly discombobulating.

Actually, it spooks me more than it should.

Saving the effort this time, I bypass the mirror and go straight to my closet. Quickly, I gather up my crimson dress and heels I plan to wear, a change of underwear, and my makeup bag. I exit my apartment and lock the door.

I can deal with that tonight when I get back.

Chapter 30

Lane arrives at six thirty on the dot. As I get in his sedan, I try to act as if everything is normal.

"You're definitely representing today," he says.

"Thanks." I lift his crimson and white "Roll Tide" tie from his chest and make to look at it. "As are you."

"I thought we might run by my fraternity house while we are there."

"You never told me you were in a fraternity at Alabama." Now that he mentions it, it is perfectly evident.

"There's a lot about me you don't know."

Given that he is best friends with Howard and we work together, I sort of doubt there's much about Lane I haven't heard. But when people say stuff like that, it's best not to contradict them. Besides, what's the point.

We pass through Bessemer on the west side of Birmingham when I find out the trip is more than Lane having an extra ticket. "I need to tell you something if you can keep a secret." His eyes shift from the road to me quickly.

I feel an uneasy turn in my gut. "Sure. I guess."

"You promise? No one can know."

At this point, my mind is racing to twenty things at once. Lane is going to profess his undying love for me, or maybe tell me that he is my dad because he had a one-night stand with my mama thirty years prior, or perhaps he and my uncle Howard have been lovers for the last twenty years—the suspense is killing me.

"Yeah. Sure." My voice does not sound like my own.

His head bobs briefly. "Okay, good. I haven't told anyone this yet. But if everything goes to plan, my DA position will be open in a year or two."

Alright, maybe I overshot it a little with the imagination. "You're quitting?"

"No, not exactly. There's a judgeship coming available, and I'm hoping to be appointed to it."

"In Guntersville?"

He steals another look in my direction. "Yes. Isn't that wonderful?"

"Yeah. But who's retiring?" Please don't let it be Judge Rossi. Judge Rossi has become my hero in the last five months. I have heard more wisdom from that woman in five months than I heard in three years of law school. At five foot two with a slight frame, wiry gray hair, and skin the color of midnight, nobody would mistake her for King Solomon. But her judgments are as creative, thoughtful, and wise.

If I could become half the arbitrator Judge Rossi is, I would consider myself a success.

"I can't say. Really no one is supposed to know yet. The judge just told me so I could be prepared once the resignation letter is turned in."

That doesn't bode well. Judge Rossi knew Lane's dad and practically raised him in the courthouse herself.

They have a standing Wednesday morning breakfast date. If she is retiring, I would be surprised if she didn't let Lane in on the secret before her resignation letter.

I try to act happy for Lane, even though the impending loss of Judge Rossi weighs heavily on my spirits. "That would be great. You would be good at it."

"I like to think so. But I also wanted to pass the favor along." A long silence ensues. Lane's eyes dart back to me again. "Do you understand?"

A nervous laugh escapes me. "Not exactly."

"You should put your name in for district attorney. We'll have to appoint an interim, which will give you a leg up on the election."

A hysterical laugh bubbles up from my gut. I have no control over it. Even though I know laughing is the least appropriate thing to do when someone is proposing you take on a position of such magnitude. "I don't think so, Lane."

"Why not? You're better at figuring out cases than ninety percent of the district attorneys I've met. You'd probably end up with more successful prosecutions in a year than most do in five."

I am finally able to get some control over my laughter. "Thank you. I appreciate the compliment."

"I'm not complimenting you, April. I'm telling you the truth. You would be awesome at this job."

This is so uncomfortable. "Except that it's in Guntersville. Lane, you know I want to leave town. I'm not trying to tie myself to the town."

Lane's ears turn a darker shade of red, and his jaw flexes. "I just thought you were trying to leave because you wanted a job with responsibilities. I didn't realize that you were too good for us."

That slaps my anger button. "Don't be putting words in my mouth, Lane Jameson. I have never said I was too good for Guntersville. I just don't want to live in Guntersville."

"Why? Your family is here. Everybody in town knows and respects you. You've got the lake and the woods for recreation. You can drive in two and a half hours to either Nashville or Birmingham if you need entertainment. You would have that important, well-paying job you've been desiring, April."

"Out of town."

My comment has the desired effect. Lane falls silent, and the driving suddenly requires all of his attention.

We have thirty minutes before we reach Tuscaloosa. That means that I have an hour of quiet to roll his question over and over in my mind.

What wouldn't it provide? Besides the out-of-town. What would I be missing? He is right. Everything I could possibly want, if I were objective, could be found in Guntersville.

Well, there is one thing missing. I still don't have anybody to spend my time with.

What if that someone is Justin Lakes? What then?

If Justin Lakes is what he seemed to be last night, he might be the one. Since he lives in Huntsville, wouldn't that put Guntersville ahead of Austin? Or am I going to assume that there are plenty of available men like Justin Lakes all over the country and I shouldn't tie myself down because of a relationship?

No. If the dry spell has taught me anything, it is that relationships should never be taken for granted. I didn't care to admit it, but I can't entirely discount what Lane is telling me. If Justin does turn out to be the one, that DA position might be just the ticket to have the lifestyle I want.

Lane starts down fraternity row and pulls up to the SAE house. "Seriously?"

"What? I was a third-generation legacy."

"Figures," I say as I get out of the car.

"We'll just swing in and say hi. We don't want to stay long."

I'm not too far removed from my sorority days to know truer words have never been spoken. Nothing is quite as awkward as folks in their forties talking to kids in their early twenties about their glory days.

"When was the last time you visited the house?" I ask as we walk up the brick stairs.

"I haven't been here since I graduated from law school."

Oh, this will be a blast.

Chapter 31

Half an hour later we exit Lane's fraternity after having enjoyed a barbecue sandwich and a beer, compliments of his younger fraternity brothers. They also pumped both of us for information about the LSAT and the bar. It seems that at least half of his fraternity has their heart set on becoming attorneys.

"I might have to start contributing more to my fraternity. I really like what sort of young men they're developing."

Geez. Lane even contributes to his fraternity? From my standpoint, my sorority got more than what they deserved from me when I was a member. I delete their donation requests from my Gmail account before I even open them.

They shouldn't start sending you those until you've paid off your student loan debt anyway. Or at least that's my opinion.

We have been blessed with a mild day for the game. The skies are clear, and the temperature hovers around seventy degrees.

As we walk the oak-lined walkways, the number of vendors, tickets scalpers, and tailgaters grows more numerous. When we are within three blocks, the roads are closed off to all but pedestrian traffic, which flows from small side streets into the main as creeks flow into the river tributaries. Soon we are being jostled by other fans and the chants of "Roll Tide" pierce the late-morning air repeatedly.

The air is electrified with the revelry of a carnival atmosphere. My own excitement builds.

I know it may be difficult for someone who is not a sports nut to understand, but there is something deliciously tribal about being a college sports fan. And the University of Alabama is at the apex of the most popular college sport.

I'm a lucky girl.

One of the downfalls of being a fan of a perennial contender is that in a typical season there are only one or two games that will even begin to severely test the abilities of your team. Unfortunately for the Mississippi State Bulldogs this Saturday, they are not one of those tests. Instead, by halftime the only hope the Bulldogs have is if they could have somebody trap the Alabama team in their own locker room during the break.

"That sandwich didn't feel me up. Are you still hungry?" Lane asks.

I start to say yes and then remember our deal. "Sure. What do you want?"

"I was going to buy."

"No, remember the deal was I would buy the food."

Sitting back, he crosses his arms and makes a show of relaxing. "Well, if that's the case. I would like two kraut dogs and a diet soda."

"How does that even work?" I ask.

"What do you mean?"

"So, like does the diet soda allow you to have the second hot dog?"

"No, the thirty minutes on the treadmill before I go to bed tonight allows me the second hot dog. I drink the diet soda because I like the way it tastes."

"Fine." I head off for the snack bar.

Sticker shock hits me as I'm waiting in line. I can't believe the prices they charge for a soda at the stadium. I'm trying to remember if that's what I paid a few years earlier, and then remember I rarely bought my own snacks.

As I debate the value of paying two dollars more for nachos versus a cheesy pretzel, a voice catches my ear. "Valerie?"

The young woman stops talking to the three even younger women surrounding her as if she is the principal source of all wisdom in the universe. Her left eye squints as she searches for my name. "April?"

"Yes. How have you been?"

Her expression turns awkward—uncomfortable. "Good. I see you've come back to catch a game?"

"Yes, one of my business contacts had an extra ticket and talked me into coming down."

"Oh. That's nice."

Thinking about how much fun we had at Lane's fraternity earlier that day I add, "I was thinking about coming by after the game and visiting everyone."

"Oh, really."

Her expression tells me she is less than thrilled with the idea. I would be lying if I said it doesn't sting a little.

"Well, it's good to see you. Enjoy the rest the game," she says as she corrals the three girls a few feet over to the right.

"Yeah, you too."

Screw the two dollars. I'm going to get the nachos. I might get a slaw dog, too.

That girl was a complete wreck when she showed up at Alabama. No friends, no style, and hopeless.

I had shown Valerie the ropes and introduced her to the right people when she showed up at our rush pledge party. And now she's going to act like it would be inconvenient for me to show up at the sorority house I lived in for four years?

"Who is she?" I hear a young female voice ask conspiratorially.

"Just one of the old girls. You know how some of them have to remember their glory days," I hear Valerie whisper loud enough for me to hear.

"That's so sad."

I keep my eyes forward and try to keep my mind busy debating slaw dog or kraut dog. The only thing that keeps me from turning around and yanking Valerie bald-headed are the security officers. That, and I don't want to run the risk of being disbarred for earning a felony in the state of Alabama.

As I hand Lane his two hot dogs and diet soda, he eyes the two dogs, nachos, and soda I keep back for myself.

"I see you took my advice on the two dogs and raised it a nacho."

"Shut up and eat your wiener." I drop into my chair next to him.

Chapter 32

There are five minutes left in the third quarter, and unbelievably, the game has gotten worse. Alabama is still scoring at will with their third-string and true freshman now playing.

Lane taps my arm. "I've got sort of a busy week coming up. Have you seen enough?"

"Yeah, I'm good."

Halfway home, Lane's phone rings. He glances at the number. "Sorry, I need to take this."

I gesture with a nod that I understand and direct my gaze outside the window as if that will allow him an added layer of privacy.

Lane's portion of the conversation consists mainly of, "I understand," "Sure we can do that," and "Yes," with the exception of when he asks, "Is that really necessary?" He hangs up.

I continue to stare out the window.

"That was Agent Taggart."

"Oh? I didn't realize you two were friends like that."

"We're not. It's business."

I direct my attention to Lane. "And?"

"And he needs to talk to your defendant, Jayron Freeman,

Monday morning."

"I have something planned for Monday."

"When it comes to the FBI, it's best to get it done as quickly as possible. Do you really want to cancel?"

"No. I'm not saying that. It's just a little advance warning would've been nice."

Lane snorts a laugh. "This is an advance warning by FBI standards. They're so used to getting their way, a forty-hour notice is extremely odd."

Great. The FBI has built this entire case around being able to read what Jayron's motives were. That would be fine if they could understand that his motivation was hunger.

Instead, they built this elaborate terrorist conspiracy theory. With no evidence of him having had prior terrorist interest or interaction, and therefore no motive. I'm sure Taggart will try to trick Jayron into saying something incriminating during an interview.

Taggart strikes me as just the type of person who would ask one of those questions that no answer will leave you beyond reproach. Sort of like that old question, "Have you stopped beating your wife?"

It is a shame. My feelings had recovered from the bruising they took from Valerie snubbing me. I really had enjoyed the road trip with Lane, even if the game had been a bit of a bust.

Taggart is really knocking the shine off my day. Something tells me it is most likely a role he relishes.

Lane pulls up to my parents' house. I notice Miles Trufant's beat-up blue subcompact in our driveway. It is then I remember Dusty planned to have Miles look into the Motlow mansion ghost. I'm very interested to learn what he found out.

"I had a fun time." Lane stops the car.

"Me too. I appreciate your offering to take me. I also had an unexpectantly great time at your fraternity house."

"Yeah, those kids are actually pretty cool about this old dude crashing in on their party."

I wish I could say the same for my sorority sisters. "Yes, that was very gracious of them."

Lane extends his right hand to shake. It catches me off guard, and it takes a moment for me to reciprocate and take his hand. "Okay. I'll see you Monday. Fill me in on Taggart's interview of your client."

"Will do."

Chapter 33

Dusty and Miles aren't in the kitchen. I open the stairwell door. "Dusty, you down there?"

"Hey, April. Come on down here." Dusty's voice floats up to me.

When I reach the bottom of the stairs, Dusty and Miles sit at one of the research tables. "Did you find something?"

"Miles did."

"Hi, April." Miles affects a voice much deeper than his natural tone for his salutation.

Miles is the first team member my brother ever hired. Well, after me.

I believe Miles has a crush on me. It's not difficult to know this. But long ago, I decided it was much easier to act like I was impervious to this knowledge.

"Hi, Miles. What did you find out for us?" I say as I take a chair next to them.

"Oh, this one's all your find, April." Miles clicks a few keys, and a picture of the model house, with smaller trees and shrubbery, appears on the wall-mounted monitor. "I must admit I wanted to start with a broad search. But Dusty told me you wanted to target females living in the house during the 1920s who were younger."

The excitement builds to a crescendo. Miles wouldn't be

going through all the theatrics if it were a dead end. "Tell me, Miles."

He clicks the mouse in his hand, and a grainy photo displays on the wall. "Sylvia Motlow, 1927."

"That's her," I whisper. I pat Miles on the back. "You found her, Miles."

"You're sure this is who you saw?"

"Beyond any doubt. Except her apparition was much clearer than that old photo." She has the same almond-shaped eyes, short bobbed hair, and sensual lips.

In my peripheral vision, Miles turns to Dusty. "This could be big, Dusty."

"Originals are hard to find. You're sure there's never been anything?" Dusty asks.

I break away from the photo and watch their discussion.

"Nothing I found so far. There's never been anything associated with the family or the property."

"What happened to her?" I ask.

"Understand, April, the available documentation is a bit spotty. For whatever reason, it seems the Motlows wanted to keep her death obscure. Most of what I found read like a sterilized Wikipedia account. Sylvia Motlow, youngest of three daughters of the Motlow family. Tragically killed in an accident. Not particularly enthralling story material."

"But she did die in an accident. Correct, Miles?" I ask.

"Yes."

"How?" I know it seems morbid, but my curiosity is getting the best of me again.

"Again, April. The family obviously had something to hide. There isn't much talk about what sort of an accident she died of."

"Nothing?" It doesn't seem right. I know the Motlows had been a big deal in Guntersville. Regardless of what the accident was, it would've been big news.

"There is one report of the accident I found. Honestly, it seems sort of salacious to me, and I've not been able to verify it," Miles says.

"What happened."

Miles is highly analytical. I like to take clues and develop a hypothesis on what might have taken place. Miles is much more cautious and wants to confirm things before he talks about them. I can tell that discussing what he has not verified is painful, and I can only assume that if he did not have a crush on me, he would not discuss it at all.

"There was a single report that Sylvia pretty much got to do whatever she wanted to do. Whether this was because she was the baby or Sylvia was just wild by nature, nobody says. But one of the reports is that she had fallen in love with a performer in a traveling zoo."

Miles stops talking and begins twirling his index finger. "Have you ever seen that act where the motorcycle runs around in the metal cage?"

"Sure, I have."

"The story goes that it was the motorcycle rider that Sylvia had fallen in love with. When it came time for the circus to pack up and leave for New Orleans, the bike rider asked her to marry him and run off before her parents could tell them no.

On the way to the courthouse that night, an awful accident happened. Sylvia had a long silk scarf around her neck. Somehow it became entangled in the rear wheel spokes of the motorcycle."

"It killed her? Oh, how awful. What a mortifying death, Miles."

"Dead is dead," Dusty interjects. "However, for family members, a decapitation would be particularly horrifying."

With Dusty's comment, the room begins to spin. I grab hold of the research table and wait for the vertigo to pass.

Like an old transmission low on fluid, the gears in my mind finally catch, and my mind leaps forward. "Her head came off?"

Dusty studies me closely as if he is checking for a concussion. "Last I checked, that's what decapitation entails."

This is awesome! Well, not for Sylvia. That must have been

an awful way to go. Messy, too. Poor girl.

What great news for me, though. I finally know why I have been haunted by a headless ghost. Through some time cross, Sylvia Motlow knew she would come in contact with me. She knew what I was and that I had resources to help her pass peacefully to her resting place. Everything is falling perfectly into place, just like I hoped.

"April."

I refocus on Dusty. "What?"

"Are you okay?"

It couldn't be more perfect if I tried. "Sure. Why?"

"I asked if you thought you had time for a setup at the Motlow house this weekend. I want to get in there before Mom sells it out from under us."

"I suppose. When? Next weekend?"

"Either Friday or Saturday night. It just depends on the rest of the team's schedule."

"I'm good either way," Miles offers.

Of course, he is. No girlfriend to mess up his weekends. I'm still holding out hope that I just located the man who can potentially mess up my weekend schedules. He can also mess up my lipstick, my hair, heck, maybe even my bed. You never know.

"I guess so," I agree reluctantly.

Chapter 34

I emerge from the basement to find Mama and Daddy curled up together on the sofa with wine goblets in their hands and the fireplace burning. The scene is *way* too intimate for me, and I immediately feel awkward.

Geez. It's only October. It's still way too warm to start a fire.

"Hey, baby. I didn't see you come home."

I stop on my way to the glass door. "Yes, ma'am. I've been home maybe an hour."

"Did you have a good time?"

"Yes, ma'am."

"Lane was a gentleman, wasn't he? I would hate to have to mess him up," Daddy adds.

"Eww."

Daddy pulls Mama closer to his chest as he chuckles. "Just thought I'd ask."

I need to walk away before the scene is burned on my brain. Still, my curiosity keeps my feet planted. "Where y'all been tonight?"

"We were over at the Rains' watching the game," Daddy says.

Daddy plus the Rainses means the Auburn game, not the Alabama game. Mama doesn't count. She's neutral.

"The Auburn game should've been over hours ago."

"It was. Chip and Diane talked us into staying for hamburgers." Mom flips her hand toward Daddy. "Then Chip and your daddy started talking shop."

Daddy and Chip are both physicists. Daddy works as a contractor for the government at Redstone Arsenal and teaches at the University of North Alabama. Chip took his physicist degree and opened up his own engineering company that does top-secret work for the government.

"Chip's company is experiencing the same issue my boss is having," Daddy explains. "There's just not enough young talent studying physics nowadays. At least not Americans. And we can't always get visas for foreign nationals. Especially not with some of the military projects we are working on."

"I wish it was that way with lawyers," I say.

"I told you seven years ago you should've gone into engineering. You're smart enough, and with all these companies pushing for diversity nowadays, there would've been a bidding war for you coming out of school, considering you're female.

"Heck, Chip was telling me that he now has a scholarship program set up at Auburn for three new high school students each year in physics. You want to take a guess at how many students he's had apply this year, not qualify, just apply."

This conversation has moved way past my cursory interest. "Oh, I don't know, Daddy. A thousand."

Daddy holds up a single finger. "One. He's had one application this year, and that's it."

A chill runs up my spine. "Daddy, is that just for incoming freshmen?"

"I think that was the intent when he first started. But it's gotten to the point where he would take any minority or female that can show a successful academic background." He grins lazily at me. "You got somebody in mind for us?"

"I might. I have to find out about the academic scores, but I might."

I leave my parents to whatever hanky-panky they have planned.

Puppy is nowhere to be found on my way back to my apartment. I'm not going to be one of those moms that worries all the time. I unlock his doggie door, so he can let himself in when he is ready to come home.

I set my purse down, kick out of my heels, and pull the comforter off my full-length mirror. I'm not afraid of Sylvia. In fact, I welcome her to come to visit me now. Now that I have a plan to help her after the team gets what they need for their story.

I slide into the crisp sheets of my bed and flip off my nightstand lamp. The pitch dark engulfs me.

I don't fall asleep.

Certain things niggle at my mind. I like the cleanness of the haunting explanations. Still, I have some questions.

If my headless ghost is Sylvia, *which it is*, how did she know Mama would be having the Halloween party at the house she used to live at? How did she know I could help her when I had never been to the home before Friday? Most importantly, what's with the knife?

If Sylvia died by a scarf getting trapped in the spokes of a motorcycle, it makes no sense that she would attack people with a knife and try to cut their heads off.

Nah. I'm overthinking it. Sylvia is the ghost from start to finish.

It all has to do with the parallel time frames Nana always coaches me on. One of us, either Sylvia or me, accidentally pierced the veil. That's all.

Chapter 35

Early Sunday morning, I call Jayron Freeman and give him the news about the FBI. He tells me I don't need to worry about giving him a ride. His brother Kenny will bring him.

I begin to mention the scholarship program but think better of it. I can talk to Kenny about that Monday morning in person when he comes to pick up Jayron.

Justin Lakes's phone number has appeared magically under my thumb on three occasions. Finally, in the afternoon, I chicken out on the phone call and text him.

My text tells him I'm looking forward to seeing him tomorrow. I know it's lame, but it is early in the game, and I don't want to seem overly eager.

Daddy cooked pot roast and mashed potatoes for the family that night. It is a charming ending to what proved to be a most restful day. The fact that it isn't my turn to do the dishes is just a bonus.

I hang out a couple hours after dinner with my family. I push Daddy for more information on the Rains physicist scholarship.

Finally, I quit beating around the bush and tell him about Kenny. Daddy seems to think Kenny is precisely the type of individual Chip is recruiting.

It's midnight when I lock my apartment door and get ready

for bed. Puppy is already asleep and snoring hard.

I pull out Jayron's case file and flip through it again. I have the entire case folder memorized. I don't believe that will necessarily help me during the FBI interview tomorrow.

Truthfully, what does Agent Taggart hope to glean from a conversation with Jayron? I have already asked him everything I possibly can, and I still don't see any malicious intent. Lord knows he isn't a terrorist.

Am I scared? You bet I am. Not for myself. It isn't like I'm going to go to jail for life. Still, if the FBI is showing interest, regardless of how minor the infraction is, you are either going to do some time or be so broke when they are done with you, you'll *wish* someone would feed you three meals a day.

Jayron is probably walking into a buzz saw. The worst part is that the person who is supposed to protect him, me, doesn't have enough experience to know how to turn the buzz saw off.

I turn off my lights and sleep through the night for the second night in a row. The headless ghost images have simply disappeared since I met Sylvia Motlow.

Chapter 36

I'm surprised to find Monday morning that our FBI meeting is scheduled to be held in the smallest meeting room. I wouldn't even call it a meeting room. It has the depth of a typical office but three times the standard width.

Jayron arrives in an ironed black T-shirt and clean blue jeans. This is a definite improvement from the bail hearing when he wore the bright orange jumpsuit.

Agent Taggart enters the meeting room and shuts the door behind him. He takes an excruciating amount of time shuffling his manilla folders and spreading them out in front of him.

"Ms. Snow, I appreciate you being here. Still, the goal today is to get candid responses from your defendant so that the government might develop a better understanding of what transpired in this event."

"What event would that be, Agent Taggart?" I ask.

His eyes reveal I'm not the first smart-mouthed defense attorney he has gone up against. "That we've established your client is working as a forward scout for a terrorist organization."

"I'm not a terrorist!"

I put my hand on Jayron's forearm so he will cool his jets.

"Best I can tell you, Agent, you haven't proved anything yet, and you've called us in for a fishing expedition."

Taggart turns his head away from me and leans in toward Jayron. "Boy, you need to come clean. I know you want to. Just tell me who else was involved with the attack, and I can get you a reduced sentence."

"There isn't anyone else," Jayron says.

"Don't lie to me, young man." Agent Taggart's intensity somehow increases. "When was the last time you traveled abroad?"

"I, never. I've never traveled abroad."

"So, all this chatter in Guntersville about the dam, and you're going to tell me you had nothing to do with it." Taggert glares at Jayron.

"I don't even know what you mean by 'chatter,'" Jayron says.

"So, this is what we're gonna do." Taggart slams his fist onto the table. I'm not sure if it gets Jayron's attention because I am too busy jumping in the air myself.

"Don't you even dare think you can play me, boy. I have stayed on some of the most powerful men in the world. They all cracked and resigned to tell the truth. You're no different than the 9/11 hijackers in my book." Taggert stops for effect. "Actually, you're worse. You're a traitor who would sell out his own people for personal gain."

"I'm no traitor," Jayron insists.

"Agent Taggart, I'm not going to allow you to just throw a bunch of unsubstantiated claims at my client in hopes of something sticking. You continue to call him a terrorist, yet you have not substantiated that claim in the least. You do not hear Jayron claiming he did not set off charges in the lake. He is more than willing to take responsibility for those actions. But your circumstantial leap to him being a terrorist—well, that's just plain silly."

Taggart's chest puffs out. "Silly? You call over thirty-five captured conversations about blowing up the Guntersville dam in the last fourteen days silly?"

"People are actually planning on blowing up the Guntersville dam? Why would anyone do that?" I ask.

"I would tell you to ask your client, but I'm sure he would just tell you some story to get you to feel sorry for him, so let me just paint it for you really quick. He was doing it for the disruption of the government. He and his handlers are one of the hundreds of cells planted throughout this country wanting to do maximum damage to our communities and sow fear and dissent."

"Are you saying some people are actually saying they would blow up the dam?" Jayron asks.

"I have to admit you're a darn good liar." Taggert throws three photos on the table in front of Jayron.

"Look familiar?" Taggert snarls. "See, we're on to you, son. You need to flip now and save yourself some serious jail time."

Jayron picks up the photos and his expression changes. "These are the folks that are planning to blow up the dam?"

"No. You were planning on blowing up the dam, Jayron. Why don't you go ahead and admit it."

"Come on, Jayron, we're leaving," I say.

"You can't just walk out on the interview!" Taggart yells as he gets inches from my face.

"I can when you are badgering my client," I say calmly.

"We have almost two hundred hours of taped conversations," Taggart continues.

"That's good," I comment. "Please don't forget to turn that in. You don't want to withhold exculpatory evidence at the hearing." I grab Jayron by the shoulder and practically pull him out of the room.

We walk down the hall together and lean against a wall to gather our thoughts.

"Anything you want to tell me, Jayron?

He shakes his head. "No, ma'am."

I steal a look at my phone. I need to get on the road to Huntsville if I'm going to make my lunch date with Justin. "Are you going to be able to make it home, alright?"

"Yes, ma'am. Don't worry about me. My brother Kenny is waiting for me just outside the courtroom."

Crud. I forgot I need to talk to Kenny, too. That will have to wait for another day. "I need to ask a favor of you."

"Yes, ma'am?"

"I need you to ask Kenny to get together his transcripts. I've got a possible opportunity for him."

"Opportunity like how."

I pat Jayron on the shoulder. "Don't worry about that now. I need to see his transcripts before we worry about it anymore. Can you remember that?"

"Sure."

I start trotting down the marble hallway in my heels. I would give anything to be in the Tinker Bell slippers I wore Friday night.

"Hey, April!"

Stopping abruptly, I nearly turn my ankle. "Yeah?"

Jayron has an unusually sharp, calculating edge to his expression. It is very dissimilar to the usual "not so bright kid" look he has typically.

"The FBI man."

"Agent Taggart," I say.

"Right." His eyes squint. "He didn't say he had caught the people they thought were going to blow up the dam."

I consider what he is asking and can't figure out where he is going with it. "That's correct."

"Which means they're still out there, planning to blow up the dam."

"Most likely. If what Taggart heard was true." I have an uneasy feeling developing in my gut. "Why are you asking me this, Jayron?"

"I was just trying to get it straight in my head and make sure I'd heard it right."

"I'm only going to ask you one more time. Is there something you need to tell me?" I ask again.

His face retains the same sharp edge as he shakes his head. "No, ma'am. All good here."

"Alright, I'll see you later this week." Despite running behind schedule, I can't bring myself to jog. Something about the conversation with Jayron is eating at me, and I just can't put my finger on it.

Well, that's not wholly true. What is making my gut uneasy is that look. That hard edge the male half of the species' face takes on when they're deciding to do something crazy, possibly noble, and often with deadly implications. The pause in their expressions as they think it through and make their decision comes from the high degree of difficulty and the danger it will expose them to if they pick up the challenge.

I've learned from my brothers that the male risk-to-reward scale is quite different than most females. In fact, I believe in many males, the scale is just busted.

There is no way I can even begin to contemplate what Jayron is thinking in that limited brain of his. Knowing he isn't the sharpest tool in the shed makes it harder to determine what project he had latched onto as a personal quest.

Still, I have no doubt about the expression. He is a man on the precipice of accepting a challenge.

Men. They're so straightforward to read as long as I pay attention to the signs. Usually, if I'm caught off guard by them, it is my fault. I've been lulled into seeing what I wanted to see and quit paying attention to their non-verbal cues.

Chapter 37

As I approach my IROC, I do a cursory check of my emails and see one from Lisa Barlow from New Day Attorneys, the firm out of Austin that I sent my résumé to. Perfect timing since I have a forty-five-minute drive to Huntsville, and as Grandpa always said, "You should strike while the iron is hot."

I'm not a hundred percent sure what he meant by that. I sure wouldn't want to be on the receiving end of said hot iron. But I know I'm thinking of the term in the proper context when I dial Lisa's number immediately.

The phone rings as I turn out of the court parking lot.

"It's a new day."

The young woman's declaration over the phone nearly causes me to laugh. Struggling mightily, I manage to say, "Hi. Is Lisa Barlow in?"

"Why yes, she is. May I ask who's calling?"

"April Snow. She sent me a recruiting email a couple of hours ago."

"One moment."

The young woman puts me on hold, and Katie Perry begins singing "Roar" to me. That's pretty cool.

I now realize that since I have been home, I have listened to very little music. No wonder, some days I do well to make it home, eat, and get a shower before I go to my next job.

Madonna begins to tell me how she is a material girl. I remember in high school, I thought that was one of the most fantastic songs ever. For some reason, the song has begun to perturb me the older I get.

Good Lord, how long do they leave people on hold? I have half a mind to hang up and call back.

When Gloria Gaynor comes on and starts singing, "I will survive," something begins to seem a little odd to me. I'm preparing to hang up when an older but equally chipper voice comes online.

"Hi, Ms. Snow, this is Lisa Barlow, your personal guide to your new day."

I'm dumbfounded. All the usual cool-headed responses I have pre-recorded in my head disappear. "Thank you," I say.

"You're welcome. I really do appreciate your quick response to our recruiting letter."

"Well, I guess the same to you on the quick response to my résumé."

"With qualifications like yours, we know there's a limited amount of time before somebody else snatches up our gal."

This "gal" wishes that were the case. Maybe the market in Texas is a lot busier than the rest of the country. I had heard Texas was a hot market.

"Ms. Snow, you have completed your internship, correct?"

"Yes. I have already defended many defendants successfully in high-level criminal trials." My canned responses are coming back to me.

"My. You are teething on granite. We don't ask any of our associates to work on cases that strenuous. We do leave that to the partners. For the most part, I would say a full seventy to eighty percent of our business is derived from women's separation issues."

I try to think through the corporate coding and then break. "Separation issues from what?"

"Well, from their spouses, of course."

"The majority of your business is through divorces?" I'm not passing judgment. It's just that divorces aren't any fun, and I can only imagine if that were the bulk of my business.

"Female divorces," Lisa corrects me.

"Isn't there usually a male and female in divorces?" I catch myself. "I mean when it's not a man and a man—or a female and a female. You don't just specialize in lesbian divorces, do you?"

"No. I'm saying that we only cater to the female side of these issues."

Austin looked really pretty when I pulled it up on the Internet. I like the idea of living in an expanding market. But I don't think I've really got my mind around this female-only thing. "So, like New Day only has female clients?"

"Exactly. That way, everybody is more at ease," Lisa pitches.

I don't know. Some girls in my sorority loved that only females were allowed in our house after nine in the evening. But I was never one of them. If I could go back, I would've spent less time at the sorority and more time hanging out with mixed groups. "So, no male clients at all?"

"Absolutely not. Besides, it's women who have been taken advantage of for the last five hundred years. It's time we band together and resist against the control of patriarchy."

I am not really sure what I said, but I think I made Lisa mad. Her speech is getting louder and faster with every sentence.

"We have to fight for our sisters to level the playing field."

No. I don't think Austin is going to be a good fit for me. I don't have an issue defending a female. Well, if I never have to see Nina Rodriguez again, it would be too soon. But I don't know how you can decide the merits of a trial case by the gender of your client.

How would I tell my brothers? I mean, can you work at a feminist organization and still like guys? I mean, I love guys.

When they aren't acting stupid.

I'm headed to what I hope is a date with a guy right now. Yeah, Austin isn't a good match for this chick.

I interrupt Lisa's soliloquy about the firm's community service. "Lisa, I do appreciate the opportunity, but at this time, I'm going to remain in Guntersville, Alabama."

"Wait now. You didn't even let me tell you about our compensation package or our healthcare," Lisa says.

Okay. I'll bite. Especially since I don't have healthcare right now, and I don't really have a set compensation package. "Okay, wow me."

Lisa laughs, and it is so fake it makes the hairs on the back of my neck stand up. "Each attorney has their base salary, but they also enjoy an annual bonus. The bonus is twenty percent of the firm's profit divided among the non-owner associates. It really is fantastic."

"How is the bonus divided out?" I'm just curious.

"The partners keep tabs on each attorney during the year. The one with the most hire recommendations minus the negative recommendations is the winner."

I only see five thousand and one ways that could be manipulated to show favoritism. "Lisa. Again, thank you for reviewing my résumé and offering to talk, but I just don't—"

"Don't say it. Don't say a word. I'm sending you a ticket for a round-trip flight to Austin. I need you to come in here this weekend and meet the partners. Do you think you could do that?"

I wasn't sure if I could get up on Saturday. Much less fly out to Austin, considering I'll be coming off the Motlow mansion research trip. I *don't* plan to miss that. "I'll think about it."

"Don't think about it too long," Lisa urges.

There are times that my brothers really aggravate me. There are times I wish they understood me better. Taking all the negatives of being raised with two brothers, I must admit I enjoy the fact they are different than me.

I don't think I ever want to limit my exposure to only one type of person again. In many ways, it is one of the things I have enjoyed about working with Howard. True story, I never know what's coming through our door next.

New Day is probably a fantastic opportunity for some wonderful attorney. I know myself well enough now that it just isn't me.

Chapter 38

Justin has arranged for Jonah to join us at Rosalina's Mexican restaurant. I was expecting a tiny hole-in-the-wall, but Rosalina owns an entire strip mall. The Mexican restaurant is made out to look like an authentic hacienda, complete with a tile fountain and large carp swimming lazily about in the November sun.

Stepping inside, it takes a moment for my eyes to adjust to the subdued lighting. The male host standing in front of me says, "I know a woman as beautiful as you is not eating alone. The man you are meeting, tell me, what does he look like?"

I hold up two fingers. "Two men."

His dark bushy mustache jerks into a smile. "But of course." He lifts a menu. "Follow me, please."

We walk through a large eating hall that has fifty tables. The majority of them have between two and four diners already sampling the lunch menu. We turn left into a small nook where there are only four tables.

It embarrasses me to say this, but this powerful physical reaction racks through my body when I see Justin. I feel like I might lose my balance.

I don't know what it is about him, but whatever it is, my body overrides any logic from my brain.

Justin jumps to his feet and pulls a chair out for me. "Did you have any problems finding the place?"

"Nope. The modern wonders of GPS," I say.

"Good. April, this is Jonah. Jonah, April."

I had not even noticed the tall, thin man standing next to Justin. He extends his hand. "A pleasure to meet you, April."

"April, I've been telling Jonah about your background and also about all your family businesses."

"You make it sound like my family is in the Dixie Mafia."

"No, the Mafia wishes they were as diversified as the Snows. Marina, real estate brokerage, law firm, and private research. That's about as diverse as it gets."

"You forgot publishing," I say.

Justin gestures with his finger. "That's right." Turning to Jonah, he says, "One of her brothers is a highly successful author."

"That's interesting. What does your brother write? I'm always looking for new authors."

"Paranormal stories."

I can tell by Jonah's expression he is caught off guard by my answer. I don't believe paranormal is his cup of tea.

"I might have to read one," he says, forcing a wan smile.

Justin redirects the topic. "I was explaining to Jonah that it was probably difficult for you to figure out what exactly you wanted to excel at. Don't get me wrong, I know you're already a successful lawyer. I only mean to say you have so many different avenues you could take given your immense talents."

"Justin never knows when to stop selling, April. You know as well as I do that work is work and practicing law is like any other job. Still, I like to believe that real estate attorneys have the best of both worlds.

"Like criminal attorneys and divorce attorneys, people are always going to be selling and trading property, so business is steady. Also, it doesn't come with the high stakes defense attorneys face, where a mistake can get someone incarcerated for thirty years. Or the dirty feeling that divorce attorneys feel when they actively break a family apart. No, real estate attorneys don't have any of those job hazards."

Jonah is speaking a lot of truth. A tremendous amount of the stress on me lately is the gravity of the criminal cases I have been assigned while with Snow and Associates. "But doesn't it get boring?"

Jonah's high cheekbones threaten to close his brown eyes by way of his smile. "Some days. Still, for three hundred thousand a year and the perks that come with it, I could do headstands in four-inch mud each day as long as I know it's only for a nine-hour shift."

I understand his point, even though I don't entirely agree with him. It would mean I'd only have to do the job for a couple of years to get my student loans paid off.

"But what about your clientele. How did you develop it?"

"Word of mouth mostly. But you can't worry about that right now. If you take care of the folks who do give you an opportunity, you'll have a larger clientele base than you can ever service before too long."

I like Jonah. He has an unassuming manner about him. In a lot of ways, he reminds me of Howard. Except he is thinner, better dressed, taller, and much younger.

"Being a lawyer is no different than writing books, building neighborhoods, or running a marina. It's business. In business, the only thing that counts is that you promise people something they want, and then you deliver on that promise each and every time without fail. Since so few people do what they promise today, your customers will pay you an obscene amount of money to keep the right to remain a paying customer of yours."

Jonah missed his calling. He should have been an inspirational speaker because I'm getting the itch to open my own business today.

Chapter 39

After lunch, Jonah introduces me to his team and gives me a tour of his office. The complex consists of two refurbished late-nineteenth-century homes adjoined by a tasteful pebble driveway and garden.

We continue our conversation about legal work for another two hours. Jonah applies no pressure for me to agree that real estate would be my best professional choice.

The few times I talked to attorneys who specialize, they possessed a maniacal need for me to affirm their specialty was the best of all law specialties. Instead, Jonah continues to ask questions about my current position with Howard, what I enjoy, and what I believe are my best strengths.

Justin, for his part, makes himself comfortable in one of the plush leather chairs behind and to the side of us. If not for the physical attraction I feel, which occasionally causes my eyes to dart in his direction, I would have forgotten Justin was in the room.

Jonah leans forward and teepees his hands in front of him. "You know what I think, Ms. Snow?"

"No, sir."

His eyes are kind, inviting. "You would be professionally successful in any specialty. Just for the record, I don't say that lightly."

"Thank you."

A brief laugh escapes him. "I can't say it's necessarily a good thing. One of the pleasantries of limitations is they often direct us to the professions that play to our strengths.

"Being proficient, even excellent, at a lot of different things is much more complicated. Since you have the luxury, or dare I say the burden, of deciding what you believe would make you the happiest."

I'm beginning to get the uneasy feeling Jonah is gonna lay some trite truism on me like "follow your heart."

"When Justin mentioned you to me, I thought you might be a suitable candidate for my firm."

I start to object, and he raises his hand to stop me. "Before you say anything, yes, you would be highly successful at this firm. I have no doubt of that.

"Likewise, I believe given your, shall we say restless nature, I would lose you in two, three years, tops. That would be fine in my mind if you took what you learned here and started your own practice. Yet, I have a feeling you would simply do something different. What would be gained for you?"

Indignation bubbles up inside of me. What I hear is that Jonah has talked to me for a few hours, and he wouldn't consider offering me a job because he now knows me so well he is sure I will be out of the industry in three years. It all feels so presumptive to me, and I don't appreciate it.

"What if I did apply for a position here?" I blurt. "Or are you saying you wouldn't hire me because you have this idea on what I want out of life?"

"Oh, I'd hire you. It's always difficult to take a pass on somebody with such a talented skillset. Still, I think I'd always be waiting for the day you tell me you have decided to quit and become an author or a law professor. I do not believe hiring you would benefit you or me long-term."

I struggle to keep everything in perspective. To be honest with myself, the reason I drove to Huntsville today was to get another chance to interact with Justin.

Talking about the opportunities of real estate is just an added bonus. Still, it was only a pretense to find out more about Justin.

Even though I'm getting pretty blasted tired of being rejected. Sure, I guess technically you can say that I turned down New Day practice earlier in the day. Still, I was only on a pseudo-information-gathering trip regarding real estate law. Without even applying for a position, I'm being rejected.

"I've only just met you, and I can't tell you what to do," Jonah says.

It seems like he is.

"Talented litigators don't grow on trees. Add to that you are not an attorney who spends all their time in the law books. You raise your eyes and look at the real world. You go through the trouble of reviewing facts from the actual crime sites, doing your own interviewing, and basically applying common sense to the case.

"Those are hard-to-find skillsets in a lawyer, and I do believe you should continue to hone those traits. Top-level defense attorneys, attorneys that get results, are highly compensated for a reason. There just aren't many people who can do it right and win."

New flash. I've been trying to get a position as a defense attorney for the last six months to "hone" my skills. Unfortunately, every law firm I interview with has been closed by the FBI or has a manager who triggers my sexual predator alarms.

"That's the type of position I have been trying to land for the last six months without any success," I inform Jonah.

"Success yet. Timing is everything. When things don't happen right away, things are only lining up for us. Besides, the experience you have been able to develop while working with your uncle is awe-inspiring. Your dream job is around the corner. You can be certain of it."

Easy for Jonah to say sitting in his two-thousand-dollar leather executive chair. Justin appears in my peripheral vision, giving me a start.

"Jonah, thank you for taking the time to talk shop with April."

"My pleasure. I always love to meet bright new professionals. It also gives me a name to call if I ever need a defense attorney, heaven forbid."

Both men laugh. I don't. I'm feeling too morose to muster a polite laugh.

Justin gestures to the door. "Walk you out?"

That isn't the worse consolation prize. "Sure."

Jonah said a lot of nice things to me. So why do I feel so dejected?

"Are you alright?" Justin leans a hand on the roof of my car as I unlock the door.

"Yeah. Why?"

"You seem a lot quieter than I remember from the other night."

"Well, tequila makes me talkative."

He laughs, and every sensor in my body leaps to total overload. "We should have had margaritas with our lunch, then. Rosalina's makes a great one."

I can smell the woodsy scent of his cologne in the air. My body is like a spring wound too tight. His face is so near. His lips, full and sensual, look so kissable.

It is an accident, I swear. I didn't plan it; it just sorta happens.

I lean forward, placing my lips against Justin's, and passion flames through my body in an instant. My hands grip his arms, pulling him toward me as my lips part.

Heat. Unbridled fire races over me as I experience the electricity of excitement firing across from *his* mind.

Leaning into me, his weight pins me to my car as his shaking hand glides up my skirted thigh, finishing its journey by clutching me tighter to him. His mouth opens as his teeth tease my now swollen lips.

Lord, I need this. I want this man. I need his body, now.

This feels so incredibly delectable I want to continue until we have quenched the hungry fires that threaten to consume us.

Justin pulls back from me. "I'm sorry. That was inappropriate of me."

I feel the loss of his body heat immediately. My body mourns the loss of contact as my hands pull at his forearms, hoping he will renew our tight embrace.

Readily I read regret and guilt flow to me from his feelings. It's wrong of me to continue reading him, but I'm confused, flustered, and hope to glean some helpful information from his thoughts on what has just transpired.

"You didn't start this, Justin. I did."

He drops his arms, effectively escaping my grasp. "That still doesn't excuse my behavior. I apologize. I don't want you to think that this was all setup to trick you into this."

What isn't he understanding? I kissed him, not the other way around.

Besides, regardless of his intent of the meeting, my goal had always been to get to know Justin better and perhaps end up right here with his weight pinning me to my car in a hot kiss.

I had a desire to know if the chemistry between us might be hot. It is. I was hoping for Tabasco. Instead, I got ghost pepper salsa so intense the flames continue to crackle across my skin.

Despite the stupidity of his apology, my body yearns for him to touch me again.

Justin moves to open my car door. "I just wouldn't want you to ever think I don't respect you. And if your mother ever found out..."

His comment makes me bark a laugh. "My mama knows I'm a big girl now. She's welcome to have her opinions about my choices, as long as she keeps them to herself."

Justin gestures for me to get in my car. "I understand. Still, I respect what she thinks, and I respect you."

Now I'm aggravated as all get out. Sexually, I am on all lights green. Except now, my prospective partner is overly concerned about how my mama would view us having a relationship? I drop my fanny onto the driver's seat and swing my legs in. Justin holds the door open as I try to shut it.

"I don't want you to think I'm not interested. I find you extremely sexy and desirable." His brown eyes are pleading.

Is he for real? He better let go of my door before my redneck comes out.

"You've got an odd way of showing it, mister." I wrench the door from his grip and succeed in slamming it with a rewardingly loud sound.

I fire up the IROC and turn my front wheel to the right as I back out. I grin when he steps back as if I were about to run over his foot.

Geez. Some men are so indecisive. I'll never understand it.

Justin telling me he finds me desirable? How did he think that was going to make me feel as he was turning me down? Of all the men in the world I have to have an animal-like attraction to, I pick the one worried about my mama's opinion if he sleeps with her little girl.

Mother of pearl! These guys are driving me crazy.

Chapter 40

As I reach Guntersville, I'm over my hissy fit. I've even developed a certain level of empathy for Justin.

The attraction between is so exhilarating I can't remember a time I have been so sexually charged. If it is the same for Justin, I can understand how it is too much to process so soon. Especially when you add in what he believes to be the awkwardness of being one of Mama's clients.

I don't want to throw away this level of magnetism over one lousy encounter. Instead, I need to cultivate and ride this relationship to its full fruition. And yes, I do mean *ride* both figuratively and literally.

I want to live out the vision I gleaned from Justin's mind the first time I touched him.

Jacob's police cruiser is in the driveway when I park at home. I hadn't seen him in a few days, and the thought of getting to talk to Jacob brings a smile to my face.

As I get out of my car, I know something isn't quite right. Jacob and my family are on the patio. The grill isn't smoking, and nobody is holding a beer. It has all the appearance of a business call by Jacob.

"What's up, Officer Hurley?" I tease as I approached the patio.

Jacob does not look like his usual lighthearted self. "I was checking with your family to see if anybody might be available to help with a search tomorrow."

"What did we lose now?"

"We think a body."

I wait for Jacob to crack a grin. Jacob is as poor of a liar as me and can't tell a lie without breaking a smile. When he doesn't even smirk, my gut rolls. "Seriously?"

"I'm afraid so."

"Who?" I ask.

"Faith Ray."

I knew the antique dealer had been missing for a few days, but nobody mentioned they didn't expect to find her alive. "She's dead?"

Jacob exhales loudly, gesturing toward my family. "Like I was telling your family, we were treating the case as a missing person. You know, maybe she needed some time away from Kyle. He's not the easiest man to be around, and I can only imagine what it would be like to live with him."

That is true. The two Ray brothers own a few trailer parks in the area. Their grandfather had set them up decades ago, and the brothers inherited them from their mother.

The life of a landlord had afforded them a good living. It also gave them way too much time on their hands, and they are, as a rule, surly and most often drunk.

"Then we found her SUV today. It was parked at the east boat ramp."

"Maybe she got a ride with a friend?" I offer.

"Our officers checked the east boat ramp parking lot at least three times since she's been reported gone. Then the SUV shows up this morning. Plus, the techs found smeared traces of blood in the driver's seat and a small blood smudge on the armrest. Other than the blood, the vehicle is immaculate."

I want to hold out hope in situations like this. However, once blood is added to the equation, all my quip explanations begin to sound like grand delusions to me.

There can be a perfectly logical reason why a middle-aged

antique owner parks her car at a boat dock, leaving traces of blood in the vehicle. And, she may have gone for a boat ride with a friend. It's not like it can't happen.

But let's be honest, the probability of winning the Powerball tonight is marginally better than us finding Faith unharmed.

"We've taken Kyle in for questioning. So far, he's holding to the story that he doesn't know where she's at. But something seems off with him," Jacob continues.

I sit down on the retaining wall next to the patio. "Well, it's Kyle Ray. Of course, something is off with him."

Jacob arches his eyebrows. "True that. But you know how this rolls. Spouses are always the most reliable person of interest in disappearances."

"Does he have an attorney?" I ask.

Jacob grins. "No, and we'd like to keep it that way as long as possible. He's presently cooperating with the police. So don't you go interjecting yourself."

"I wouldn't dream of it."

Jacob turns his attention back to my family. "I can count on all four of you?"

My parents and brothers nod in affirmation. Chase pats Jacob on the back.

Jacob looks at me.

I consider it for a moment. The idea of traipsing through the woods and finding a dead body doesn't seem like something I want any part of at the moment. If anything, I believe I'd try to avoid that family outing like the plague.

Jacob doesn't press me. "Great. I can't tell you how much I appreciate your help, folks. We'll see you at two at the east boat ramp."

Jacob begins to leave, and Mama asks, "You're not going to stay for dinner, Officer Hurley? We have plenty."

"No, ma'am. Thank you for the offer, but I have too many irons in the fire tonight for a proper meal."

"Are you sure?"

"Mama, let Jacob be. He's busy."

Chapter 41

I feel terrible Jacob missed dinner. Daddy had cooked country-fried steak, biscuits, mashed potatoes, and gravy. This is also referred to as the "widow maker closer" and is one of Jacob's favorite meals.

I ease my conscience with the knowledge that by cutting Mama's objections short, before she could turn her full charms on, I saved Jacob from a future coronary.

Which is more than I can do for Puppy. He wiped out a super-sized plate of everything Daddy put down for him and promptly trotted off to our apartment. Surprisingly, he was still able to fit thru his puppy door.

"You're going to have to cut him a bigger door if you keep feeding him like that, Daddy."

"I can always make it bigger. Just not smaller." Daddy replies without looking up from his plate.

"If you keep feeding him people food, we might just need to close the dog door permanently. Because I won't have a dog."

Daddy favors me a look that makes me wonder if I have stepped over the line. Daddy rarely loses his temper, but when he does, it's ugly.

Mama puts her hand on his forearm. "April, it's been forever since we had a dog in the family, and I believe you're right. Perhaps if you could get some literature from Dr. Rains on what people food does to a dog's longevity, we can convince the men to quit feeding him things he shouldn't eat."

Dr. Rains? As in my nemesis, Jackie. Mama used the title "Dr." on purpose. Not to mention her saying we can get the *men* to quit feeding Puppy people food is rich. Considering I caught Mama sliding Puppy a plate of lasagna a few months back.

Nope. I'm not going to take the bait. The new and improved April does not have the need to argue.

I smile and pick up my plate, then proceed to pick up everyone else's. "I'll load the dishwasher. Daddy, thank you for cooking tonight. It was delicious."

"You're welcome."

I smile pleasantly and go into the kitchen. There, that was easy.

Chapter 42

Besides helping Jayron navigate the FBI interview earlier this morning, I really hadn't done any work. Yet I'm totally exhausted.

Me letting my emotions run at the top end of my RPM all day must have worn me slap out.

Stripping down to my underwear and pulling on an oversized T-shirt feels divine. I consider going directly to bed, but a guilty inner voice makes me open my laptop.

There is no containing my joy when I see an email from Mr. Kenny Freeman. "To whom it may concern. Please find attached the official transcript from Etowah County Junior College."

I open the transcript PDF. What? I've told you I'm nosy.

It becomes immediately apparent that Kenny is attempting to earn an Associate's degree in "crazy smart." He has completed physics, chemistry, and calculus classes the last semester alone, each with an A.

I end up having to revise the email to my daddy six times before it feels right. Reading it one last time, I attach Kenny's cover letter and transcript to my email.

Here's to thinking positive thoughts. I tap the send button and feel a surge of happiness.

Further down in my emails, I see an excellent follow-up note from Jonah Lynch. *April, I enjoyed meeting you today. Please, if I may be of any assistance during your employment search at regional firms, I am here for you. All the luck in your bright future. Best regards.*

The email brings our lunch back into clear focus. I remember how attentively Jonah listened when he asked a question. More impressive is how he was able to take our interview process and know my needs and desires so accurately. I like him, and he has a true gift as a mentor.

Unfortunately, Jonah's email also reminds me of the awkward interaction with Justin. I do feel marginally guilty for reading his emotions. It was cheating, I'll own that, and it was also probably wrong of me.

Still, I was desperate to be sure what we had was real, and when I touched him, his mind was an open window. It plainly showed passionate, erotic visions quickly through my mind.

So, what was that at the end? Why did I end up in my car driving home rather than us going back to his place or a motel? Too weird.

What in the world am I going to do about Jayron? Agent Taggart has him in his sights. Suppose it's true that the FBI has conversations from actual terrorists talking about blowing up the dam. In that case, Jayron may be in a classic "wrong place at the wrong time" situation.

Watching him today, I know if there is some way I can help him get into the service that he would be an asset for the military. I guess the best thing I can do to help him is to prepare his case and get Jayron's sentence reduced to a misdemeanor or dropped in its entirety.

The knock on my apartment door startles me. I start toward the door, then decide to pull on my robe in case it isn't Mama.

I blush as I open the door. "Jacob?"

His eyes scan down my robe and rest on my bare legs for too long. "Sorry. But I need to talk to you about tomorrow."

"Jeez. Let me put some shorts on." I locate a pair on the top of my dresser. I give a quick check to make sure Jacob's head is turned. Satisfied with his usual chivalry, I pull the shorts on quickly. "I know you have my stupid number."

"I do. But I'm pressed for time, and this is something I shouldn't ask over the phone."

"You can turn around, you big lug. I'm decent now."

Jacob's eyes go directly to my legs again, and his ears turn red. What's gotten into him tonight anyway?

"You might not like what I'm about to ask," Jacob says.

"Less than you crashing my door at bedtime?"

Jacob shifts his weight as his eyes lock on mine. "I need your help tomorrow."

I snort a laugh. "Yeah, no. You don't need me in the woods. If you were going to court or the mall, yes, I would go with you if you asked. But I don't really do woods."

Jacob's eyes narrow. "That's not why I'm asking, and you know it, April."

He continues to watch me as if he gave me a clue, and I'm supposed to answer his riddle. I respond with a shrug of my shoulders.

"You're gonna make me spell it out?"

"I suppose I am. Because I don't have a clue what you're talking about, Hurley."

"Your gift."

My body tenses. A single bead of sweat traces down my spine as I attempt to lie by denial. "What gift?"

Jacob makes a circular gesture with his finger. "Your ability to see things and hear things other people can't."

"Where did you hear that nonsense?" I laugh, but it sounds contrived.

Jacob's facial features harden. "Aren't we past that?"

"I guess I don't know because I don't have a clue what you're talking about."

"Listen, April. If you just want to say no, then tell me no. But don't be blowing smoke up my butt. I read Dusty's work, and I know everybody on his team. And even though the books are written where the team has pseudonyms, you really think I can't figure out that Alora is your character's name."

There is a long awkward silence between us. Our eyes are still locked as if we are playing a game of blink.

"I've got some hundred people lined up to walk the grids out from the east boat ramp tomorrow. Do you know what I will find out by the end of the day, in all likelihood? Nothing. Absolutely nothing. There's just way too many places to hide a body around here."

"So why do it?"

"Because we can, should—It's not enough to sit around and hope. Come on, April. You know it's about getting up and making it happen on certain days."

We glare at each other. Jacob releases a frustrated groan. "Oh, forget it. I don't know why I thought this would work. You don't ever do anything you don't want to."

"Hey, that's not fair," I holler at his back.

He pushes my door open. "You're what's not fair, April."

"I'm sorry. I would if I could, Jacob," I plead.

He stops but does not turn to face me. "You know all those times I help you out, April? I don't think I much care for this one-way street relationship."

I sputter and shake. Before I can answer, Jacob steps out of my apartment and shuts my door.

What does he expect from me? I can't get in front of the whole town and reveal my powers. That would be idiotic. "Hello, Guntersville, I know you've always thought I was a bit odd. Well, the reason is I'm a full-fledged clairvoyant. Oh, and I practice witchcraft, too."

Yeah, that would go over like a turd in the punchbowl. I know it's my goal to leave Guntersville, but I'd prefer not to be run out of town.

Jacob really knows how to kill a girl's carbohydrate overload glow. I was feeling pretty content and happy before he knocked on my door.

Now I'm just becoming more agitated with each passing moment. I don't like the fact that my best friend knows about my powers. I love having at least one close friend who believes I'm normal.

I'm also angry at myself.

Jacob is right. I've never asked him to do something where he failed to do for me. My answer should've been an immediate yes. Having told him no is embarrassing to me.

The worst is that in the end, I know I'll cave and try to help him with my powers. So why say no? It's like getting the worst of both worlds.

Fine. It must be my fantastical day of missteps with guys.

First, I do something to scare Justin during a passionate kiss, and now my best friend thinks I'm a selfish jerk. Well, technically, he would be correct in light of my wrong answer.

There's always tomorrow, and I'll redeem myself then.

This is all making my head hurt. It will be surprising if all this stress doesn't bring on a migraine soon.

I pull my shorts off, flick out my nightstand light, and slide into bed.

Moments later, I feel Puppy hop up on the bed, circling three times before lying down. He rests his chin on one of my ankles. The one that persistently itches.

Chapter 43

The smell is musty and dank. My bed has become extremely hard and is hurting my back.

I arch my spine to relieve the pressure momentarily. When I draw my knees up toward me to stretch my legs, they strike something hard. I can't lift them more than a foot above me.

Something is terribly wrong. My breath quickens as I fight to keep my composure. I can feel the air becoming moist and oxygen-poor from my fast panting.

Puppy has moved up the bed. I feel him snuggled against my right arm while my left arm is pressed against the wall.

That can't be. This must be a dream since it would be my right arm against the wall. It's impossible for my left to be against the wall when I'm on my back.

Ever since I had the dream that left me temporarily in the void, I don't much trust my dreams. The best thing to do is wake as quickly as possible.

I sit up quickly and strike my head against a solid surface that forces me to fall onto my back with momentum. I lift my hands to find a flat surface less than a few inches above my face. I run my hand quickly up and down the smooth surface and am unable to identify it.

My hands search for grips, handles, creases, or cracks. I find none and let my hands drop back to my side.

I'm in my jeans? I wouldn't sleep in my jeans.

Keys! I jam my hands into my jeans pocket and find my keys. I fumble then drop them. Recovering them with my right hand, I quickly find what I'm looking for. I press the back of the small penlight.

A glossy surface is directly in front of my face. But this isn't the void. This is something horrifyingly different.

At least I have Puppy with me this time. He will keep me safe.

I pan my vision to the right as I flash the penlight in Puppy's direction. It isn't Puppy.

The flesh packed tightly against my left arm is the headless woman who brandished a knife at me a few nights back. I scream.

When I don't wake from my dream immediately, I scream louder. Faintly I hear Puppy's bark.

Concentrating on Puppy, I pull and claw my mind toward him. It is like swimming upstream in a fast-flowing river.

My eyes pop open.

A woman steps out from my full-length mirror, holding a severed head in her left hand and a large butcher knife in her right. The mirror is surrounded by an unnatural light-green mist.

The apparition stares out over me and then turns its attention to Puppy, who continues to growl. All the hair on the back of his neck stands up.

The Lord's Prayer rolls haltingly off my tongue while Puppy continues to work himself up into full-fledged attack of dog barks and growls. I'm not clear if I thought prayer might work, but I'm momentarily out of ideas.

A wicked smile takes root on the knife-wielding ghost's face. When the spirit lifts the severed head of her victim, my prayers catch in my throat.

The eyelids of the severed head flip open. My lungs stop working.

The severed head asks, "Why didn't you help me?" I nearly

pass out from fright.

Puppy continues in wolf mode, snapping twice in the direction of the mirror before he flies off the bed charging at the mirror.

As he nears, the ghost and head disappear, leaving only a tiny amount of green smoke to retreat back into the glass.

Puppy snaps once more as I quickly throw a comforter over the mirror. Thoroughly confused now, I turn on my overhead light.

While waiting for my heartbeat to normalize, I call Puppy to my side and crush his fur in my hands. He pushes harder against my hand.

This makes no sense. Miles's research showed that Sylvia died from a scarf decapitating her. Not some crazy woman with a butcher knife.

Help her? How was I supposed to help her? Time travel and help her find her pearl necklace rather than allowing her to wear the scarf?

Nope. Not going to happen. I'm not going to risk being caught in the void for some spoiled rich girl who died nearly a hundred years ago. Where is the logic in that?

Where was the logic in knife girl, though? Her style looks a lot more like 2021 than 1928.

Too many things do not make sense to take anything literally. In all honesty, the "why didn't you help me" line is probably me feeling guilty for not offering to help Jacob. But I'll set that right first thing in the morning.

I begin to turn my light out and think better of it.

Chapter 44

Poor attitude is the name of the game Tuesday morning. Because I turned down a prospective job in Austin yesterday. The FBI is railroading my client. I was the worst of friends to Jacob the night before, too. And lastly, despite identifying my ghost as Sylvia Motlow, she still has the need to haunt me and keep me up during the night.

I feel really old, like forty or something.

Howard pops in the front door. "What? No biscuit this morning?" The day has little sign of improving anytime soon.

He shakes his head. "Sorry. I'm going down to Mobile next month and need to keep this sexy figure."

"I see what you mean."

Howard turns sideways for me. "Are those protein shakes already working? Wow. I wouldn't have ever imagined they would work that fast."

Now I feel terrible for being sarcastic. It serves me right. "She won't know what hit her."

Howard walks toward his office, saying over his shoulder, "We're closing down at two today. I want to help search for Faith."

I don't want to search for her but owe a friend a favor, and I intend to make good on it. I pull out my cell phone and hit speed dial.

"What are you thinking about right now, big guy?" I say with the sexiest voice I can muster with my present mood.

"I think if I had been smart enough to set my phone to airplane mode, I could have had a three-hour nap before I go to work. What do you *need*, Snow?"

Ouch. Jacob is furious. The accentuation of the word "need" is not lost on me, either. "I just wanted to tell you I will help this afternoon."

"Oh, please. Don't let me inconvenience you."

"I want to help this afternoon."

There is a brief pause. "Do you really, or are you just saying this because you don't like conflict."

I don't have a problem with conflict. "I want to help because my friend asked."

"What was that all about last night, then?"

"I don't know. It's just weird. I don't like everyone in the world knowing about it. Especially you."

"Why me?"

"'Cause you're normal. I don't want to scare you off with my weirdness."

He laughs, and it makes me feel a little better. "You've never been normal, Snow, but there's also nothing you can do to scare me off."

I'm glad one of us is sure of that. "Good. So, two o'clock?"

"Actually, can you meet me at the precinct at one? I would like you to talk with the husband, Kyle Ray, before we go to the site."

"Okay—"

"Good. And, April?"

"Yeah?"

"Thank you."

I smile. "You're welcome."

It is a slow morning, all things considered. I take care of a couple of contract adjustments for Howard and begin reading the report of Nina Rodriguez being taken into custody in Georgia.

It looks like she moved up to the big leagues and will be looking at a long sentence. I suspect it will be hard for her to justify why she shot at two officers. I'm just pleased not to have to be her defense attorney.

The office is so quiet my ears begin to hum. Usually, that drives me crazy and I'll sneak an earbud in and play some music, but something about it is therapeutic today.

A lot has happened in the past few days, and there is a lot for me to unpack. The first order of business is this Justin deal. The more I've had time to think about what happened yesterday, the more I'm inclined to cut the line on that one.

I don't have the time or the inclination to chase a guy. Is Justin hot, and does he ring my bell? Absolutely.

Still, I'm not desperate enough to start seducing men into wanting me. I much prefer it when they seduce me.

Besides, something is wonky in the universe with my guy attractor lately. It's probably best if I give the cosmos time to correct itself.

Even though it can be great fun, there's nothing that says I *need* a guy.

My phone rings. I'm alarmed when "Daddy" shows on caller ID. Daddy doesn't call me very often. I worry that someone might be hurt or sick.

"Daddy?"

"Hey, Pumpkin. I just want to thank you for sending in the application for the scholarship. That Freeman kid you recommended has been called in for an interview this Friday."

Tears of joy swell in my eyes. "Really, Daddy?"

"Yes. Kenny has an interview with the director. If he likes him, it should be a done deal."

"Do you really think he has a chance?" I really want this for Kenny and his family, but I also don't want to get too excited. I know Daddy will give me the truth.

"I would say he has an excellent shot. I understand the director was impressed with his transcript, and the past science fair entries are a big plus..."

His voice trails off, and I know this is trouble. "What?"

"One of the requirements of the scholarship and internship is community service. Kenny doesn't have any listed, and the director is old school about those requirements."

"But his family is in bad financial straits. He wouldn't have much time for community service."

"Whoa, Pumpkin. I was just giving you the skinny. Don't kill the messenger."

"You're right, Daddy. I'm sorry. That really is good news, and I appreciate you sharing it with me."

Kenny would be so great in the Redstone Arsenal internship program. I would hate for something as stupid as a community service requirement to keep him out.

"April, I'm going to go grab a late lunch with Colonel Sullivan. If you leave, put the sign on the door and lock up," Howard announces.

"Okay," I say absently as he slides out the door.

Late lunch? I check my phone and see it is twelve forty-five. Bless it! I'm supposed to be at the precinct at one.

I grab my purse and sling my backpack over my shoulder. I lock up and turn my car toward the precinct.

Jacob looks at his watch pointedly as I trot toward him, my heels clicking on the marble floor. "Sorry. Sorry."

"We'll just need to make it quick. We have to be to the east boat ramp by one forty-five for the setup of the search teams."

Jacob opens the heavy metal door and ushers me in.

I give a start when I see the anger in the jade green eyes of Kyle Ray. He is a towering hulk of a man, and his face reveals his extreme displeasure of being where he is.

"You need to speed this process up, Officer, or I'm going to walk right out of here."

"You can do whatever you want, Mr. Ray. But you would be back here in an hour after I get the warrant for your arrest."

"You're a liar, you little punk." Mr. Ray stands, and he is even bigger than I thought.

"I'd think twice about what you're doing. Some things can't

be undone." Jacob's words sound more like a taunt than sage advice.

I finally get my head around the situation and reach for Jacob's arm. "Jacob. How about you step outside for a second. This won't work with all the hostility in the air."

His brows draw together. "Are you crazy? I'm not leaving you alone in here with him."

"Am I safe with you, Mr. Ray?"

His bloodshot green eyes lock on mine, and he smirks. "Perfectly safe."

His words send slight tremors of fright up my spine. "See, Jacob? All good."

Jacob glares at me and then Kyle Ray before he snorts and stomps out the door.

I turn my attention back to Mr. Ray, who is still standing and grinning like a Cheshire cat. I motion to his chair. "Please, this will be easier if we both sit."

"Sure."

I sit across from him and take my time studying his face. Once my body is relaxed, I push out toward him with my mind as I ask, "Did you hurt your wife, Mr. Ray?"

"I got no reason to hurt Faith. She's a bit flighty, not so bright at times, but she's a pretty good woman all-in-all."

"You didn't answer my question. Did you hurt Faith?"

He grins as if to say "well played," but he never answers me.

"Well, I'm waiting." I lower my chin as I raise my eyebrows to give him my best "are you going to waste my time" look.

"No. Like I said, I have no issue with Faith. She's easy on the eyes, good in the sack, can cook, and is pretty laidback as far as women go."

"Has she ever cheated on you?"

His expression sours immediately. "No."

"No guy friends that are maybe too friendly? Always hanging around."

He shakes his head, and I can feel the anger he is controlling just under his skin. "What if there was? You'd best be asking me why they came up missing. Not my Faith."

Fair enough. "You got any idea where Faith might be?"

He exhales as his shoulders slump. "Nah. Truthfully that's one of the reasons why I'm down here talking to these butt wipes. I know they won't get serious about looking for Faith until they clear me as a suspect."

"Just to make sure, because I'm getting in on this late, you've checked with all of her girlfriends and other family?"

"Yeah. I called Faith's mama and her sister straight off. She will hang out over there every once in a while and forget what time it is. Never for a full night, though. She just can be forgetful at times. Other than that, the only other place she goes is the antique store she and her friend Chelsie own."

Kyle's eyes no longer look angry, just tired.

"Can I ask a favor of you?"

He squints his eyes. "What kind of favor?"

Here we go with the freak reveal. "I'd like you to put your hands in mine and let me ask you about Faith again."

"For real?"

"Really. Sometimes it helps me focus on the person we're looking for."

He frowns, then extends his large hairy hands. I lay my hands in his. "Kyle, did you hurt Faith?"

"No, ma'am."

"Do you know where she is?"

"No, ma'am."

I'm getting no visions of violence or location. All I get is a fuzzy image of a woman's face just before the picture dissolves into darkness.

"Do you miss her, Kyle?"

He drops his head, revealing his male-pattern baldness. "I do. I really miss her."

Being a clairvoyant can sometimes leave me feeling dirty. I know the information is critical, as is the ability to eliminate Kyle as a suspect. But I can't stop the depths of the visions. I could've done without seeing the whole of a man sitting on the side of his bed broken and sobbing.

I lift my hands from Kyle's. "Thank you."

"Did your focus thing work?"

"Sorry. I didn't get any of the gut feelings I sometimes get," I lie.

He wipes at his nose. "Okay. Thank you for trying."

I step through the door when Jacob opens it for me.

"What do you think?" he asks.

"The husband doesn't have anything to do with it."

"Really?" Jacob's tone is speculative. "Well, that will only change, like, *all* the current theories."

"He said there were no lovers or boyfriends."

"No. Faith wasn't like that. She had plenty of guys who were interested in her, but she only had eyes for the big beast in there."

"I'm pretty sure the feeling was mutual," I say.

"I don't know about all that," Jacob grouses.

I'm too emotional to argue with Jacob and am not prepared to explain the vision I had seen of Kyle crying on his bed. "So now what?"

"In police work, an elimination is sometimes as good as a solid lead. We'll head over to the east boat ramp where her car was found and see if you or the search team can find any new clues."

I follow Jacob in my car. The east boat ramp is three miles from the middle of town but takes fifteen minutes to get to because it's out on a peninsula.

The drive allows me to get my emotions back in check. Lately, it seems everything I come in contact with is emotionally charged. Everything is about the extremes. I get thrilled, then frustrated, and the next moment despondent. It's enough for a girl to self-diagnose herself as bipolar.

Clairvoyance allows you to see with complete clarity some things I'm sure we're not supposed to see. From Jacob's reaction, it is apparent that he believes Faith is in a relationship where her love was not reciprocated. He believes that by marrying Kyle, she, in essence, set in motion her own death.

I find it odd how people with good intentions have feelings about relationships that are none of their business. More importantly, they can't possibly understand. They can't know a husband considers his wife as his only real friend. That his wife is the sun his world revolves around.

That is Kyle Ray. Everyone sees a huge, angry man, but inside he is shattered and scared to death that the anchor of his life might be lost forever.

Chapter 45

Over fifty people are at the search site when we drive up, including my family, and the Neal, Rains, and Bates families. Jacob stops me as I start toward the rest of the group.

"Hey, if you don't mind, stay here. Let me get the teams working on their grids. I'll come back to you."

"Yeah, sure." Jacob's logic doesn't make any sense to me, but I'm not in the mood to be social at the moment anyway.

I wave at Mama as Jacob lines the teams up and explains the grid maps. I'm thankful that I'm not going to be traipsing through the woods after all. At least not working the grid with a map in my hand.

The vision from Kyle is still eating at me. In some ways, I would've been more relieved to have gotten an image of him choking Faith so that we had our answers. No, that isn't true. There is something else aggravating about the brief vision, but I just can't put my finger on it.

It is like I get close to identifying what is bugging me, and then it will move a little further away from me. My mind keeps being distracted by the giant man crying on the bed, but that isn't it.

Focus April. Focus on it.

As it often happens, it comes to me in a rush. The vision of the woman. Her face was elongated and strong-jawed. Sylvia's face, the ghost from Motlow, was round with delicate features. Oh, man. This can't be right.

I trot over to Jacob as he is sending the last team to their grid. "Jacob, do you have a photo of Faith?"

He looks over his shoulder at me briefly. "In the squad car."

"Is it unlocked?"

"Uh—no. I have a small arsenal in there."

"I need to see her picture."

He holds up a single finger in my direction and returns his attention to the last team.

My anxiety level is building to a crescendo. How could I've been so stupid? How could I not notice this earlier? More importantly, what does it mean?

Jacob finally finishes with the last group and comes over to his cruiser. "I swear, Snow. If your mama had only named you Patience."

He opens his cruiser door and pulls out a manila folder. From that, he lifts a photo, stares at it briefly, then hands it to me.

The dizziness hits me immediately. I put my hand against the cruiser to keep from falling over. Jacob's arm slides under mine to help support me.

"What's the matter with you? Do you need water?"

The very first face in the mirror at the precinct. That's what I see in the photo. Faith Ray was the floating head all along. It never was Sylvia Motlow.

How could I have missed it? They don't even have similarly shaped faces.

Of course, I may have been focusing on the fact her head was severed rather than on her facial structure.

"April, what is the matter?" Jacob asks.

It makes me sick to think about it. It makes me even sicker to know that if I could've put it together earlier, I might have been able to effect change. "Jacob, I'm pretty sure Faith is dead."

Jacob pins me against the side of the cruiser with his right hand as he reaches into the car and pulls out a bottled water.

"Here, drink this."

I don't want the water, but I take it from him anyway. "Did you hear me?"

"Yeah, I heard you, April. And frankly, given the blood in her vehicle when we found it... Yeah, you're probably right."

I open my mouth to explain my vision to him. But describing how I now know that Faith is somewhere minus her head, and I knew it would happen a few days before it took place, doesn't seem like something I can easily explain. Besides, if he already believes she is dead, my vision won't add anything helpful to his hypothesis.

I open the water and take a drink.

I'm upset with myself for not having figured out this clue earlier. It is also disconcerting to think that there is a killer on the loose in our town. A killer who, given what Kyle reported, couldn't possibly have a motive.

Oh no. What will Kyle do when he learns the news?

"Can you go on? Do you need to rest?" Jacob asks.

"I'll be okay soon."

His speculative frown tells me he doesn't believe me.

"I will. I just got upset by the last vision."

"Is that common?"

"More than I like." But especially when I realize I could have prevented a murder.

I screw the cap back on the water. "So, what's my part in this big shindig?"

Jacob shrugs. "I don't know. What does it take for you to get one of those visions? Maybe with the murderer in the picture this time?"

"I'll need to touch something with Faith's spirit residue still on it. The residue could be highly charged given she may have died violently—" I take in Jacob's horrified look.

"Can you take me to where they found her car?" I ask.

"Sure." Jacob gestures toward the water. "Can you see this residue?"

"I haven't ever before. But I'm not going to say that it's not possible."

Jacob stops in the middle of a parking space on the row closest to the water. "This is it."

I center myself as much as the emotions of day will allow. For extra help, now that I know, I focus on Faith's face, too.

Pushing out with my mind, I hold her vision steady in my mind. For confirmation, I check a second time. Nothing. Not a single energy tickle.

"She's not been here, Jacob."

"But her car was here, Snow."

"I hear you. But Faith wasn't in it when it was here."

"Well, there goes more theories of what happened to her."

"I'll add another theory for the ones that dropped off your list. Faith was never at the east boat ramp."

Jacob leans against his cruiser. "You think dumping the vehicle here was a decoy."

"That, and it would have been hard to explain if her vehicle was found in the killer's driveway."

"Yeah. True that." Jacob frowns. "That means that the search party—"

"Isn't going to find anything except a collection of chigger and tick bites on their legs," I finish the thought for him.

Chapter 46

Jacob wouldn't allow me to leave the boat ramp until I promised him I would help tomorrow afternoon. He has a few more places he wants to take me and see if I feel Faith's presence. Given my caseload has lightened in the last few days, it didn't seem like much of a sacrifice. It will also allow me to tally up more "good friend" points

I'm in the lake house den flipping channels when my family arrives back at the house as it turns dark outside. We each pick our favorite flavor of canned soup from the pantry. As we warm the bowls of soup in the microwave, Daddy pulls out his extra-large skillet and makes his grilled cheese sandwiches that put Prozac to shame.

Entering my apartment after dinner, my curiosity gets the best of me, and I pull the comforter off my full-length mirror. Puppy walks over to the mirror, circles it twice, sniffs it, and begins to lift his leg.

"No! Don't you even think about it, young man!" I yell.

With his leg half hawked, he looks at me as if to say I've lost my mind. Maybe I have. Either way, he drops his leg and pads out through the puppy door.

I sit down on my bed and stare at the mirror. I'm genuinely conflicted.

On the one hand, I want to see the severed head again to

confirm it is Faith Ray. Still, what fool wishes for a ghost to appear in their room.

I lose interest after twenty minutes.

The day—well, week—has been so emotionally stressful I decide it best to go to bed early. I strip and slip in between my cool, soft sheets.

Thankfully my dreams are a complete blank.

Blank, except for the sound of bells ringing in the distance.

They stop and then begin again. I can't see in the pitch dark or feel anything against me. I consider if I may have slipped into the void again, but none of my danger senses are triggered.

Just the bells. Are they church bells—no.

The bells clang louder this time in my mind, and my consciousness wrestles control from my subconsciousness. There's no mystery here.

I open my eyes to the light vibrating on my nightstand. Ugh … It's my phone. I've got to change that ringtone in the morning.

Lifting the phone from my dresser, I note the time as the call rolls to voicemail.

"Who calls at two thirty in the middle of the night?"

Before I can check my voicemail, the bells ring again as the phone vibrates in my hand. It's an unidentified number. I answer, "Hello?"

"April, this is Jayron. I need your help."

My gut tenses as I sit up. "How did you get my number?"

"You gave it to my mom. Back when you came out to see Kenny."

I don't remember having done that. Maybe I did? "What's the matter?"

"I can't talk about it on the phone. I need you to come and see."

I yawn. "Okay, Jayron. I've got kind of a light day tomorrow. I can meet you at nine in the morning."

"You're not listening. I need you to come here now," he says excitedly.

The sleepy haze is beginning to wear off of me. "You need me to come to meet you somewhere at two thirty in the morning?"

"Yes."

"That's not really in my job description, Jayron. Call a friend."

"This is important, April."

"So's my sleep, Jayron."

"This might keep me out of jail," he says.

No … did he just play the "get out of jail" card? There is no way as an attorney with no credible argument to help Jayron's defense I can turn down anything that may exonerate him. I cradle the phone between my ear and shoulder as I pull on my jeans.

"How?" I demand.

"April, I'll show you when you get here. I need you to trust me."

I'd prefer he inform me what I am going into rather than rely on the blind trust of another person. What I do trust is my assessment of people. I know Jayron is a protector, and he would not hurt me or put me in harm's way if possible. "Alright, if you're not going to tell me how this helps your case, where do I need to meet you?"

"The north shoreline approximately a quarter mile before the dam," he says.

What the heck. My wild-eyed client has gone back to the dam for a second terrorist charge? "Jayron, you really can't be at that dam."

"It's all good. At least, I think with some help from my attorney, it will all be good."

I'm feeling uncomfortable on so many levels. "It will take me twenty minutes to get there."

"Try to hurry if you can. I don't want us to miss this."

I start out of my apartment. "You should at least tell me—" The line drops. I redial the last number as I get in my car.

The call goes straight to Marcy Freeman's voicemail. Well,

that explains how Jayron was able to call me. Marcy will probably tan his hide when she finds out, but the more significant concern is if Agent Taggart collars him at the dam. If that were to happen, I'm sure Jayron is done for.

I never should have gotten Jayron out of jail. I should have left him there until his court date. It is so predictable that he would only get himself into more trouble if I got him released. *Foolish, foolish girl. Mama was right from the start.*

My lights cut through the dark of the tree-canopied backroads leading to the north shore. The homes are much sparser on the north side, and many are not much more than shacks. Consequently, Guntersville's utility and transportation departments are stingy with the street lighting.

I obviously only have one oar in the water. What was I thinking when I decided to post bail for Jayron? His bail will be revoked. Worse, the bond can go into forfeiture, which means not only do I lose my five hundred dollars cash, I stand to lose the restored Z-28 I have been enjoying.

I'm so stupid. Why do I have to be such a sucker for these hard case boys that can't keep themselves out of trouble?

I'm fit to be tied. I plan to give it to Jayron with both barrels —even though I know it'll just bounce off his thick skull.

The old Stokes General Store comes up on my right. All that remains are a few charred roof timbers and portions of its concrete block wall jutting into the air like decayed teeth. I knew it closed while I was in college but had not heard about the fire.

The memory of all the Ding Dongs and Goo Goo Clusters my brothers and I bought when we were younger makes me sigh, thinking of easier times as I survey the damage slowing my car to a crawl.

The old general store is a quarter of a mile from the dam's lock. I angle my car to light the gravel driveway across the road from the store leading up to the dilapidated pier where kids used to tie up their boats while they came in off the water to shop.

Jayron must be close. There are no other clearings to the lake between here and the TVA fence line. I continue onto the small gravel parking lot, and my lights illuminate the flat black tailgate of a small pickup truck I failed to notice at first.

My danger senses pique. Jayron's truck is an old beater. This isn't his. I've never seen this vehicle before tonight.

I sit in my car and contemplate my next move. My curiosity is telling me to get out, take a look at the truck, and see if I can locate Jayron.

Forget that! My rational brain is begging me to turn this car around, make an anonymous call to the police, turn my phone on airplane mode, and sleep in until nine in the morning.

Common sense wins the argument easily, and I begin to back out of the lot.

My headlights flit across the lake's surface, silhouetting a figure loping toward me. My foot is about to crush the accelerator when Jayron waves a thin arm, his pale face coming into view.

I pull my car back into the lot as he closes the distance. His eyes are wide as he taps on my window.

Lowering my window, I ask, "What's going on, Jayron?"

His charged energy leaps off him and stuns my senses, their power momentarily disorientating me.

"Come quick, April! We need your help."

We? He has the oddest concoction of exhilaration, fear, and anxiety swirling in the air like a tornado. "Who is 'we,' Jayron?"

Jayron pulls at my door handle. Still locked, the handle slips from his hand when he pulls. "Kenny and me."

For Pete's sake. These two knuckleheads have finally done it. Kenny is lying on the side of the river with his hands blown off, if I have to guess. There ought to be a law against brothers being left alone.

Jayron steps back as I push open my door. "Where is he, Jayron?"

"This way!" He gestures with his hand as he takes off in the same odd lope toward the lake.

He leaps over a mound of vegetation, cuts between two

water oaks, and disappears behind sawgrass that skirts the edge of the lake. I turn on my small penlight, which is of little help.

I should call Jacob. Maybe Deputy Gray, too. It wouldn't be a bad idea to call my brother, either.

Everything tells me we will need some help. Jayron's energy level and the unidentified truck tell me this is not something we should take lightly.

Bless it, that boy is fast. If I don't start after him now, I'll lose him in the sawgrass.

I jump over the mound of vegetation, and my tennis shoes sink into the muck. There is a loud sucking sound as my shoes are nearly pulled off my feet.

I'm tearing through the vegetation, willow branches scratching at my face and sweat running into my eyes. While I run, I visualize what I will do to those two dummies when I catch up to them.

Confusion sets in as I come around a clump of particularly tall sawgrass, and I see a man holding a shotgun on two men on their knees. I scan my penlight beam on the armed man's shadowed face. "Kenny?"

"Hi, Ms. Snow."

I run the small beam of light over the two men on their knees. I don't know them. They aren't from Guntersville. "Kenny, what's going on?"

"A citizen's arrest, ma'am."

One of the restrained men turns toward me. "Help us, please. My brothers and I were just fishing, and these crazy men attacked us."

I stare in a stupor. It is as if I'm having an out-of-body moment.

Actually, I believe at this moment my mind is shattered. It is difficult to hold a coherent thought as the last of my sanity floats into the mental health heaven in the sky.

I see Jayron pull off one of his muddied boots and yank a threadbare tube sock from his foot in my peripheral vision. He grabs the man by the back of the hair and makes to stuff his dirty tube sock into the man's mouth.

"Enough of your lies. You have the right to remain silent," Jayron yells.

I grab his arm. "No, Jayron!"

He looks offended. "He can still breathe out his nose."

I ignore him and look at Kenny. I gesture to the men on their knees. "You need to explain to me what is going on, and you need to do it quickly."

"Isn't it obvious?" the man Jayron released says.

"If it were, I wouldn't be asking, mister," I say.

Kenny clicks his tongue. "Hello. Terrorist."

Seriously? A couple of out-of-towners on a late-night fishing trip? "Kenny, this is serious business. You can't just go detaining people like this."

"But Agent Taggart said there were terrorists in the area. That's why he wants to put me away," Jayron explains as if I hadn't been present at his bail hearing.

Oh, Lord. The stupidity is going to make my head explode. I can't save these two from themselves. "Just because they aren't from here doesn't mean they are automatically terrorists."

"I can prove it." Jayron jogs away from me.

"If you don't let us go, I will sue you and take all your money!" the spokesperson of the two threatens.

I glare at the man Jayron wanted to gag. Maybe he would be safer with a dirty sock in his mouth because I'm fighting the urge to kick him. "Threatening us isn't helping, and besides, nobody here has any money anyway."

"But you can go to jail," he says.

I look around the area and notice it absent of any fishing gear, not to mention this hour is a *way* early start to a fishing day. "What sort of fish were you trying to catch at night anyway?"

The man looks as if I asked him to solve a quadratic equation. "Salmon?"

What? "There's no salmon in this lake."

"Yes, there is," the man argues.

"*No*. There's not," I say.

"I told you he was a terrorist," Kenny says coolly as he racks his shotgun, sending a cold chill up my spine.

The seriousness of the situation has increased exponentially. Looking at Kenny, I get the distinct impression he's not prone to bluffing. "Kenny, put the shotgun down."

"Kenny, put the shotgun down," the man on his knees repeats.

"Shut your mouth," Kenny and I say in unison.

"This proves it!" Jayron runs toward us, oblivious to the willow branches striking him. He holds up a large, plastic storage bin.

His feet tangle in the sawgrass, and in what seems like slow motion, he tosses the container into the air where it turns upside down, and small bricks fly out, taking flight.

"Eeeiii!" the two strangers scream as they dive face-first into the mud.

I examine the small, wax paper-covered bricks stuck helter-skelter in the muddy lakeshore. My eyes lock with Jayron's. His eyes are even crazier than usual. I wouldn't have thought that to be a possibility.

"Don't move." Kenny's voice is smooth and calm. "That means you too, Jayron."

"Okay." Jayron stands so motionless I swear he's stopped blinking.

"Kenny, what am I looking at?" My voice sounds tinny and thin to me. So much for sounding authoritative and taking control of the situation.

"You don't want to know," he says smoothly while passing by me toward the spilled contents of the container.

"Kenny," I drawl his name out for several syllables.

He bends over, carefully plucking the first brick from the mud. "C-4 explosives."

Words I never wanted to hear. Kenny was correct. I didn't want to know. Too late now.

I begin to sweat even more profusely. "Can I help?"

"Probably best not to," Kenny replies.

I watch Kenny work with the controlled patience and steadiness of a surgeon. I'm duly impressed. I'm also grateful. I may be able to see ghosts, but I'm not ready to be one.

Kenny puts the last plastique brick into the container and seals the lid.

"You want to tell me why I'm involved in this, Kenny?" I ask.

"Number one, you know the law. Number two, I don't trust Agent Taggart further than I can throw him. You're the best witness I could hope for."

This will not end well. Even if the C-4 doesn't accidentally create a Jupiter-sized crater where we stand.

I dial Jacob. "Hey."

"Dang, Snow. Can't you call at a reasonable hour?" His voice is still thick with sleep.

"Can you come down to the river?" I ask.

"Why would I want to do that?"

"Because we've solved the Guntersville terrorist issue."

"I thought you were defending the Guntersville terrorist," Jacob says.

"Ha, ha. Can you just come out here and help me?"

He sighs. "Keep your britches on, Snow. I'll be there in a few."

"Thank you."

I hang up and dial Agent Taggart. As the phone rings, I pull both men back up to their knees via the scruff of their neck. We are in enough trouble. I don't need them to asphyxiate on river mud before the authorities arrive.

"There's a third one behind the truck," Kenny only now informs me.

"Hello?" Agent Taggart says.

I cover the phone. "Seriously?" I hiss at Kenny.

"Hello?"

I best get Taggart handled first. "Agent Taggart, April Snow here. Yes, sir, I definitely know what time it is."

Chapter 47

Taggart must sleep in his suit. It isn't ten minutes later he's sliding down the embankment toward us to see for himself. His hand jerks to his hip momentarily before he asks Kenny. "Is that shotgun loaded, son?"

Kenny pans the shotgun off of his hip and fires it in the general direction of the lake without uttering a word.

"A simple yes would have sufficed, son," Taggart says as he kneels and begins to wipe the mud from both men's faces. "Just like I thought."

Smiling like the little boy who got to open his Christmas gifts first, Taggart says, "Bill Hassam and his little brother. I've been following them all over the state."

I clear my throat and move closer to Taggart's side. "So, what about my client, agent?"

"What about him?"

"Can we expect you to drop his charges?"

Agent Taggart's brow furrows. "Why would I do that?"

To borrow Billy Hassam's words: "Isn't it obvious?" If it were, Taggart wouldn't still be asking. "Because the terrorists you heard on the radio have been captured. It never was my client."

"Ms. Snow, it is quite probable that there are multiple cells assigned to take out the Guntersville Dam. It is common for a second cell to be activated in short order after the failure of the first cell to eliminate the target. Besides, Mr. Freeman must be held accountable for his prior actions."

Jacob must have some clairvoyance skills of his own. I feel the heavy weight of his hand holding my right shoulder down, preventing me from moving forward. This is good since I was about to go all rabid raccoon on Agent Stick-up-my-Butt.

"Let me give you a hand getting these two into your SUV, Agent." Jacob pushes me further back as he moves forward.

Jacob lifts the hundred-and-eighty-pound man easily from a kneeling position in the mud to his feet. I feel better about him being able to immobilize me with one hand on my shoulder.

The boys and I fall in line behind the two officers of the law and their prisoners.

"I'm sorry, Jayron. Any reasonable person would have dropped the charges." I don't bother to whisper. I don't care if Taggart hears or not. He is a heartless jerk.

"It's okay, April. Kenny and I made our country safer. That's enough of a reward."

Oh, he is killing me. I have to get this boy an opportunity to join the service.

"It was pretty fun, too," Kenny adds.

Jayron flashes a toothy smile. "Kenny made this cool HAM radio from scratch, and—"

"Yeah!!" A madman with blood streaming from his forehead charges Taggart with a fourteen-inch butcher's knife out of the shadows. The tiny sliver of moon glints off the blade as the entire world slows down once again.

Taggart freezes as he watches the crazed man come from behind the black truck brandishing the knife. Jacob draws his service revolver, and his prisoner slams into his side, causing him to stumble forward.

Kenny, on my right, swings the barrel of his shotgun but does not have a shot as Jayron and I are in the scatter path.

Without thought, I thrust the heels of my palms toward the assailant. The knife flies out of the attacker's hand and over his shoulder in a flash of blue light.

He turns sideways to watch the knife's flight. I bring my right hand violently across my body. The knife man's head jerks to the right, his legs managing two more faltering steps before he falls, face first, unconscious onto the gravel parking lot.

I feel all eyes on me.

"What was that flash of light?" Taggart asks.

"What light?" I ask innocently. "I didn't see any light."

"The light from your—" Jayron hushes when I raise my brows.

"I think you may have saved Agent Taggart's life, Jayron."

"I did?"

"He did?" Taggart asks.

"I don't think I have ever seen anyone disarm a knife-wielding man that smoothly. What do you think, Agent Taggart?"

"Oh yes. Quite an impressive young man." His eyebrows knit together as he looks from the assailant to Jayron.

"It seems like the least a man could do is show a little leniency toward the young man who saved his life. Especially when he helped bring in three *known* terrorists."

Taggart stops and hangs his head.

I expect he will dismiss my comment out of hand. I don't feel any positive juju flowing.

"You're correct, Ms. Snow. Without the Freemans, these bad actors might have very well sent millions of gallons of water flooding through Guntersville. I promise you I will talk to Judge Rossi tomorrow about dropping the charges against Jayron."

It is embarrassing to say, but I let out a squeal when Taggart announces his decision. Jayron and I practically leap into each other's arms for a hug. Then I hug Kenny. I jog toward Taggart to give him a hug because he always looks like he needs one, and he's a good guy after all.

He stops my progress cold by holding out a hand as if he were posing for the Heisman. "I'm really not a hugger."

As if the world didn't already know. I extend my hand, and

Taggart does accept that. "Thank you."

"No worries. He earned it."

Yes, they did.

Well, this just dills my pickle! I'm so happy I'm beside myself. My crazy silly boys have somehow extricated themselves from a terrorism charge. It doesn't bother me one bit that none of it had to do with my ability to defend Jayron. In some ways, the fact the boys were able to free themselves is even sweeter.

It only proves that they are the resourceful young men I have come to believe them to be. How can they not be a success in the future?

Taggart sits his prisoner in the center of the long bench seat of his sedan. He attaches the prisoner's cuffs and anklets to the hook in the floorboard welded to the car's frame. As he finishes securing his prisoner, I touch his shoulder, and he jumps.

"You know, Agent Taggart, that both Kenny and Jayron had a lot to do with capturing these criminals for you. Is there any chance I can get you to do one more favor for one of them?"

"What kind of favor?" he asks with a suspicious tone.

"Neighborhood watch is a form of community service, wouldn't you say?"

"I would," Taggart agrees.

"Well, Kenny." I point in the direction of Kenny. "The tall boy in the back. He is the one who developed the radio that clued them in to where this was taking place. Without him, there may have been a tragedy in the *community*. Except he was *watching*."

Jacob jostles past Taggart and secures his prisoner in the sedan. The first light of the new morning creases the sky, lighting it into beautiful orange and powder blue.

"I would say you're correct, Ms. Snow."

"Since Kenny helped you—I was wondering if you would write a note talking about how much help he has been to you on the community watch."

"Why?"

"Because he needs a letter about completing some community service to win a slot on the Redstone Arsenal intern program," I say.

Taggart looks shocked. He steps past me. "You've got the grades to qualify for Redstone Arsenal's internship program?" he asks Kenny.

"Yes, sir."

Taggart smiles. Who knew he could do that?

"Why didn't you just tell me what you needed. That is a wonderful program. If you think a letter from a bureau agent would help—well, count me in."

"Oh, thank you." I jump into the air and make to hug Taggart a second time. A second time he lifts his hand to stop me.

"Not a hugger. Got it," I say.

Chapter 48

I call Howard, and he agrees I deserve to play hooky today, given it's nearly seven and I'm just now leaving the north shore. Our caseload has been light, and by getting Jayron cleared, I now have a wide-open schedule. Besides, I need some rest most desperately.

I'm struggling to keep my eyes open on the short drive home, no matter how loudly I play the radio. I can feel the stress flowing out and away from my body. But like fiberglass patches can hold a rusted car together, adrenaline and anxiety are the only things keeping me awake, and they are dissipating fast.

I unlock my apartment door and fall onto my bed, fully dressed. Remembering that my tennis shoes, now ruined, are caked in mud, I push them off with my toes. The *clunk-clunk* sound of them striking the wooden floor makes me take a deep breath as I know I am all clear to slide further up in my bed, burrowing my face onto my pillow.

My bed embraces my exhausted body better than any lover ever could. I'm in ecstasy.

The phone ringing doesn't confuse me this time. Having answered another call just a few hours earlier, it is becoming more of a regular thing than I care for. At least I know it's not anything to do with terrorists or guns. Thanks to the Freeman brothers, that has been handled.

"Hello?" My voice sounds as fuzzy as my teeth feel.

"April?"

The familiar voice has me sitting up so quickly my head spins. I wanted this call but had not expected it.

"I didn't wake you, did I?"

"No." Why am I lying? "I was just getting the day started looking at some transcripts."

"Oh." Justin doesn't sound convinced. "I needed to call and explain the other day."

Hmm … If you ask me out on a date, I'm good with that. But reviving an uncomfortable situation while you give me an excuse? Yeah, not really interested in that.

"No, you really don't have to," I say.

"I think I do. I don't want you to get the wrong impression. I think you're the sexiest woman I have met in my entire life. Then when you were talking to Jonah, I realized not only are you sexy, but you are also brilliant and talented."

Okay, so sue me. My ego is in need of some stroking, and the man has my full attention. And yes, I hear the "but" coming.

"But, right up to the moment you kissed me, I thought we were only friends. Think about it, April. Your mother and I work together. That makes it extremely awkward, and my brain just short-circuited."

While he's been talking, I have been preparing my in-depth rebuttal in my mind. I plan to tell him there are lots of people who have work and intimate relations. Also, he needs to quit worrying about what my mama thinks. If he is afraid of what she will think of him, that makes him some sort of a weenie, and I don't date weenies.

"I'm sorry, and I would like to make it up to you if you let me."

There went my rebuttal. "How do you propose to do that? I have to admit I'm not really feeling it right now."

He laughs. He has a sexy laugh. "Dinner at the Coach House. I'll reserve a room at the Hilton, just in case we want to hang out afterward. That way, we don't have to drive home if we're not in good enough shape to."

"Sounds like you're working an angle, mister." I think I like it.

"Maybe. Probably. But no pressure. We'll just see where things lead."

Oh, I know where this will lead. "I don't know."

"I give an awesome deep tissue massage."

Justin plays hardball! "I suppose we can do dinner and see if there is anything there. When do you want to make a date?"

"I was hoping for tonight."

What? Who asks for a date only twelve hours in advance? Besides, it seems like I'm supposed to do something today, and it isn't to rearrange my sock drawer. It is important. I just have forgotten it like everything else lately.

"April?"

"Wait a minute. I have to check my calendar." I switch our conversation to speaker and go over to my calendar app. Darn it, I'm working with Jacob this afternoon on the Faith Ray disappearance. "I've got an appointment today I can't get out of."

"What time will you be done?"

"I'm not sure. Maybe six."

"Perfect, I'll make the dinner reservations for eight. That will give you plenty of time to change and get up to Huntsville."

No, it won't. "But..."

"I won't take no for an answer, April. Don't you want to know if there is a spark between us?"

Oh, I know there's more than a spark. There is something more akin to a firebomb. "Okay, but I may have to call and cancel if I'm delayed."

"I understand this is last minute, and the window is tight. But, April."

"Yes?"

"Don't cancel on me. Come late if you need to, but don't cancel. You are definitely worth the wait," Justin says.

He is definitely working an angle. I must admit, it's sort of working, too. "Okay. I'll see you tonight."

"I'm looking forward to it."

I stare at my phone for a minute after we disconnect. I grin, then pump my arms in the air. "Yes! I've got my mojo back."

My extended sexual dry spell had dinged my ego. I was starting to worry somewhere, seemingly overnight, I had lost my sexual appeal.

Nothing had really changed. I was the same April, but the recent series of near misses and relegation to "friend" status with men I was interested in had me wondering.

But the six months in the desert of lonely souls is *over*. I'm on a roll to the promised land now.

I need to confirm that my commitment to help Jacob with his investigation doesn't interfere with leaving on time for my date with destiny in Huntsville.

I hit Jacob's speed dial number. "Hey, can we do the psychic thing earlier in the day?"

Someone is speaking Spanish loudly in the background. "Hold on." He must have covered the phone. I hear him say, "Give me a minute," but it is muffled.

The Spanish becomes louder and shriller. "What time did you have in mind?" Jacob asks.

"I don't know. When can you go?"

A door slams, and the Spanish stops. "I can come over now."

I begin to object and then think better of it. "Okay. But you might have to wait while I finish taking a shower."

"Cool. I'll get your back for you."

I have a quick flutter just below my belly button, and I swear I blush. "I got one of those back scrubbing brushes years ago," I lie.

"Well, that takes the fun out of things."

Probably. "I'll leave my apartment unlocked."

"See you in a few."

When I turn my shower off, I hear an awful noise that sounds like a herd of caribou crossing through my apartment.

This is followed by a loud crash, and the door to the bathroom shakes.

Immediately my mind goes to the knife-wielding ghost from the mirror. Panic sets in when I consider the fact I'm trapped in the bathroom.

My anxiety only grows when I further contemplate that if the knife-wielding ghost has her way and decapitates me, I'll be found. Not the way I want to be found, if I must die.

"Hello?" It sounds stupid when I ask it. Like a murderous ghost is going to answer me.

Still, I hold out hope that I'll be lucky enough to hear a familiar voice say hello back. Suppose I'm unlucky and a spirit answers me. In that case, I'll save it the trouble of killing me by just dying of a heart attack before she gets the opportunity to lop my head off.

"Hey, sorry about that."

"You scared the tar out of me, Jacob!"

"I was just playing with Fang, and he got a little rambunctious."

"His name is Puppy," I holler back through the bathroom door as I wrap a towel around me.

"Chase told me his name was—"

"He's not Chase's dog," I interject before he can finish.

I hear a ball bouncing on the floor, followed by the sound of a cow on roller skates giving chase. Then somebody or something's body slams another wall. I better hurry up, or those two bozos are going to tear my apartment down.

"Why did you take a shower anyway?" Jacob asks.

"Because I was dirty. Might have something to do with trudging around by the lake with the Freeman boys last night."

"That ended pretty well for everyone."

Yes, it did. Well, except for the real terrorists. "Yep."

"You think Kenny might get that internship?"

What sounds like a tennis ball bounces off my bathroom door, and I hear more nails across the floor, a chair being knocked over, and a bark from Puppy.

"Hope so. Daddy seems to think Kenny has an excellent chance now."

"I'll keep him in my prayers. That family deserves a few breaks."

Aww. I have the sweetest best friend in the world. That reminds me. "Hey, how's it going with Dominique?"

My question is met by silence, except for the slow bounce of a tennis ball and Puppy's whimper of displeasure. Interesting.

I run a comb through my hair and step out of the bathroom. When Jacob looks up, I make a twirling motion with my finger, and he and Puppy turn their backs to me.

"You didn't answer me."

"Chica loca," Jacob grumbles.

"Well, that's sweet of her to help you with your Spanish."

"Nah, she's all right. But she's got some peculiar thoughts about relationships. She's telling me we should be getting married now."

I can't restrain my laughter. "Sorry, that's not really funny."

"No, it's messed up, is what it is. The bad thing is I really like Dominique, but it's not like I'm gonna just jump in and get married before we date for a year or two."

"What did she say about that?" I pull on a sports bra.

"She said she wouldn't live in sin that long."

"You're religious. You should be able to appreciate that."

Jacob grumbles something I can't hear.

"What did you say?" I ask.

"I said I'm not that religious."

I drop one of my older cotton dresses over my head and check myself in the mirror. Cute. "Sounds like you have some expectation differences. I hope you two can get them resolved if you like her. As for me, I have an uber-hot date tonight."

"Seriously?"

"Don't sound so shocked."

"No, it's not like that. It's just I hadn't heard you mention anybody."

"Sort of like your Dominique relationship with me. You

never mentioned her to me before I asked you to watch Nina's house."

"That's different. Guys don't go disappearing on dates with strangers."

"Thank you for confirming you're sexist, Hurley."

He clicks his tongue. "If it's factual, it's not sexist."

"You really need to learn to shut your mouth when you're digging a hole," I say. "Okay, you can turn around and not worry about the vision of my naked body being burned into your retina."

"Thank the Lord. Wouldn't want that to happen." He flashes his boyish crooked grin that I love so much.

"So, what are we doing today, boss man?"

He tosses the tennis ball into Puppy's bed. "We're going to the shop Faith had with Chelsie McDermont, Truncated Journeys."

I roll my eyes. "I got cleaned up to go look through a dusty old antique shop?"

"That's why I asked you why you were taking a shower."

"You can at least take me to breakfast first since I am presentable."

"Waffle House?"

"Sure." Waffle with bacon coated in syrup sounds pretty good this morning.

Chapter 49

Truncated Journeys is all but deserted when we pull up to the front in the police cruiser. It's not unusual for the local shops to be a little slow during the weekdays, especially during the off-season. Still, the only car in the lot is the one we know to be Chelsie's.

There is a lot of energy to pick up on. I develop an uneasy feeling, and my feet plant on the front porch as Jacob opens the door.

"Are you not coming in?"

"I'm thinking about it." I had been here only a week earlier, and I hadn't felt this level of disturbance. Even when I'm not looking, I'm usually a spirit magnet because my mind can act as a portal from one to the other. "I just need to prepare you, Jacob, because you've never been involved in this before. Something evil is going on at this store."

His lips form a tight line. "Okay. I'll take that as a good sign that maybe we'll get somewhere with this case during this visit." He squeezes the handle on the door, and nothing happens. "It's locked."

"It should be open." I point at the hours of operation posted on the old door.

"I called her to tell her I was coming."

I don't want to say anything to make matters worse, but

calling and announcing your arrival might be the first mistake. "Maybe you should call Chelsie again?"

"Yeah." Jacob begins to dial her, and the front door of the store opens.

"Hello, Officer Hurley. I was in the back. I hope you didn't have to wait too long."

The woman is attempting to cover her real character, but the rot of an evil soul wafts on the wind like five-day-old road-kill in June. There is something else disconcerting about her, but her rotten spirit overwhelms me initially.

"And you brought—"

"April Snow, an attorney from Snow and Associates."

Her face and ears flush red as she moves to extend a welcoming hand. "Loretta's granddaughter?" Her face is now as red as the last time I saw her when she was arguing vehemently with her partner, Faith Ray.

"That's me." I wave my hand in a swiping motion. Her eyes narrow.

"As I told you on the phone, this is all unnecessary. I've already talked to the other detectives regarding the case and told them everything I know," Chelsie insists.

Jacob listens patiently before answering. "Yes, your interviews are all on the transcript for us to review. This isn't really about getting additional information from you as much as it is to familiarize ourselves with Faith's workplace, home life, and other personal preferences."

Seemingly impossible, Chelsie's face turns a darker shade of red. "How's that supposed to find her?"

Jacob gestures with his thumb in my direction. "April does profiling for some of the different agencies. Just like the FBI profiles serial murderers, sometimes we can develop a profile on a missing person that will help us locate them."

I'm very impressed with Jacob's impromptu story. It's the first time I've seen him pull off a fib without cracking a smile. I'll have to make a note of his improvement.

"The FBI profiles housewives now?" Chelsie asks incredulously.

"Of course not." I pick up the storyline. This is actually fun. "This is strictly an after-the-event study. We have found if we answer the hundred and twenty-seven different variables that take place in an individual's life, we can accurately determine a slew of probabilities. Within one standard deviation, we can determine where the person will live, their profession, and what they will die from. Most importantly, we can determine where the individual would go if they ever decided to disappear from their current life." I air quote "disappear."

Chelsie eyes me suspiciously. Some days it's hard to con a con, but with steady eye contact, she finally relents and gives a one-arm shrug. "It sounds boring."

"We're just gonna start having a look around at personal effects. I'll give you a call if we need you to open anything," Jacob interjects.

Chelsie's shoulders shiver, and her face blanches. "Oh, I will be more than happy to walk you around."

"No. We can hunt around on our own," Jacob continues.

"It really is no bother. I would prefer it."

I wave a single finger in front of my face. "You don't understand how this works. If I have you in the same room, it can color my perception of how Faith would answer the hundred and twenty-seven questions. I can't have you tainting the survey."

Chelsie's mouth opens, and I watch her eyes dilate. Oh, she is hiding something. I'm not sure if she is hiding a dead body or a money-laundering operation, but she is definitely scared.

Grabbing Jacob by the elbow, I pull him toward the hallway on our left. "Let's go, Officer Hurley. I have other cases to get to today."

Jacob follows me dutifully down the hallway, and we bypass the first four consignment rooms to make sure to put some distance between Chelsie and ourselves.

"She's hiding something, and it's *bad*," I whisper.

"No kidding, Sherlock."

"What do you think?"

He raised his eyebrows. "That she's hiding something. And since I am not the IRS, I'm going to assume it has something to do with Faith's disappearance."

"They had a huge blow-up the day she disappeared."

Jacob grabs my wrist and pulls me to a stop. "Why haven't you mentioned this? That's sort of, like, important. I know you understand opportunity and motive."

"Duh." I favor him with an exaggerated eye roll. "And I just remembered it. So, sue me."

Jacob smirks. "Just now? Right now, you remembered?"

"Yes. Besides, slow your roll, cowboy. You might have motive and opportunity, but no dead body. Until we either find Faith alive or recover her body, everything you just mentioned is speculation."

"Now you're deflecting."

Yeah, but I was also sorta kicking myself in the butt for not having remembered earlier. Lately, I feel like I've been getting early-onset Alzheimer's. "If I had remembered, I would've told you. I'm sorry."

My apology seems to quell his frustration. "It's cool." He scans side to side. "Are you still picking up vibes or wavelengths or whatever it is you feel?"

There is an extreme level of energy in the shop. But it is chaotic, making it difficult to understand the low rumbling of voices or develop any visuals in my mind's eye. It is as if the spirit has a tremendous amount of power but is ineffective at harnessing it.

It is a young spirit. Full of vitality and no knowledge of how to use its power to best communicate. "There might be a little something here."

"Okay. I'll just follow your lead and try to stay out of your way until you need me."

I nod my head without looking directly at Jacob. Moving to our left, I enter the fifth consignment room.

I'm not entirely clear on how to proceed. When I'm working

with Dusty, we're trying to locate the spirits and make contact with them. This is one step further where I will need to extract information. We need to know where to find Faith, whether she is alive or dead.

The volume of the feedback in my mind doesn't change as I walk through the first consignment room we entered, touching items that draw my attention. At this stage, I cannot be sure if it is my own personal preference bringing me to the article or if a spirit is guiding me. I make sure to touch each of them in case there is any residual energy imprint.

Complete with the first room, I walk to the room directly across the hall and follow the same pattern. Again, with the same results, nothing.

Except I picked up a headache that has begun to pound at the base of my skull. Thankfully it's not a starburst migraine like I can often experience while playing in the paranormal, but it threatens to get worse.

Still, I can't get discouraged. We're at the stage of Faith's murder sliding to a cold case forever. If there is any chance I can help prevent that, I need to soldier through the task.

Further down the hall, just before the hallway turn, I enter a consignment room that consists primarily of old glass bottles. The low rumbling of voices suddenly increases. My head snaps to the left, and I become obsessed with a large, blue oval-shaped bottle with a flat bottom.

Encouraged, I walk quickly to it and lay my hand on it. Immediately, the vision of a mahogany desk pops into my head. The large bottle, that I now hold, sits on the table next to a tumbler. The angles are all wrong. Then I realize the point of view. The cup is filled, lifted toward my vision, and replaced on the desk in short order.

There is a revolver to the right of the tumbler.

Let it go, April. Not today; this is not about today. I push back against the vision and try to clear the harmful residue from my mind by thinking about happy thoughts. Puppy in the lake and Daddy's jambalaya come to mind, and I step out of the room, quickly turning the corner in the hall.

"April. Are you okay?" Jacob asks.

"Sure. I'm fine." No, I'm not okay. Some days when I think about the hurt and pain in the world and how some people decide to handle it, it tears at my seams. I know, fundamentally, it's part of the human experience. However, seeing other people in pain still hurts me, even if they've been dead for several decades.

We walk into a large room that used to most likely be the old school gym, and the unfocused energy I felt earlier throughout the building pounds against my head. It is as if someone were to blow an air horn in my ear at the exact moment I have a migraine attack. "There's something here, Jacob."

His eyebrows shoot up. "Really? What do you need me to do?"

I struggle to filter the energy that is crashing against my mind. I gather all my energy into the center of my core and quickly push out with all my power. At the same time, I straighten my arms in the direction I feel the most activity. "Be at peace. I am here," I send through my thoughts.

The volume lowers. So, I *can* communicate with it. That is good.

"April?" Jacob is at my side. "I asked what do you need me to do."

As the shock of the migraine pain leaves the back of my head, I open my eyes and take inventory of what is in the room. There are hundreds of old lamps, antique executive desks, and other furniture pieces in varying states of repair and chalk painting. But my eyes are drawn to the far right, where there are several stacks of antique traveler's trunks. The collection looks to be twelve units deep and ten boxes across.

I point toward the trunks. "We're going to need to open those."

"All those?"

I can't explain it to him, but the feeling is inescapable. I *need* the lid of every one of those trunks opened now. "I'm pretty sure."

Jacob shakes his head as he walks toward the stack of trunks. "This could take all day," he grumbles.

He is right. There are over a hundred trunks, and although it might not take all day, it certainly will take the better part of the day.

There are too many spirits in this building if the consignment room with the empty bottles has shown me anything. I can't be sure I'm tuned into something that will ultimately be helpful with Faith's case.

I steady my breathing and focus entirely on Faith. Once I have her picture centered in my mind, I cocoon the vision with love and empathy. "Where are you, Faith? Please give me a visual. Where are you?"

My eyes are closed, but I hear the clasp of a trunk pop open. All the noise that has been assaulting me since I stepped into the antique store suddenly falls away.

Only the *snap, snap* of Jacob opening up trunks one by one remains.

With all going silent, I half anticipate hearing Faith's voice instructing me where to find her. I concentrate even harder on her face, but no voice comes to me. All I hear is more clicking from Jacob's search.

I open my eyes and realize I had them closed so tightly my sight is blurred. As my vision clears, my eyes play tricks on me.

The stack of trunks the furthest to Jacob's left appears to have a tiny green streamer dangling from the ceiling above it. The banner sways side to side despite the lack of breeze in the room.

Walking toward the stack of trunks near the streamer, I notice that this has an air of familiarity. As I get nearer, my chest constricts as I realize what I'm witnessing.

Smoke. A tiny tendril of green smoke floats upward from the back row of the trunks. A familiar, green smoke. The same color that leaked out of the mirror in the police annex building last week.

"Jacob! Quick, over here."

I jog to the far stack and begin to tug at the first row. The trunks are heavier than they look.

"What's up?" Jacob helps me pull the first row clear.

I point upward. "The smoke." I pull on the second trunk. It doesn't budge. I look over my shoulder, and Jacob is staring in the direction I pointed.

"What smoke?" he asks.

I stand and point again at the green tendril floating to the top of the ceiling forming a small puddle on the white acoustic tiles. "That green smoke."

Jacob's face twists, and he lets out a short laugh. "I don't see what you're talking about."

I start to argue then realize he might not be able to see it. "Never mind, just help me pull this out. We need to get to the back row. We're close now."

Jacob leans over to help me pull the trunks, then falls forward on his face. He makes a "humph" sound as the impact forces the air out of his lungs.

Turning, I freeze. The red-faced, red-haired Chelsie stands in front of me with a baseball bat in her hand. Jacob might've been right about her having opportunity and motive now that I consider it in light of her present actions.

"Aaargh!" She screams as she brandishes the bat at me over her head.

In an attempt to backpedal, I catch my heel and land on my fanny, rolling onto my back. Chelsie straddles me and is preparing to bring the bat down when I flick my hands upward. The bat explodes into flames.

Chelsie throws the flaming bat to the side and pulls her burnt hands to her chest. She turns to escape. As she pivots, I kick up at her knee, sending her to the floor.

Without thought, I roll over onto my knees and dive on top of her back. As she struggles to get away, I clutch her clothes and slide up her back until I have both my hands wound tightly in her red hair. I then pull my knees up, tucking them neatly into her armpits as I pull her head back further by her hair.

The room is filled with animal-like noises. I'm not sure if it is Chelsie screaming in pain or me growling as I wrestle with the desire to slam her face repeatedly onto the hardwood floor. I want to kill her for having hit Jacob with the bat.

Despite all the screaming, I hear a metallic click and look to my right.

Jacob places his left foot between Chelsie's shoulder blades. "Let her go, April. I've got her."

The red battle tint dissipates from my vision as I calm. Reluctantly, I let go of her hair and push back until I'm sitting on her buttocks. Jacob finishes cuffing her.

I immediately burst into tears.

"Aww, come on, Snow. Don't cry."

I can't help it. The flood starts in earnest, and I begin to hiccup. "I thought she killed you. And then I thought she was going to kill me."

Jacob helps me up and envelops me in his arms. I can feel his chest heaving as he's trying not to laugh. "And I thought you were about to kill her by slamming her head on that hardwood floor."

"I wanted to."

"You're crazy, Snow. But thank you for having my back."

Chapter 50

Jacob calls for backup. Our worst fears are confirmed an hour later when we find Faith's plastic-wrapped body packed in a trunk filled with deodorant kitty litter.

I'm grateful they had already taken Chelsie to the station when Doc Crowley arrives and pulls Faith's body from the packaging enough to identify her. By this time, I seriously want to hurt Chelsie.

A motive was found at the bottom of the trunk in front of Faith. Fifteen thousand dollars in cash. Most of it dyed blue and unusable. Who kills a business partner over fifteen thousand dollars?

Despite being read her Miranda rights, Chelsie kept explaining to Jacob on the way out that it wasn't her fault. They had found the money in one of the trunks, and Faith wanted to report it to the police. Chelsie, who had a considerable amount of credit card debt she was trying to hide from her husband, wanted to see if they could get the dye out with an oxidation laundry product.

When Faith called the police, the bat "appeared," and Chelsie wasn't sure what happened next. She claims she blacked out.

With friends like that, who needs enemies. Right? I sure am glad Jacob is my friend and not that wackadoodle, Chelsie.

Chapter 51

I seriously want to cancel my date with Justin, but I believe it might be therapeutic to have something "nice" in my life today. Honestly, now that I have his interest and my dry spell is broken—well, I don't want to break the momentum.

By seven forty-five, I'm at the Carriage House. I look sharp in my jade green dress and heels. I have butterflies in my stomach as I walk in and say hello to the maître d'.

Justin hasn't arrived yet, but the maître d' leads me to our table and brings me a glass of Pinot Noir while I wait for him. It tastes expensive.

Ten minutes later, I get antsy and check my messages to ensure I have not missed one from him. He isn't late, but I sort of feel like maybe I was a bit overeager now.

I know the twenty-four roses covering the maître d's face as he approaches my table are for me. No, I'm not the least bit pleased. I know what they mean before I open the sizeable cream-colored envelope attached to the ostentatious ribbon around the neck of the vase.

"Thank you," I whisper as I favor him with a brave smile.

He dips his eyes, then offers his own brave smile. What do you do? These things happen. He retreats to his station.

For several minutes all I can do is stare at the luxurious, overflowing floral arrangement in front of me. It is impressive.

Something that could easily be used for the centerpiece floral arrangement of a classy wedding.

The thought of a wedding turns me bitter. I won't have to worry about any wedding plans for quite some time.

Why, and when, did I start to care about a wedding anyway? All through college, I believed a man would simply slow me down from what I want to accomplish in life.

Screw it. I down the last of the Pinot Noir, slam the fluted glass to the table, and rip the envelope from the vase.

What is it this time? His mom in Peoria needs him to move in. He just wasn't into me? If I'm a betting girl, he probably thought our relationship would be too complicated since he contracted Mama to sell in his sub-division. Cowardly slug.

The card has the most beautiful calligraphy. "I'm Sorry" is written across the front. Yes, you are, mister. You are incredibly sorry to drag my butt all the way to Huntsville just to stand me up.

Pulling the card open, I almost tear it in half. I don't even know why I'm reading it. If Justin doesn't think it is important enough to tell me face to face, it isn't significant enough for me to waste my time reading.

April, I will never be able to tell you I'm sorry enough. I am a cowardly and dishonorable man. You deserve better.

Yes, I do. There's one thing we can agree on.

You are the brightest, most engaging woman I have met in my life. I also find you incredibly sexy, and I am drawn to you like a moth to a flame.

Except for tonight. The moth didn't show up.

I am ashamed of my behavior and the fact that I led you on. Understand, I want to be with you more than anything I have ever wanted in my life. When I called you today, my mind was set on one great goal: ultimately earning your love, body, mind, and soul. But I took a vow ten years ago and have three children.

I have to reread the sentence to make sure I read it correctly.

Although I am sure my happiness lies with you, I must keep my word. I truly am sorry if I have hurt you. Love, Justin.

Love? What the heck, you psycho, two-timing lecherous cheat. Love. *Please.*

PS. I have instructed the restaurant that I will pick up your tab tonight. Please enjoy your dinner.

Oh, the nerve! Like I got cleaned up and drove an hour to Huntsville for a free steak. Really? You know what? I dodged a bullet. I could have been in a long-term relationship with the freak—if he wasn't already in a long-term relationship.

I dip the corner of the card into the candle tumbler. I can feel my teeth grinding as I hold the offensive communiqué in the air. I probably look like a crazy woman, grinning as the blackened paper curls ever closer to my fingers. Heck, I am a crazy woman.

The maître d' appears out of thin air, sliding a bread plate under my hand. "It can burn completely on the plate without damaging your manicure, madam."

I drop the last corner onto the plate and turn my nails toward me. "I like this color pink."

"It is a splendid shade, madam."

He is a suck-up, but I sort of need someone to suck up to me right now. He also has kind eyes and a gentle voice.

"I hope you will still be dining with us tonight. The filet mignon is second to none."

"No. I seem to have lost my appetite." At least for food. "But can I take the rest of the bottle of wine home?"

"Ah, but I am sorry. I certainly would let you, but the city will not allow it once a bottle is opened." He holds up a finger as he arches a brow. "But you can take an unopened bottle home. And there is more in a sealed bottle than an opened bottle."

I can't help but laugh at his teasing. "I would like that."

He puts his fist to his chin. "Sometimes bottles are not so easy to carry. They are sort of long and cylinder-shaped. Very easy to drop."

"Yes, they are," I agree.

"But in a case of six—the nice square box is much easier to carry."

"I agree. Excellent point."

Chapter 52

Carriage House is supposed to be a nationally acclaimed steak-house. I still can't attest to the quality of their steaks, but their service is second to none. They even carried the case of wine to my IROC for me. With an eighteen-hundred-dollar wine bill and a four-hundred-dollar tip, I figure Justin is getting off dirt cheap.

Lucky for him, I'm not the type of woman to call his wife or re-mail the cheesy card he had written me to their home. The woman already has enough issues to deal with if she is married to him, and she has saved me from a huge mistake.

Who knows, maybe it was a one-time almost indiscretion on his part. In that case, I wish them many years of happiness.

As for me? I'm windows down, music blaring, with one hand out my IROC hoping to take flight and float. Relax and float with the breeze, just like Grandpa used to say.

I hit speed dial. "Am I interrupting anything?"

"Nope. Just me, Bud, and Jack hanging around having a discussion about women."

"I thought you might be over at Dominique's."

"You know what they say. You can't eat the same thing every night."

"Oh, for Pete's sakes!"

"What? Was that over the line?"

"If you have to ask, you know it was," I say.

We're both silent, listening to each other breathe. I finally break the silence. "Am I weird, Jacob?"

"How do you mean?"

"I don't know. I just have all these desires, and a lot of the time, they are in conflict. It drives me crazy, and sometimes I think it drives the people around me crazy."

"You worry about stuff too much. You always have. You're, not weird, April—you're just figuring it out, you know. Trial and error."

"It sucks."

"Nah. It could be worse."

"How?" I ask.

"You could be an old woman who has to hike her boobs up into her bra."

"How do you know that's not the case?"

"Because I saw you change today."

"You had your back—"

"The glass in the picture frame by the front door. Perfect reflection."

"You dog!"

"I turned my back like you asked."

It is another foolish desire, but I have to ask. "I scored some excellent Pinot Noir tonight. I'm willing to share if you'll let me come over."

"Uh, no on the chick wine, but you're welcome to come over and bad mouth men if I can unload my overbearing girlfriend story on you."

"Deal. I'll see you in ten." I hang up, push my hand out the window allowing it to float on the rushing air while I laugh. Life would be a grind if it weren't for good friends.

The End

Never miss an April May Snow release.

Join the reader's club!

www.mscottswanson.com

April's story continues with

Foolish Expectations

Click to read.

Have you read the prequels? *The Gifts Awaken* stories are the prequel series to the *Foolish* novel series of April May Snow.

Click to get your copies today!

The Gifts Awaken Prequel Series

Throw the Bouquet

Throw the Cap

Throw the Dice

Throw the Elbow

Throw the Fastball

Throw the Gauntlet

Throw the Hissy

M. Scott lives outside of Nashville, Tennessee, with his wife and two guard chihuahuas. When he's not writing, he's cooking or taking long walks to smooth out plotlines for the next April May Snow adventure.

Dear Reader,

Thank you for reading April's story. You make her adventures possible. Without you, there would be no point in creating her these novels.

I'd like to encourage you to post a review on Amazon. A favorable critique from you is a powerful way to support authors you enjoy. It allows our books to be found by additional readers, and frankly, motivates us to continue to produce books. This is especially true for your independents.

Once again, thank you for the support. You are the magic that breathes life into these characters.

M. Scott Swanson

The best way to stay in touch is to join the reader's club!

www.mscottswanson.com

Other ways to stay in touch are:

Like on Amazon

Like on Facebook

Like on Goodreads

You can also reach me at mscottswanson@gmail.com.

I hope your life is filled with

magic and LOVE!

Made in United States
North Haven, CT
07 September 2022